Higher Ground

Higher Ground

Anke Stelling

**Translated from the German
by Lucy Jones**

SCRIBE
Melbourne • London

Scribe Publications
18–20 Edward St, Brunswick, Victoria 3056, Australia
2 John St, Clerkenwell, London, WC1N 2ES, United Kingdom
3754 Pleasant Ave, Suite 100, Minneapolis, Minnesota 55409, USA

Originally published in German as *Schäfchen im Trockenen* by Verbrecher Verlag in 2018

First published in English by Scribe 2021

Typeset in Adobe Garamond Pro by the publishers

Printed and bound in the UK by CPI Group (UK) Ltd, Croydon CR0 4YY

Scribe Publications is committed to the sustainable use of natural resources and the use of
paper products made responsibly from those resources.

9781925849905 (Australian edition)
9781913348014 (UK edition)
9781950354627 (US edition)
9781925938760 (ebook)

Catalogue records for this book are available from the National Library of Australia
and the British Library.

scribepublications.com.au
scribepublications.co.uk
scribepublications.com

Listen, Bea, the most important thing and the most awful, and the hardest to understand — but if you somehow manage it, also the most valuable — is this: nothing in life is black and white. I have to get that off my chest at the start. Because I keep forgetting it. And I probably keep forgetting it because what I want most is for things to be black and white, and realising they aren't is painful. But at the same time, it's comforting.

How can something painful be comforting? There you go. That's exactly the kind of ambiguity I mean.

Like when I say: 'I love you', for example. Oh, yes, I love you. It's incredible. You're incredible! You're so beautiful, clever, and alive. I want to kiss you and argue with you, and you're the best thing ever. You're the best thing that's ever happened to me, and at the same time, I'd rather you didn't exist, because you being alive is unbearable. I'm so afraid for you, and I'm afraid for me, just because you were born. And my advice to you, quite frankly, is to get away from here as quickly as possible. Run as fast as you can, put some distance between you and me, and grow up fast. I'm toxic for you, see? Families are a hotbed of neuroses, and the ruler of this particular hotbed, our nest, is me. I'm the eagle with claws and a protective, feathery bottom, a screechy voice and a vast wingspan, and I'll peck out the eyes of anybody who comes too close to you. I'll circle above you, teach you how to fly, and be a step ahead of you in everything you do. I'll show you the beauty and dangers of the world, and when you fly away, I'll wait behind in the nest, indulgent, begrudging, and proud.

You already know what I'm talking about.

You shuddered recently when you came home. 'Jesus, it stinks in here!'

And you're right, darling. It stinks. Of us. Of family. So luscious, cosy, and disgusting; so, get the hell out of here! Let me hold you close to my breast. And remember — you have to get away.

Everybody knows that

I'm a very late starter. Or is it the same for everybody? Do we all realise halfway through life how much we've failed to understand even though it was staring us in the face?

I always thought I was clever, understood the world, and was a good judge of character. After all, I could read before I started school, could express myself well, and was good at doing sums in my head. I knew I had to steer clear of Frank Häberle and the caretaker, and I could rely on Simmi Sanders and the needlework teacher. But as for the bigger picture, structures and power relations, I didn't have a clue — that my life might have been different, for example. That must be what they call security. Feeling safe. A happy childhood.

I can still remember the exact moment when I realised: *Fuck! If my parents had lived somewhere else, we'd have had a different kitchen floor.*

I was in my twenties when this flash of insight came to me, after I'd already moved several times — first out of my parents' home to Berlin, and then a few times in the city.

This time I'd landed a really fantastic kitchen floor: dark green, 1930s pulped chipboard in excellent condition.

My parents had 1960s West German PVC tiles, thirty by thirty with a streaky grey pattern — which meant that it kept changing direction. There was nothing wrong with that floor: I had grown up on it just fine. And it was easy to clean. You practically had to get stuck to it before my mother said: 'This could do with a mop' and then I would shake some scouring powder over it and scrub it with a bare brush, amazed at how black the water was that I poured down the toilet afterwards.

The floor was the floor. And if people had a different floor, it was because they were different people.

The toilet cistern had a black lever on the side. I would push it down to flush away the dirty water. It was never renewed, not even when all kinds of water-saving flush systems became fashionable, or when the mechanism got so old that it broke, and the lever snapped off from wear and tear. My parents never told the landlord. In all the years that we lived in that flat, I never once saw the landlord. Perhaps that's why it took me so long to work out that there were flats you rented and flats you owned — because my parents treated their rented flat as if it were their own, calling a plumber if there was no way round it and paying him out of their own pocket. Why? To avoid arguments, I imagine. To pretend they were free.

'Why are you so angry?' Renate, a friend of my mother's, asked me when we were sitting together in a café.

I flinched because I thought I was very composed, sitting there drinking my tea and talking to her about all kinds of things. She, however, only wanted to talk about the book I'd written, in which I accused mothers like mine of saddling their daughters with their

4

dreams of freedom, without giving them a clue how to put them into practice. Renate had taken my book personally. Rightly so, I thought, even though I hadn't been thinking of her in particular when I was writing it.

'No generation can avoid being blamed by the next,' I answered.

'Well then, good luck with your own children,' she said, and I nodded.

'Yes, thanks a lot.'

I am a last-word freak. But so is she.

'You're welcome.' She said it with *that* facial expression: poorly disguised smugness, fake meekness.

I can do that expression too. Mothers pass it down to their daughters, along with their unfulfilled dreams. In fact, this expression tells of your dreams while your lips stay tightly pursed, and you say nothing. Lips pursed, chin jutting forward slightly — Renate is a pro at that expression. But so am I.

And Bea has started doing it too, and I can't stand how some things just keep on playing out forever. I'd rather be angry, talk, write, and spit in Renate's tea, so she really sees for once what being angry means.

'Do you remember the floor tiles we had in our flat?' I asked.

'No, why?'

'They were ugly. And it didn't have to be that way! But I had to work that out for myself. You didn't talk to us.'

'Of course we did, all the time! Don't pretend we didn't.'

'Not about floor tiles and why we had them.'

Renate raised her eyebrows and gave me a derisive look. That's another thing she's good at: making you feel that you're out of your mind.

5

She used to do it back when she came over to visit my mother, and I would join them and tell them some story — about school, friends, or the injustice of the world. Renate would raise her eyebrows, along with doubts about what I'd said, pointing out things I'd overlooked, doing her best to unnerve me. And I let her, instead of using her objections as arguing practice.

These days it's different. These days I argue back. So I told her I was now convinced my mother had thought the floor tiles were ugly too, but had accepted them because they were all she could afford, they just happened to be there, and had nothing to do with her. But that's where she'd made a mistake; now, the floor stood for her. Well, okay, maybe that was a slight exaggeration: for me, my mother is the woman who stood on that floor.

Renate's eyebrows stayed raised.

'Don't you get it?' I asked, furious. 'I should have known what she *really* wanted, and how we ended up with the things I thought were normal, and what other options there might have been, and why she didn't take them!'

'And what has that got to do with you?'

'Everything! Because I stood on that floor too!'

Renate shook her head and ordered more tea. Went to the bathroom, clearly didn't want to talk about it. But now she has to, since my mother can't: she died before I realised what I needed to ask her, where I needed to dig deeper because, as I was to find out from Renate, her silence was deliberate, not an oversight. Neither Renate nor my mother wanted to burden their children with anecdotes and old stories, especially not ones about their lack of options, unfavourable starts in life, or lesser evils.

'We wanted you children to be free to follow your own path.'

'Yes, exactly,' I said. 'Clean slates all round.'

Renate wasn't in the mood for my irony. She preferred to be the one to tease.

'Your mother would have obviously preferred terrazzo flooring in a chalet on Lake Geneva.'

Yeah, yeah. Obviously.

List for Bea: pulped chipboard floors are my personal favourite, but they're ridiculously expensive these days because they're so niche. Pulped chipboard has become a luxury for enthusiasts only, so forget it.

Floorboards in the kitchen might look nice at first, but they're prone to grease stains, and all the dirt falls into the gaps. You know the kind from our flat: a floor like that is very hard to clean.

On the other hand, a tiled floor, which is easy to mop, isn't exactly low maintenance either because you *have* to mop it every day. It doesn't absorb or hide anything unless it has a streaky or speckled pattern — and then, Bea, it's absolutely hideous. Even worse than PVC, in fact, because tiles are cold underfoot, except if you have underfloor heating. Let's just say that neutral terracotta tiles with underfloor heating are okay if you have a cleaner who takes care of them all the time.

I've never had a cleaner. I've worked as a cleaner, but that isn't part of my list about floors — or is it?

Of course it is. Definitely.

———

I've decided to tell you everything. Nothing is natural; everything is constructed and connected; everything helps or harms somebody or other; and anything that's taken for granted is particularly suspicious.

Bea is fourteen and needs to be taught the facts of life. She has to be initiated and introduced to the world of kitchen floors, the division and distribution of labour, cleaning jobs, labour costs, accommodation costs, basic and additional costs, cost-benefit calculations, and the whole business of setting off and settling up, both financially and emotionally.

Unlike my mother, I won't presume that she'll find out everything she needs to know in time; unlike Renate and her friends, I won't hold back for fear of having a negative influence on my children, of discouraging them or stunting their development. Quite the opposite: I imagine arming them with knowledge and stories, so they don't go out into the world as naïve, carefree souls, but are, instead, loaded with insights and analytical powers. Munition and weapons are heavy.

Speaking of weapons.

A letter came for me. It's addressed to me and contains a neatly folded sheet of paper, which is the termination of the lease on our flat. No, that's wrong. It's a copy of the termination of the lease on our flat for my attention. Because our flat is really Frank's; Frank's name is on the contract, and he's terminated the lease.

We've lived here for four years. When Frank and Vera moved into K23, we took over their flat. A stroke of luck, because ours was already too small with three kids — and by then, we had four.

What a stroke of luck that we knew somebody with an eighteen-year-old lease who no longer needed it.

But what comes around goes around.

This letter is a comeuppance for what I've done, and that's why it's not addressed to Sven, or to us both, just to me. This whole mess is my fault. I put Frank in a position that made him do it. I only have myself to blame for everything that's happened, and that's what I'm doing here in my broom cupboard, my two square metres next to our old-style Berlin kitchen, which is really the pantry, which is really the rear section of the loo that it shares a window with. The kids are at school or childcare, and Sven is in his studio, which he's only temporarily able to lease, until the investor has reworded and resubmitted the rejected planning application. It all comes down to the wording. I stare at the letter.

Dear Sir/Madam it says impersonally, addressing the housing agent, and for me, there's an extra stamp saying: *For Your Attention*, and no salutation whatsoever. Just the green rubber stamp. Very official and very strange, because Frank isn't an official, he's an old friend. Where on earth did he get that stamp? Couldn't he have phoned?

No. Frank doesn't want to talk to me.

'There's no talking to you,' Vera would say.

Vera sent me an email months ago, which said: 'This is where we part ways.' Which I hadn't interpreted as: 'You better figure out pretty quickly where you're going to live, because I'll get Frank on to you next.'

I'd understood that she was terminating our friendship, and didn't want to see me anymore.

She'd also written 'I love you', and it wasn't until the termination of the lease arrived that I realised there are two ways of saying this: simply and passionately, because it's true. Or threateningly, to show that action will be taken. Parents talk like this. And gods.

When I held that termination letter in my hands, I realised Vera had been using it in the second instance, because even though I'm not her child, I'm a very, very old friend, a member of her chosen family. In other words, family rules apply to me too.

In Vera's family, love was always emphasised very strongly, no matter what horrors were going on at the time or followed later. Vera's declaration of love should have made me suspicious; after all, I had 'seriously broken the rules' and therefore 'shouldn't be surprised'.

The rule I had broken was: 'Don't wash your dirty laundry in public.' It's a nice phrase that holds families together. 'Laundry' stands for privacy, 'dirty' for 'unpresentable', and 'wash' for spilling the beans, snitching, and telling stories. And when I say that telling stories is my profession, Ulf says: 'You can't use that as a smokescreen.' Because in the end, I chose my profession.

There's a children's book by Leo Lionni that defends the profession of the artist. The book was a bestseller forty years ago and is now a classic, but that doesn't mean its message has sunk in.

In the story, a group of mice is busy collecting food supplies for winter, and it's hard going. One of them lies in the sun all day and says he's collecting smells, colours, and impressions. Will he have the right to eat from the supplies when winter comes? But behold: at some point, during the darkest, hungriest period towards the end of winter, the lazy mouse's moment comes, and he saves the other mice by describing the colours, smells, and tastes out there in the world. 'You're a poet,' say the other mice, and the artist mouse blushes and nods.

I wonder whether Leo was also chased out of his flat because of his story? I bet some of his friends with full-time jobs recognised themselves in the depiction of the humdrum gatherer mice, and his ex-wife said how arrogant he was to recast himself from failed breadwinner to world saviour. But who knows? Perhaps they all laughed, and Leo's book was a favourite birthday present for friends and relatives; perhaps they were proud, and grateful to him for managing to express their ambivalence and their never-ending struggle with life choices.

In any case, Vera, Friederike, Ulf, Ingmar, and the rest were not grateful to me for finding words for the mess we were in. Quite the opposite, in fact: they even thought 'mess' was an unsuitable description. Because everything was fine.

What's good: to have made it this far. To have made it to higher ground — or, at least, to have got your kids into the school of your choice, which is better than the local school in any number of ways.

Everybody's still healthy. And cheerful — or, at least, not bad-tempered enough that something has to change. We're still at the stage when taking out your bad temper on others is enough — on the ones who don't behave the way you think they should.

What sucks: calling this good life 'a mess'.

In the darkest moment, instead of telling stories about the sun and the colours, I talked about how dark the moment was. Only some mice found this comforting, whereas others didn't; and some, who played a role in my story of the darkness, felt betrayed and exploited.

'Who do you think you are to impose your views on others?' they asked. 'And who, may we ask, gave you permission?'

I gave myself permission, the poet mouse.

In the darkness, it's dark, and in my broom cupboard, it's lonely.

The statutory period of notice on a lease is three months. We have to leave this place by the end of the year.

Do you even know, Bea, that the lease is in Frank's name? I'm afraid I've left you as much in the dark as my parents did me. I'm afraid you might also take our kitchen floor for granted.

I took a gamble on the flat. And lost. Only myself to blame. What comes around goes around.

No one talks about things, at least not the important things, such as personal hardships and your own part in them. Twenty-five per cent of the whole sum — I wonder what that is in euros?

I can write what I like. The only sound I can hear is the humming of my laptop. The humming is disturbingly loud these days. Who knows, maybe it'll give up the ghost soon. I need a back-up, a security copy.

Did you know that writing provides security? It's an insurance, a reassurance, a linchpin for the future. There it is in writing, see? Yes, I remember!

I can't provide you with a house, Bea, not even a flat; but I can tell you everything I know.

———

I don't care if you want to hear it or not. I'm Resi, the narrator of this story and a writer by profession. Sucks for you: why did you choose a mother like me?

Because that's another widespread myth: that children choose their parents. That before they're born, they are little souls floating on their way to find the right couple. It's like the idea that parents get the child they deserve — or need — to become real grown-ups.

Do you like stories like these? I don't.

But you see, I've heard people telling them and seen their effects. That's another thing I realised too late: the strength of stories and the power of telling them.

I remember that parents' evening at your school a few years ago when things got slightly out of hand, and men with greying temples and strident voices kept interrupting each other — late-in-life fathers who, as I found out later on, were all journalists for big broadsheets.

Of course! I thought. Some people are journalists because they like the sheer power of it. It isn't just the medium of choice for introverts and stutterers. It can also be a way of hammering home your point, opinions, and analyses.

In any case, the tone of the statements at that parents' evening was: 'I'm going to wipe the floor with you', and the circle of chairs formed an arena into which the talkers stepped and flexed their muscles to scare off the others. In their children's best interests, it goes without saying.

Back then I didn't have a book to my name yet. No one said afterwards: 'That's Resi, the writer.' They said: 'That's Resi, Bea's mum', and that should have meant I was qualified to have my say at the parents' meeting. But no. In groups randomly thrown together by fate, who you are is what counts. And who you are is nothing less than the extent of the power you possess — which is especially depressing when the points on the agenda are: 'Treating each other with respect', 'How to stop bullying', and 'Each person is an individual'.

You know, Bea, I'm a late-in-life mother myself these days. I notice how I run out of steam, especially at parents' meetings. I'm not optimistic or curious like I was when I used to go to parents' evenings at your kindergarten. I was in my early thirties then and all enthusiastic about being a mum. Now I'm in my mid-forties and want these dickheads to leave me in peace. I despise them, really. Fear seeps from their pores, and they throw their weight around and stir things up and try to find something in common with people who will protect their interests. They form little cliques, exclude the weaker ones, and lie in wait for the others to make fools of themselves.

I'm exactly the same.

There's nothing you can do, it's the fear. There's nothing worse than groups randomly thrown together by fate, and nothing more terrifying than a bunch of people who think they have to come to an agreement at all costs.

But staying away isn't an option. I have to protect you by marking my territory as a parent — and not just any old parent, but one with power! Enough power at least to get through a parents' evening! Yes, that's right, darling. It's a vicious circle.

When it comes to being power hungry, children come in very

handy. You can use them as a shield, even when they're not your own. The line about it being 'in the best interests of the children' always works: who wants kids to suffer? The hypocrisy of it is shocking.

But what should I do? Stop going? Avoid parents' evenings? Avoid parents' social nights? No one seems to realise the irony of calling them 'social nights': they're the most anti-social gatherings I've ever been to.

'Don't be like that, Resi!' they say. 'It's just a name.' 'Don't be so negative!'

I now know the power of words, clichés, and stories; but the solution can't be to stop using them. I'm a leftie — in other words, pro-justice, pro-respect, and pro-everybody-being-equal — and I think the world still has a long way to go. But if everybody is equal, that doesn't settle the question of who is right and who gets to decide. Quite the opposite, in fact. People mistrust claims to power, so much so that they sometimes prefer doing nothing than being suspected of claiming power. Lefties are terrified of blame, precisely because they are so pro-justice and pro-respect. But the opposite of power is powerlessness, and the opposite of having your say is letting others have it.

'You abuse words,' says Friederike. 'You use them to wipe the floor with people.'

Is she right?

At parents' evenings, I do see my words as a weapon. It's calming to picture myself later describing how insane it all was, and to imagine shaking up the world with my report.

But that's ridiculous: that's not how it works.

Exactly the same thing will happen at the next parents' evening; or, as Erich Kästner put it: 'You can't prevent the catastrophe with a typewriter.'

I'm just holding myself together. I write for my sake, no one else's, or at any rate not for Friederike, who thinks my writing is mired in clichés. Why do the journalist dads have to be greying at the temples, for God's sake?

And if I go even further and say that the people in the group who said nothing all evening were the young women in yoga pants and tailored fleeces and Birkenstocks made of vegan leather, then, Bea, you'll think it's beside the point. But these are important indicators of reality and have to be included in a text, even if they make it unbearable; even if it pinches, and bites, and bursts with clichés.

I would have preferred things to have turned out quite differently.

I could start writing sci-fi. Fantasy.

As I was going up the stair
I met a man who wasn't there.
He wasn't there again today
I wish, I wish he'd stay away.

I can't do it, Bea. No matter what I do, it always comes down to the same thing. I like rhymes — and it's comforting when a word reminds me of my childhood.

Bähmullig, for example. Do you know what a *Bähmull* is? A tetchy — or just pretty annoying — fourteen-year-old, say, but possibly even forty-year-old, who turns up her nose at everything. A perfectionist who quickly gets in a huff. In a word, a fusspot.

Maybe it's my vanity that makes me want to preserve this word in literature. Somebody else could do it; after all, there are enough books, millions of stories, so why does it have to be mine? But if you start thinking like this, you could start asking: What's the use of me? There are enough women. The world is overpopulated, on the verge of collapse.

'You don't have to write,' Friederike said. 'Please don't act like it was anything but your own, selfish decision.'

She had recognised herself, and she didn't like what she saw. No one wants to be a fusspot.

'Don't be like that,' Ulf said to me in the same café where I had sat with Renate, as well as Friederike, Ulf, and Ellen. I met them one after the other and had to explain the reasons for what I'd done. Ulf just wanted to be a go-between, he said, because he hadn't been as deeply affected as the others.

'Affected by what?'

'You know exactly what.'

I said nothing.

'Imagine somebody wrote about you.'

'Okay.'

'How would you like it?'

'I wouldn't have to like it.'

'You've exposed people's private lives!'

'I'm sorry.'

'It doesn't seem that way to me. It seems like you'd do it again at the drop of a hat.'

'Yes, I would. Because I think it's necessary.'

'Hurting others is necessary?'

'Yes, I'm afraid so.'

'And then you're surprised when they stop talking to you?'

'Yes. I'm surprised that they don't understand. I was just using them as examples. But it was about the bigger picture.'

'About you.'

'Of course it was about me! I'm the one condemned to silence!'

'That's what I was worried about.'

'What?'

'That you'd make yourself out to be the victim.'

Ulf, my old friend. Not as deeply affected, but at his wits' end all the same.

Speaking of wits. Ulf was top of the class, even did Latin. He studied it as a hobby when he was still at school. Always make sure you pick the A-class boys, Bea, forget the B class! My parents thought that only applied to Benzes.

Ulf believes in good. I'll have to make a show of understanding or else there'll never be peace.

Peace comes when people agree on a story, on who plays which role and what the script is. Things can't settle down while everybody is fighting for the role of victim. As long as I decide who's who.

So, there's Friederike. The fusspot. The princess whose whims everybody tries to satisfy. She can't help herself. It's her role to be the fusspot, and it always takes two: one (usually a woman) to say no to everything and another (usually a man) to keep making new suggestions and do everything right. Fusspots and do-righters belong together like peas in a pod. You could almost write a rhyme about them.

And then there's Ulf, my go-between, with whom I went to primary school and who was my first proper boyfriend. Back then, at *Gymnasium*, our university-track secondary school.

That's where we met Friederike, who nowadays says I should have thought beforehand whether I could afford to have children. 'Everybody knows that,' she said when I complained how expensive school excursions were.

Friederike has two children, Silas and Sophie, with Ingmar, the doctor she met at Christian's wedding — the same Christian who also went to *Gymnasium* with Ulf, Friederike, and me.

Vera didn't. She changed to a private school after fourth grade.

Vera went to primary school with Ulf and me, and then joined the same tennis club as Friederike and Christian.

Vera and Frank also have two children, Willi and Leon.

Ulf doesn't have any children: he has Carolina and his architectural firm.

Christian and Ellen have three children: Charlotte, Mathilda, and Finn.

I'm wondering whether this type of list is of any use to anyone.

I bet the only person who sticks in your mind for longer than two seconds is Friederike — because she has such a great nickname that sums up her character. Like in a school yearbook: 'Friederike, the Fusspot, "Everybody knows that."'

When we did our A-levels in the early 1990s, some of our classmates made a yearbook because they'd watched too many

American high school films. Ulf, Friederike, Christian, and I were grouped together on a page and called 'The Brains'.

I had to explain to my mother that it meant we were intellectuals but that it probably wasn't meant nicely. There was also a page for the 'Knitting Betties' (the girls who always got out their knitting gear in class) and the page for the 'No Names' (the people no one could come up with a name for.)

'Fusspot' can be translated as 'having high standards'; and at eighteen, we were all fusspots, of course — snobbish intellectuals in the eyes of our simpler classmates who liked to party. And then we all moved to Berlin where anyone who thinks they're someone ends up.

That's really how basic it is.

And yet it's true.

Speaking of true.

It's a battle cry, Bea. I'm using it in a crude effort to make my story seem plausible. It'd be smarter to assume that it seems true by itself. Because you know Friederike! And you understand the thing with the show-offs ending up in Berlin.

The truth is: these are all just words. True words, of course, because why would I write rubbish?

Another story you'll hear again and again, ad nauseum (or until you're ready for the gas chambers, as my anti-intellectual classmates would have said, not understanding why that was problematic) is that, sooner or later, the truth will out. Concealing the truth doesn't work, and hushing it up definitely doesn't either, and sweeping it under the carpet means it will come back to bite you in the bum. So I'm not even going to try.

I learn from stories, you see.

It's better than following the principles of a mythical 'social consensus', which we call 'common sense' in a crude effort to make it seem plausible.

'Hey, everybody knows that people grow apart, especially when you're over forty and have kids.'

Yes, exactly. In my case, that means we'll all be out on the street in January, or our rent will be three times as high.

'Everybody knows that children cost money, grow up, and need more space. You should have thought about whether you could afford them in the first place.'

Yes, exactly. I've lived beyond my means, and now it's my problem where that leaves me.

Not in Zone A, that's for sure.

Living in the city centre is not a human right, as a member of the Berlin Housing Department put it. And in a couple of years, perhaps even months, this too will be incorporated into 'common sense'; and anybody who thinks differently is a late starter.

I'm not going to complain. Pity is for the meek; and for mice whose idea of contributing to the common good has been misunderstood. Those who complain and those who are out of touch steal empathy from the others.

There's no way I'm going to want something I can't have. I don't want to be a victim. I'm strong. I can get a grip on my feelings, and, if need be, tell myself lies, like the fox who says the grapes are 'too sour' because he can't reach them.

Another one of those stories, Bea.

We're surrounded by stories.

'Everybody knows that' is one too, albeit a very short one.

As long as Friederike tells hers, I'll tell mine, in which the main character takes 'Everybody knows that' to mean 'Shut your mouth, bitch, and just deal with it.'

I know you hate it when I swear. You're the one thing that keeps me in check, my sweet angel, you're my better self—

No. You're just my daughter. And I'm afraid for you. Of you? They're probably the same thing.

I want you to be happy, or at least not be blamed if you and your brothers and sister make a mess of your lives. But how do you measure a successful life? What do you all need from me? What should I give you? What should I spare you from? What the hell should I *do*?

'No matter what you do, it's wrong,' as the perennial adage for parents goes. It's supposed to remove blame, but the effect doesn't last. Because in the long run, every parent wants to do what's right.

One way is to do the opposite of your own parents. Even if they did nothing wrong, you're bound to find something, because no matter what parents do, it's wrong, so they definitely did something wrong. Which you, in turn, can do differently, and rightly. Wrong again.

Tell me how it's possible not to lose your mind over these things.

Speaking of losing your mind.

Ingmar has decided I'm mad. And that touched a nerve, because he's a doctor and has the authority to put people into psychiatric wards.

When people annoy me, I often say they're mad too, of course, like Ingmar, for example. But it's different when I say it, because it's just my way of stating that I don't agree with his opinions and don't like how he expresses them, especially considering what might happen to me as a result of his opinion — i.e., being committed to a psychiatric ward.

Ulf replied that I shouldn't make myself out to be the victim. I started it, after all, and now it was enough.

'But it's not enough.'

And off we went again.

'You're not the one to decide that, Resi.'

'Who does then?'

'Everybody has to decide for themselves.'

'Exactly. And I'm saying that it's not enough for me.'

'We know that. You made sure we all knew that.'

'Who's "we"?'

'You could have been a part of it.'

'But I didn't want to.'

'Why not?'

'Because it wasn't enough!'

And again, from the top.

'That's just your opinion.'

'Yes, exactly.'

'Keep it to yourself.'

'I'm a writer.'

'Then write about yourself.'

'That's exactly what I did! I. Didn't. Think. It. Was. Enough!'

And so on, and so on, until one of us gives in or starts a fist fight.

Frank raised his fists. He saw my story as a declaration of war and threw everything he had at me.

For the record, after my book was published, I was so shocked when I found out who felt humiliated and who felt insulted that I thought I'd have to stop being a writer. I hadn't meant to hurt anybody, but then it occurred to me that I hadn't expected Ingmar to stop being a doctor.

No matter what you do, it's wrong. Power gives you responsibility, and if I stop doing what I do now, it'll be my fault for not having done anything.

People who want to avoid this dilemma have to die. I mean, withdraw from life. And definitely not have children, even though children are a reason to ignore the dilemma and keep going to the best of your ability and conscience. Somehow. By doing the opposite of what your parents did, or by telling stories to help you understand how the world works. Either because of or despite these stories, I had you all vaccinated. And who did it? Ingmar, of course.

Idea for a TV film: the main character, Resi — a writer who has withdrawn from professional life because she's afraid of abusing her power, using the wrong words or being narrow-minded (and who now devotes all her time to her family and their best interests) has her toddler vaccinated by Dr Ingmar; the child suffers brain damage and falls into a coma.

The worst part is that Resi was against any kind of vaccination to begin with — Too risky! Just more profits for the pharmaceutical industry! — but let herself by persuaded by Dr Ingmar.

Resi didn't want to be lumped together with anti-vaxxers who are just stay-at-home mums with nothing better to do than look after sick kids.

She sues Dr Ingmar but loses, because she signed a form listing the possible risks and side effects, and she only has herself to blame.

I'm a writer. I just do what I think is right. (And what was it again? To vaccinate? Or not? Talk? Or shut my mouth? To act or do nothing, reject or endorse, do things the same way or entirely differently?) And anyway, my children have chosen me, and they'll have to stick with me through thick or thin, because they know me and care for me.

Whoops. No. That's exactly what I expected of my old friends.

A message to all my old friends: you won't like this. 'This is where we part ways,' as Vera wrote in her break-up email to me. I think it's sentimental and twee, but on the other hand, I imagine that's exactly why you all like it. And you're bound to believe it's better than anything I have come up with, so please stick it up your arses.

Bea hates it when I swear. She's my eldest, but still just about young enough to love me anyway. To want to see and somehow understand me, in other words.

She has no choice; she's still dependent on me.

Is it violent to address my text to her?

Maybe. But I also had her vaccinated. She could have died.

Only yourself to blame

Bea was born on a cold morning in Leipzig, over fourteen years ago. I could grumble and call it 'one of those winters' as if I were looking back on the old days.

Back then, the winters were still winters, and people heated with coal brought by rattling diesel trucks, which was lugged down into the damp brick cellars by men with soot-covered faces wearing aprons. Can you imagine that, Bea?

No. Fourteen years is a long time for you — your whole life. For me, it's short, because I can remember exactly how our cellar smelled, and how I stole a second coal bucket from our neighbour's cellar towards the end of my pregnancy so I could balance the weight of the coal evenly. I had one half-full bucket in my left hand, another in my right, and you in my belly in the middle. It was minus 15 degrees outside, and the pavements were covered with thick ice.

It wasn't the old days; it was the Noughties, the start of a new millennium, with mobile phones and cyberspace, geothermal underfloor heating, and cellars made of reinforced concrete. But where we lived, everything still looked like it had done in the past, and that meant low earners like Sven and me could afford to rent a flat there.

I could have given birth to Bea in a modern hospital, but a midwife with an ear trumpet came to our house instead. Because we wanted it that way. You can't leave matters of life and death to machines, or to people who have turned themselves into extensions of machines. That was crossing a line, Bea, we thought. Bea, are you listening?

The midwife held the ear trumpet to my belly and searched for your heartbeat. With her hands, she felt your position, and said everything was fine — you were lying the right way around and would come out easily — and she was right.

Sven had a decent fire going. Twice as many briquettes in the coal stove as usual.

Sven cut your umbilical cord, Bea, you hear me? That's important. There were three of us present at your birth: the midwife, Sven, and me. And although you were born using methods from the olden days, the whole thing still cost a whopping 300 euros in surcharges. Whereas if you'd been born in the hospital, using all sorts of hi-tech equipment and with five doctors present, it would have been covered by our health insurance.

You only have yourself to blame, you might say, but that's not true. Some decisions take you down one path, and others another; I want you to know that. What's covered and not covered, what's paid for and isn't, is open to negotiation. It's all about power. It's never too early to realise that the circumstances in which you live are not arbitrary and certainly not inevitable. They are based on decisions and beliefs, and the next thing you should ask is: whose?

My mother, for example, was told by the midwife in the modern hospital where I was born that breast milk was harmful and nursing would ruin her breasts. She should use formula instead. And then the nurse pulled out a sample she'd been given by a rep from a food company that had global operations, even back then, and gave it to my mother. The rep's briefcase contained not just samples, but the results of a scientific study too, which was why he didn't need to pay a commission to the midwife for getting new mothers addicted to his product. The midwife was convinced she was doing the right thing. My mother ate nothing but semolina for weeks on end to be able to afford the exorbitant formula while her breast milk dried up.

'Okay,' you say, 'it's a pity that Granny couldn't afford to buy herself a steak back then.' But just a moment, madam, I'm not finished yet. Yes, it was a pity for Granny; but for the children in Kenya and Kuala Lumpur, it was fatal, because *their* mothers diluted the formula to half the required amount for their babies' feeds, and their children starved. And, of course, you could also say: 'They only have themselves to blame' and 'Why didn't they listen to what the midwife told them and while they were at it, why didn't they stick to what it said on the leaflet?' And that's exactly what the food company lawyer said too, adding that their study proving the harmfulness of breast milk wasn't manipulated, but well founded. Because contaminants *had* been found in breast milk — such as fertilisers and insecticides for the corn that was needed to feed all those cows whose milk was the basis of formula. Do you see what I'm saying, Bea?

———

Bea sighs. Gives me that look that still has a touch of the newborn about it: I wonder when it'll disappear once and for all, and whether I'll scare it off with my stories.

Maybe I will. But I've made my decision. I'm going to teach Bea the facts of life, no holds barred. I'm going to tell her everything I know.

So — January 2003; Leipzig.
A freezing winter morning back in the old days. An expensive, self-imposed home birth. The coal stove was so hot I almost wanted to yank open the window. A little girl, my first child, was born.

There was Sven who cut the umbilical cord, his face rigid with concentration. His expression changed to delight when the midwife handed him his new baby so she could sew up the tear in my perineum. Oh, I nearly forgot. Do you know what a torn perineum is, Bea?

Bea covers her ears and sings. She doesn't like me going into this much detail, but a torn perineum provides the perfect opportunity to talk about the female sex organs. I am determined to do this more often in the presence of my children, even if I can't find the words. And how am I supposed to find them? No one gave me any.

The midwife strapped on a headlamp. The kind that campers and rock climbers wear. So that she didn't have to put on the overhead light and dazzle the baby, but could still see what she was doing.

I don't know if I can get across how much this woman between my legs with the lamp strapped to her forehead meant to me, and the fact that her expertise didn't need any bells and whistles.

The midwife borrowed her idea from outdoorsy people. She came up with an ingenious solution to satisfy her need for bright light and the baby's need for dimness. She used her head not once, but twice or three times over, kept her hands free, and looked so lovely with those elastic headbands crisscrossing her hair. The midwife made me realise that the airs doctors put on when attending to patients — which I'd thought were intrinsic to being a doctor — were just that. Instead of putting on airs, she put on her headlamp. With her bottom lip sucked in, she wondered whether three stitches would do: and then decided they would.

I really don't want to torture you, darling. In a moment I'll get back to the part about how sweet you looked in Sven's arms, and how happy we both were to have you.

Just one more word about my torn perineum. After two days, I looked at it using a hand mirror. I was terrified of what I was going to see because my muff — sorry, not a nice word either — no longer felt as if it were mine. It felt swollen and deformed and very alien. Much more alien than it looked. It took a while for the bruising to go down and the tear to heal completely, but then my muff was mine more than ever, probably because we had been through so much together.

Sven gave you back to me, and you started to feed. From my breast, which I don't want to emphasise too much because, in the meantime, the propaganda has done a U-turn. Breastfeeding is a must these days, an opportunity to test whether you've understood what it is you have to do. What if you feel there's no alternative to breastfeeding? That's right: immediately stop and think. Who says so, and why? Who stands to gain from it and who to lose? What path might have led you there?

It might have been me, for example, with my speech on formula: a paving stone on the path to breastfeeding. My voice, telling you it's not only convenient and cheap but intimate and beautiful too. Ask Sven, and he'll tell you a different story. Like, no sooner was I sewn up than he had to give you back. Or perhaps he was relieved to hand you over? You see? I have no idea what he thought.

When you were born, I didn't know anything. It would have put the fear of God in me had I believed in Him and His Grand Design, but I'm a heathen. It wasn't Him who gave you us; we made you. And then — Pow! Pow! Pow! — your brothers and sister too.

But if there is no God, and everything is our own decision, and we choose our own path, we have a huge responsibility to bear. Then when I hear you say: 'You only have yourself to blame', it's an echo of my own terror, and instead of forbidding you to say it, I should thank you for the tip. Thank you, darling, so far, so good! But now please take your hands away from your ears.

I thought children liked hearing about their births. In my mind, I see families sitting together in harmony, celebrating the myth of their origins, ideally all cuddled together on a sofa, ideally in autumn. In the hearth, a wood fire crackles — no, too much fine-dust pollution. They are nestled close together by candlelight, eating biscuits and drinking hot chocolate. They're thinking back to the white-hot stove in Leipzig that winter morning long ago. They say: 'You were our bundle of joy. That's why we called you Bea — it means "happiness".'

But you're angry with me. Your happiness isn't showing. Everything gets on your nerves — the sofa is too small for the six of us. The thing about autumn is true: next week the half-term holidays begin and everybody, literally *everybody*, is going away. Apart from us. Yet again we'll be stuck at home in our cluttered flat where I'm desperately trying to find some candles. Wait, Bea! I'm not finished yet!

Don't worry. You'll come round in the end.

At Christmas, if not before, we'll turn into that family from the hot-chocolate ad, and then even you like to be in the bosom of your family, because without happy families there is no Christmas.

We will gather in the stable, with Mum as the medium, and the little child as the saviour, and both will be so adorable and silent—

Jesus Christ, no, that's wrong: at Christmas, we won't even be here. Our flat isn't ours, it's Frank's, and he's decided to terminate the lease, and that's that.

It can't be true.

I just can't believe it.

'Nothing lasts forever.'

'Children cost money.'

'It's a dog-eat-dog world.'

And: 'We've made it.'

Want to hear any more pearls of wisdom, Bea?

Bea isn't listening — she's at school. School isn't over yet, so I can still sit here and write in peace and quiet.

I sit in my broom cupboard, which is actually the pantry no one needs anymore. These days, most people use it for their washing machine. But not in our flat. This is where Resi sits and smokes. Smokes and types on her laptop, which is going to give up the ghost any day now. The clock has already stopped, and that's the simplest component of a computer, right? The Wi-Fi is always on the blink, but that's normal. Networks are fragile — I should know, I used to be part of one.

'Sounds like you're making yourself the victim again,' grumbles Ulf inside my head.

Yes, that's true. I stand corrected: I only have myself to blame. My laptop is twelve years old, and everybody knows that devices like these need replacing at least every five years, because they're not built to last.

'O-U-T spells OUT!' the children chant. They do it in unison when one of them is picked up from childcare.

'Nah-nah — your mum's here!' and 'O-U-T spells OUT!' Because when you're picked up, you're out of the game.

Somebody has to be out, after all.

When the kids sang this, I managed to keep a grip on myself. I bit my lip to stop myself snapping back at them.

Kids, I thought, sing all sort of things at the end of the day, and in day care, the day is seven hours' long, and the kids can only get through it by being a team and singing at the top of their lungs — any old thing, all kinds of rubbish.

What, for example, is a cakehole?

'Shut your cakehole' passed without comment for years too. But I don't give kids the benefit of the doubt anymore, nor do they get concessions for ignorance. I've stopped using silent calming techniques to soothe the loud buzzing in my head. None of that works anymore, Bea, do you hear? It's not comforting — it's torture.

From now on, I'm going to avoid pacifying phrases like 'Of course I understand', 'It's going to be fine', or 'It's enough now.'

'It's not enough' is now my motto, or 'It's the last fucking straw' or 'It's all got to come out in the open.'

I'm going to call things by name, and there'll be no more holding back.

In the short time I still have before the landlord rings the bell and shows hordes of potential successors round our flat, I will tell the truth all the time. I can already feel the good it's doing me. I don't give a shit about the time being wrong in the taskbar of my computer, I light another cigarette and—

The school is already on the phone saying that Jack has a headache.

'Oh, really,' I say.

'Yes, really,' says the school secretary. 'He's even crying.'

'Okay, well,' I say, 'he has a cold.'

'You'll have to come and pick him up. He's not allowed to go home on his own.'

When Jack cries, I'm powerless. When the secretary asks me to come in, it's better to do what she says. Perhaps my memory is playing tricks on me, but I seem to remember going home on my own as a kid, no matter where I ached, armed with nothing but a dismissal slip. Maybe I'm wrong. How was it back then?

No truth without proof, as they say. In my case, there are no ready witnesses I can ask, and even if there were, the rules are different today. I'm no longer the child, I'm the mother. And I should be bloody happy that it's nothing more serious.

Here they come again, those pacifying phrases. Without them, I'd never make it to school — where things turn out to be more serious after all.

Jack and I have barely left the secretary's office when he starts crying in earnest and shows me his broken braces.

When Jack cries because he's afraid of my reaction, I'm left with one possible response: to play it down, make light of it.

Maybe his braces used to be worth something. Perhaps I built a wall of threats and sighs, and furrowed my brow bad-temperedly when I was studying the bill from the health insurance in the orthodontist's waiting room. But this wall collapses the moment I see him bawling his eyes out, his bottom lip quivering. I take it all back. I'll do and say and pay anything if he please oh please would just stop crying.

And he stops.

Jack goes to bed to sleep off his headache and the shock. I phone an orthodontist and make an appointment.

Of course I can afford new braces. I can also cope with sitting around in the ugly waiting room reading *Top Gear* for a few more hours, or staring at the fish swimming back and forth inside the green panes of the aquarium, or watching the receptionists creeping about on crepe soles to the break room to take a quick bite from a sandwich or send a text.

During that time, my bad temper will solidify into a new foundation for the next wall of threats, and that's just mine and Jack's fate. It's what connects us: parental concern and childish dependency.

What did I expect, for God's sake?

'Everybody knows that a kid will get sick once in a while.'

'And that dental braces break.'

'And that waiting rooms aren't nice.'

Yes, that's right. And anyhow — we're talking about my Jack! A poster boy for maternal feelings, with braces on his teeth and traces of tears on his dirty cheeks! A real, living boy — how cool is that!

I'll save what I wanted to write for this evening. I have to go and pick up Lynn from childcare. The days are short when they're interrupted by secretaries and orthodontists, eaten into by part-time day-care arrangements—

'O-U-T spells OUT!'

No one forced me to have children.

Except they did.

But I can't go into that now. I have to set off from my broom cupboard; there I go, hurrying along the pavement. Parents come strolling towards me with the children they have already picked up, along with baby brothers or sisters in buggies, and then stop at the baker's where a crowd has gathered.

And I think: thank God I joined the ranks of parenthood. Because who else will buy me a bread roll when I'm old? Or take me by the hand when I have to swerve around crowds? I'd have to risk falling into the gutter with my walker or wait until somebody noticed I wanted to pass.

My kids are my insurance in old age. First, I guide them; later, they'll guide me.

My kids are my gang. I'm the founder and the leader, and at some point, I'll be an honorary member when they take over the business.

When I go into the garden at the childcare centre, I feel that this transition is already taking place. Like a shy au-pair on her first day, I stand at the edge and wait until Lynn notices me, tells the nursery teacher on duty that she's leaving, and takes me to fetch her coat from the cloakroom.

Ten years ago, when I used to pick up Bea from this same centre, things were different. Back then, I marched through to the garden in full possession of my maternal powers, waving wildly, talking animatedly to the other mothers and then stopping off with them on the way home at a nearby playground: a group of tight-knit efficiency, courage, and responsibility for the next generation. When on earth did that change?

'Friendship and money don't mix,' I say to Lynn when we're outside and she's unlocking her bike, just to hear what it sounds like. She doesn't react. Without a story, these kinds of pearls of wisdom don't stick.

Lynn gets on her bike and coasts off in front of me. Her scarf is hanging so far down that it could get caught in the spokes at any minute. Warnings won't help in this case either; the accident will just have to take its course — or I'll have to tell her how Isadora Duncan died. I run after Lynn, catch her up, and wrap her scarf around her neck.

She brakes in front of the crowd at the bakery.

'Oh, all right,' I say. Even though the paediatrician warned me at the last check-up to stop giving her snacks, or she'll fall off the 'norm' curve.

Still, there's no lift in our building, so she'll probably burn off half a mouthful of her roll just by climbing the stairs.

List to self, to be worked on at the next opportunity:

Define 'free will'.

Research the psychology of disillusionment.

Find out whether it is a paradox or simply logical that late starters are especially good at teaching third parties the facts of life.

Find out what data is used at children's health check-ups to establish the 'norm' for weight curves.

And, for once and for all, stop referring to our flat as 'ours'.

I am sorry that everything is so disjointed. I'd like to be stricter, have a more straightforward narrative, and be a comfort for all those in need. But I am who I am, and I won't pretend that I have the same conditions as, say, Martin Amis.

I can refer to the wooden board that I screwed into the crumbling walls of my broom cupboard with plasterboard screws as a 'desk'; I can keep referring to 'my' broom cupboard and in that way make it mine. I am the main character of this story, and a writer by profession to boot!

But before I can blame myself for losing my flat and having children, I quickly have to fix dinner, clean out lunch boxes, check schoolbags, cut fingernails, yell quite a lot, enforce rules, give a few lectures, read aloud, supervise toothbrushing (twice to be on the safe side) and replacing the cap on the toothpaste tube, hang up towels, and yell a bit more. Apologise for yelling, pick up and fold clothes that have been chucked in corners, shake out lumpy quilts, fetch glasses of water and, of course, look for cuddly toys and give goodnight kisses. Don't worry! I'm not complaining; I only have myself to blame. Why did I have these children? I can answer that question when they're all asleep; I can assert who I am when I have time to write again.

That's why this is exactly the opposite of a well-formed, elegantly written novel.

'Well-formed and elegant.'

Well-formed with proportions of 90 x 60 x 90, an ideal for which Demi Moore had two lower ribs removed, and which looks elegant in silk stockings and a shift dress, an outfit that you not only have to wear but also know how to move in.

My name is Resi, my husband is Sven, and our kids, who are fourteen, eleven, eight, and five, are Bea, Jack, Kieran, and Lynn.

We were bonkers to have them: it was our decision, so we only have ourselves to blame.

We had Bea because we thought it would be wonderful to have children. Then Jack, so that Bea wouldn't be an only child. Kieran, so that we didn't seem like a typical family. And Lynn? You could call it hubris. Or cabin fever?

Two artists without two pennies to rub together with four children. I have no idea how we manage, but recently I realised that 'How on earth do you manage?' isn't a question or a compliment. It's a euphemism that shows the person asking doesn't think your life is manageable, and that you're stupid to even try.

'I wouldn't want to be in your shoes,' is the real meaning behind 'How on earth do you manage?' and it doesn't make it any easier to realise that all those friendly fellow mums and non-mums, journalists and editors, colleagues and friends who asked this question in the past were actually bloody glad not to be in my shoes.

You can talk yourself into believing that life is exciting with so many children, that it's all fun and one big adventure. Because they're wonderful human beings; and it's wrong that that sounds sarcastic, because they really *are* wonderful human beings.

Children can't be a mistake, despite the fashion of regretting motherhood these days. And I don't want to hear 'Surely there's no law against saying …' — because no, there isn't, but you still can't say it. Not if we believe in the dignity of all people.

It's best to follow the rules of what you can say about refugees, and keep it low-key, such as: 'Logistically, it's quite a challenge', which is absolute rubbish because the state pays, and the state is rich, and there aren't that many in the end. The reason I call them 'the hoard' or 'the brood' is just to cast myself in the role of an extremely valiant animal trainer, who really does 'manage' somehow.

We weren't forced to do what we did. We could have saved our money and spent our time doing something else. This intergenerational exercise in maximum stress could have been prevented through the use of condoms! But I thought it would be nice. I'd read too many glossy mags, watched too many Astrid Lindgren films; Angelina Jolie and her clutch of kids. *Midsummer Night in Noisy Village*. Arnie Grape's birthday.

But in our family, the music is somehow missing, and the film just carries on playing. The soundtrack and pictures aren't in sync.

As for the dialogue:

Child: 'Is there anything to eat?'

Mother: 'Don't talk to me in that tone of voice.'

Child: 'What? I'm just asking if there's anything to eat.'

Mother: 'You're not just asking, you're snapping. How about saying "Hello" first?'

Child: 'Hello, is there anything to eat?'

We're all stuck in the making-each-other-happy trap. And woe betide us if we don't.

Mother: 'Turn it off and tidy your room.'

Child: 'I just need to finish this level!'

Mother: 'Turn it off. I'm going to count to three.'

Child: 'Bloody hell, you're so stupid!'

Mother: 'One, two—'

Child: 'No!'

Mother: 'Yes.' Grabs tablet from child. 'You'll never stop unless I take it away. You're addicted.'

Child (in a flat tone): 'You haven't counted to three yet.'

Mother: 'What? Clear up your room now. It's disgusting. Don't you realise that animals are breeding in among all this?'

Child touches the pile of stuff with the tip of one toe.

Mother: 'Come on. Get a move on.'

Child's tears fall onto pile of stuff.

Mother: 'What's the matter?'

Child doesn't answer. In his world, he's probably died or lost a bunch of diamonds and skills. Mother has no idea about the child's world, child's life, or child's skills.

Mother: 'I have to tell you to clear up. And if you only ever sit around playing with your tablet, you'll turn out stupid and fat, and your tendons will get shorter, and your feet won't touch the ground in the real world, and animals will breed in here. Do you think I enjoy doing this?'

Child: (in a flat tone): 'Yes.'

Mother: 'Really! So you think I clear up after you all day and spoil your fun because I enjoy it?

Child: 'No.'

Mother: 'Well. I don't. I don't enjoy having to say the same thing all the time, not one little bit! "Turn that thing off, clear up, lay the table, brush your teeth!" Maybe you could do it without me asking for a change? And why on earth are you crying?'

Child: 'Because you're shouting at me?'

Mother: 'But why am I shouting at you?'

Child: 'Why should I brush my teeth in the middle of the day?'

Somehow this scene didn't come up in the pictures that flashed through my mind when I thought of the word 'family'. But I can't say I was innocent either. After all, I grew up in a family, and it was definitely nothing like Lisa's in *Noisy Village*.

I was the child, not the mother.

Is that the secret?

The good thing about having four children is that, as a rule, at least one of them seems happy at any given moment.

But then you start wondering if it's real, or just necessary so that the system doesn't collapse. And in truth, it's the happy child who suffers most — subconsciously, from the pressure of having to keep up the harmony. That's the child who will be horribly damaged in the long run.

Keeping the emotions of six people in check at the same time is impossible. And still, it's my greatest wish.

At least Sven understands me, so well that he can tell me what not to do.

Mother to child: 'You have to write your end-of-year letter to Kerstin. It's due in by tomorrow.'

Child: 'Not doing it, don't feel like it.'

Mother: 'It's not about whether you feel like it. It's homework.'

Child: 'So? It's bullshit homework.'

Mother: 'If you don't do it, you'll get into trouble. Believe me, I know about these things. Better to do it quickly and forget it again just as quickly. Just pretend you don't mind.'

Child (after a brief pause): 'I'm not talking to you anymore.'

Mother: 'What's it got to do with me? I didn't think it up as homework! Okay, I told you to do it, but only because I know how things work. You could write that you think it's a stupid exercise.'

Child: 'So I should just write "bullshit homework"?'

Mother: 'Well, at least that's honest. Write a real letter from person to person. From Kieran to Kerstin.'

Kieran: 'I'm not talking to you anymore.'

Kieran presses his lips together. His eyes fill with tears, but he manages not to let any run down his cheeks. His lips are completely white.

Me: 'What's the matter? What did I do? Sven, say something!'

Sven: 'Like hell I will. I'm staying out of it.'

Me: 'Great. Leave me with the problem.'

Sven sighs. 'Sorry.'

Me: 'What are you sorry about?'

Sven: 'You and your problems.'

Me: 'I don't have any problems!'

Sven: 'Are you sure?'

Me: 'My only problem is that Kieran isn't talking to me anymore. I always get walked over!'

Sven: 'Then stay out of it.'

Me: 'And then what? Who's going to make sure that Kieran doesn't get into trouble?'

Sven: 'It seems like he's already in some.'

Me: 'And it'll only get worse!'

Sven doesn't say anything.

Me: 'Go on, say it!'

Sven: 'No, I won't! I'm not going be dragged into this! It's enough that you're being dragged into it!'

Me: 'You make it sound like it's a weakness! But it's me who keeps this whole show on the road!'

Sven: 'You keep yours on the road. Kieran keeps his. I keep mine, Jack his, Bea hers.'

Me: 'And I'm the one who keeps everybody's!'

Sven shakes his head.

I've been conned. I don't know by whom, and I'm not blaming anybody.

What I do know is that I couldn't have known. No one told me the truth about having children; how humiliating it is not to be a role model for them, the madness of family life, the prison of marriage, and the misery of being a parent.

I want my children to be happy. Is that too much to ask? Yes.

I make supper. It calms me down to think about going into my broom cupboard later when everyone's in bed and writing all this down. I'll scribble about how it feels to slice an entire loaf of bread, how my arm nearly falls off and I wonder why I didn't buy sliced bread in the first place. It wouldn't go stale — everything gets gobbled up here in an instant. I'm clearly in denial about the obvious: I have four children who need feeding. And not with just any old food! So why is there nothing but saturated fat to put on their sandwiches? Everybody knows it's unhealthy, that ninety per cent of peanut butter is palm oil, which is made by cutting down rainforests, which are supposed to make the oxygen we'll breathe in the future. Do I want to suffocate my children? It doesn't matter if they like peanut butter — you're not supposed to give it to them. Just like liverwurst, which is made with the waste from mass factory farming and is contaminated with antibiotics and artificial preservatives. What the hell am I doing?

I make sandwiches, secure in the knowledge that I'll be back in my broom cupboard in a couple of hours, transformed into the Resi who can find words for this madness and sort it out or get even more entangled, get it under control or blow it apart. The Resi who is most herself.

Not everybody knows that

As for my birth, I've no idea what it was like. Natural, of course! My mother and father were married, and, being the second child, I was definitely wanted. A modern hospital with modern neonatal care; the criminal story about the formula only came out much later. And even when my mother, Marianne, eventually told me about it, the message wasn't that she'd been duped by Nestlé's greed for profits, but that *not* being breastfed hadn't done me any harm. She was trying to produce certainty, and the name of the game was 'Making Children Strong'. I was the focus of most of her stories and, as far as my birth went, there wasn't much besides being wanted, conceived, born, and healthy.

Renate shakes her head indignantly. To her, I sound ungrateful. What's that supposed to mean? Would I have preferred a more tragic fate?

No.

But my perspective on my birth is a bit limited. What about the others? What worries and desires, hopes and concerns did my parents, sister, relatives, friends, and fellow citizens have? I never found out. I wasn't told about them. Until I had children myself, I had no idea how powerless and power-drunk becoming a mother can make you. What if I hadn't been healthy?

I asked Raimund, my father. He looked at me as if I was setting a trap for him before he said: 'Well, we'd have done everything in our power for you.'

'What was in your power?'

'I don't know. Thankfully we didn't have to find out.'

'Did Marianne have nightmares before I was born? That she might give birth to a monster? Or a headless child?'

'No idea. And even if she did, what do you think that would have meant?'

'I just want to know what you felt!'

'We looked forward to having you.'

My parents didn't have much money. She was a bookseller, he a draughtsman: both worthy jobs with low salaries. But highly regarded jobs, associated with intellect and creativity rather than sales and services. Marianne might have owned the bookshop she worked in or have studied German philology, and Raimund might have descended from a long line of architects but just have been the more practical type.

My brother, sister, and I were all healthy. None of us needed special aids, prosthetic limbs, or anything else that would have been expensive. The desire to move up in the world was enough, a good disguise; we definitely weren't poor. The poor were people who had never heard of Le Corbusier, the people for whom he built his brutalist buildings.

We lived in Stuttgart in a 1960s house that had been converted into flats. Above us was an old couple, below us a teacher who lived on her own, an orthopaedic surgery, and an accountant's office. I would have liked there to have been more children in our building; I didn't know why there weren't, and it never occurred to me to ask.

In the kitchen, there was the aforesaid, preordained West German PVC floor, and wall-to-wall carpeting everywhere else. My parents eventually removed it in their room because it had been laid over a herringbone parquet floor. The wood was loose in places, and the adhesive strips that had kept the carpet in place at the edges couldn't be removed without using solvent, which would have corroded the varnish, so they left them there, collecting fuzz.

No one wanted to bother the landlord.

There was woodchip wallpaper on the walls, which was repainted every couple of years by my parents. Marianne liked renovating. Raimund didn't, but he acquiesced.

And I learned all the necessary skills: how to use masking tape, stir and apply paint, wash out the brushes. Window frames, paint, hand-me-down clothes — there was always enough to go around somehow.

DIY is seriously back in fashion. But not for me, Bea, d'you hear? For me, it's part of the cover-up. Perhaps you *can* do it all yourself, but there are differences as to why you do it: out of snobbery or to save money, to relieve boredom or because your bank account is empty.

Making babies is part of the same thing. And having them. And breastfeeding.

You can buy human organs on the darknet and breast milk on the internet, and there's a service for peeling asparagus at the local supermarket, and there's Friederike asking me whether I could cut Silas's and Sophie's hair too, because it's really great that I know how to do everything myself.

For a long time, I was proud of this. I looked down on people who didn't know how to decorate a room, cook, or repair the toilet; people who always asked their parents for money, who even had them buy their prams, despite eBay. Yes, the second-hand ones have ugly patterns, obviously, but then, add a new cover and you have a one-off! So much cooler than an 800-euro model! Dishing out 800 euros for something like that, how pathetic. Needing parents even though you are one yourself.

I was so practised in DIY to compensate for my non-existent budget that I not only ignored the reasons and limits of these home renovations, but also forgot to ask who stood to gain from them. And now it's up to me to cobble together a new flat, perhaps out of egg cartons and pipe cleaners. I'm left thinking how much further I might have gone. Perhaps I'd have breastfed Silas and Sophie if Friederike had asked me? Been a surrogate mother?

'Everybody knows that,' Friederike said when we were sitting outside the café in the sun.

It was autumn three years ago, when things had already become quite tricky between us, but we still met regularly. No longer at their house, though; preferably outside, in public. We sat there and chatted, and I complained that I had to pay for two childcare and two school excursions in one month, and Friederike replied, 'Everybody knows that. You have to think about whether you can afford children in the first place.'

I stared at her. She didn't return my look but gazed instead at the people walking through our neighbourhood, past the boutiques that stocked designer clothes. It was impossible to tell who could afford them and who couldn't, who did DIY or paid for the services of others. Friederike and I probably looked the same too, except, at that moment, I might have looked aghast; incapable of responding, in any case. Was that the beginning of the end of my friendship with Friederike or the beginning of my switch to reality? Because she was right, of course. Children cost money, and you shouldn't buy what you can't afford.

Vera was also sitting at the table and stared at her plate, dabbed up her cake crumbs, and said nothing, which was okay because she might not have heard. Since Leon's birth, Vera had mostly been caught up with herself, on the verge of collapse and constantly mulling over all the wrong decisions she'd made, so perhaps Friederike's statement wasn't directed at me but at Vera and all the other mothers who always complained and moaned and looked for sympathy. Everybody had too little money, too little sex, blocked drains, and slipped discs. They all should have known! Money doesn't grow on trees, partners lose their appeal, and desk jobs ruin your back. Things you flush down the toilet don't disappear forever just because you can't see them anymore!

I should have known, and wondered why I didn't, whereas Friederike obviously did. Was she more intelligent than me? Had she done the maths to check whether she could afford to procreate? Ingmar being a doctor was a coincidence, in my opinion: handy, without a doubt, but not part of her calculation.

It wasn't until I'd thought about it for a long time — in the sanctity of my broom cupboard — that I realised Friederike had known since the age of fourteen what it meant to build a family: you had to pay attention to the foundations.

The Bible quotation she picked out for her confirmation was about the foolish man who builds his house on sand.

And mine? The one about beholding the birds who don't sow or reap, but who God feeds anyway.

The house in which Friederike and Ingmar and all my old friends have lived for four years has a three-metre-thick concrete foundation and no cellar. It doesn't need one, Ulf said, they could easily cut corners there. No one stores potatoes these days, and a cellar wouldn't protect them in the next war; it would only flood after heavy rain.

The rooms have custom-fitted built-in cupboards so that you can store your stuff upstairs, and anyway, it's outdated to own everything. The sharing economy is on the up. Friederike and Vera had a clear-out before they moved. If they need a drill, they borrow one, and children's clothes that don't fit anymore go straight to the Syrians.

I'd like to be like that.

I like minimalist rooms and clean surfaces, but Sven keeps all the boxes just in case something breaks, and we have to exchange it or make money on eBay. And I can't complain. I save the zips from ripped trousers and buttons from torn shirts. Who knows, you might need them again, and you'd be glad to have them.

Our cellar is bursting at the seams with precautions against all kinds of eventualities.

Our cellar isn't our cellar either — why can't I get that into my head? DIY has its limits when it comes to building a house.

As a writer, I should at least have married the heir to a fortune or a high earner: it's an either/or situation, self-fulfilment or marrying for love. The two don't go together, at least not in times of declining resources and rising sea and rent levels.

I'm a late starter, Bea. Honestly. I've fallen for romantic dreams and look where's it's got me: a low-wage job and four children, a rented flat that obviously doesn't belong to me, an adorable but equally low-earning husband, and a flooded cellar full of soggy boxes and rusting zips.

'You're all doing fine,' Renate said.

'What do you mean by "all" and how do you define "fine"?'

'My mother had eleven children. Nine made it into adulthood.'

She looked at me, now serious, her eyebrows no longer raised derisively. As if this statement was the answer to all my complaints, the final retort, the last word in wisdom.

Eleven children, two dead: that probably did say everything.

But then I thought of my four births and how I had enjoyed them. In any case, each delivery had been easier than the one before, and it was probably possible to extrapolate from this. The bigger problem to me seemed to be how to see each child as an individual later on, and how to have room for them all in your thoughts. On the other hand, perhaps this ambition ceased after the fifth child, and you went back to seeing and thinking about yourself.

'What exactly are you trying to say?' I asked Renate.

'I'm certain I wouldn't have wanted her kind of life. And I didn't have it either.'

'Are you sure?'

'Absolutely.'

'How do you know what kind of life she had? Did she tell you? Or is that obvious from the number of children she had?'

'She worked all the hours that God sent. Had no quiet place of her own, no privacy. Never travelled, never met up with women friends, and didn't have any male friends except for my father—'

'You don't know that. Perhaps she led a double life!'

Renate laughed. 'When? Where?'

'In her head. At night. In a secret diary, which she later burned.'

Renate shook her head.

My mother left a diary when she died. In it, there's just one sentence:

'Ate way too much again.'

It's only natural to take this sentence at face value. Ever since I can remember, Marianne had been on a diet. But it could also be a code, heading, or place marker for something completely different.

Hunger has more than one meaning.

And a diary containing one sentence is no diary at all.

Here is an accusation aimed at my mother, Renate's mother, Renate, and all the others who believed it was better to stay silent, put the needs of others first, and place their bets on their daughters' futures: *you were mistaken.* By keeping quiet, sucking it up, and hiding things, you didn't spare us. You just kept us in the dark. And what's more, you made social inequality a private matter, because we saw you weren't enjoying your lives, but we thought it was due to personal reasons. Like you couldn't cope or weren't strong, beautiful, clever, or assertive enough. Or, even worse, that you had us and were forced to sacrifice everything else.

We went out into the world assuming that, unlike you, we were completely free, equal, and architects of our own happiness. And unsuspectingly, naïvely and defencelessly, we walked into the same trap that you had walked into before us. Because you don't really believe anything has changed, do you? Or is that what you want to believe?

I think so.

'That's enough!' was one of your favourite phrases when we argued, as if it was within our power to stop things.

Please remind me, Bea, never to tell you: 'That's enough.'

'I've had enough,' would be the correct thing to say or: 'I'd like it to be enough, so please be quiet now.'

I know how difficult it is. How much we long to have 'made it', no longer be us, and therefore never have to talk about ourselves again; but to speak for and about everybody else instead, and to lead a black-and-white life in which everybody feels, wants, and sees things the same way.

When Vera and Frank were the last to move in with the others from the building group, we sat together in the back garden, staring into the flames in the fire pit that had been lit to mark the occasion, and Vera said: 'All I need now are two cats and I'll be perfectly happy..'

When asked why she wanted two, she replied: 'So that they can play together.' Having two cats must be like having a minimum of two children; the second prevents the first from being lonely. I was reminded of the card that Friederike sent out when Sophie was born, which said: *At last we're a proper family*. Which they evidently weren't when there was just Silas.

So there *is* a recipe for completeness and properness after all, and for the happiness that results from it. Strange how we had always resisted those kinds of recipes until then.

'Each to their own,' we'd said. 'I know my limits.' 'Children? Maybe', and 'Marriage? No way.'

For my fortieth, Vera gave me a card that said: *Congratulations on a new decade!* And underneath, *At forty, you're older and wiser than the rest*, which means looking after number one, rather than number two or three. I'd always assumed that Vera meant that card as a joke, but sitting around the fire that night, I wasn't sure anymore and asked, 'Where are you going to get the cats?'

Vera said: 'Why do you ask?' and I told her about the farm cat I'd had when I was twelve. It came to live in our city flat where there were only bluebottles and silverfish to catch, and so it stared sadly out of the window down at the road, which it wasn't allowed to explore in case it got run over, which would make *me* sad.

Vera frowned, and Ulf said cats couldn't look sad and that I had read this into the cat's expression.

'That's inadmissible anthropomorphism,' Ulf commented, and I shut up, not wanting to ruin the atmosphere with my hair-splitting, which would be construed as envy anyway.

Because, of course, the flat was super, and the house was an ideal place to bring up kids, and everything had gone so smoothly to bring it to completion, and the move and party and friends—

Everything was just perfect.

And if something is perfect, it should, of course, make you

happy. After all, if it's perfect, it's complete. No one can get in the way, and nothing like doubt or ambivalence can get in-between. Do you see, Bea?

And perhaps I *was* envious. I was definitely afraid that you might be, Bea, and that's definitely a sign. Freud calls it 'projection'.

While we were baking the cake for the moving party, I had been very vocal about our new flat — Vera and Frank's old one — which we would soon move into. And how near the building group's garden would be, and that you were always over at Ulf and Carolina's anyway, and that their flat was the nicest in the whole building because they were the planners and architects.

I was trying to convert any possible envy you felt into a feeling of superiority: you might not live in the building, but you were friends with the architect. Not Corbusier in this case, but Ulf: your mum's ex-boyfriend and your godfather.

And, in fact, as soon as we arrived, you did go up to Ulf and Carolina's, so you probably missed the madness of the housewarming.

May 2013; Vera's move and housewarming.
The move and housewarming were on the same day to make it feel like the old days, when we helped each other move, and would celebrate the new place or phase of life or just the good weather with pizza and beer once we'd finished — in the old days, when everything we owned could fit into a Golf or a small rental van.

But that time, a moving firm had to be hired, with two trucks, a furniture lift, furniture covers, and four strong men; and while that was going on, a crowd of guests arrived and exclaimed 'Ah!' and 'Oh!' as they did a tour of the finished rooms, deposited bowls of fruit salad on the polished surfaces, and simply *had* to chink glasses with the new homeowners.

I'd barely stepped through the door with my cake and my boys in tow when Leon jumped out and thumped Kieran in the stomach, but just then Frank appeared, thank God, and said: 'Come into Leon's room, I have something to show you.' Distraction is still the best means to stop violence, and Frank is so good with rough 'n' tumble boys.

He was supposed to be directing the removalists, but somebody else quickly took over. Vera was nowhere to be seen among the throng of guests admiring the flat. Where could she be? Really nice kitchen, by the way. The exposed concrete behind the cupboards set off the shiny doors a treat—

I was fiddling around with a drawer where I guessed I might find a knife to cut the melon and the cake. But the drawer had a child safety lock, of course.

'What are you up to?' asked Vera. At last, there she was, in rolled-up jeans and a colourful scarf around her head. She was out of breath, sweaty, with rings under her eyes and a cold sore on her lip. But she laughed, fell onto the unopened boxes and slipped the clogs off her feet. 'First, a toast!'

There was chaos everywhere, but the cut-crystal glasses appeared as if by magic. 'Cheers, my dears!'

Of course Vera was shattered. The past few weeks had been exhausting, what with Frank putting together the kitchen every night, and she on her own with Willi and Leon, who still couldn't fall asleep unless she lay down with them.

But finally, it was all done, and the big day had arrived.

The sun was shining.

The windows had been cleaned, the sister-in-law had taken care of that; she knew what was needed in all that chaos — sunlight streaming through polished panes, conjured not by magic this time, but by a Swabian-Berliner-by-choice with a kitchen cloth.

The boys were in the kids' room. Frank was helping them make suits of armour from cardboard boxes and duct tape. They were still fighting, but now it was funny and creative. Frank got a beer as a reward. He couldn't drink it, though, because Kieran jumped on his back: once the group leader, always the group leader. Frank had to go back into the fray or else there'd be tears: he did seem a bit reluctant though. Off you go, Frank! No flaking out now! On to the next round! Give a whoop and chase Kieran back into the hallway!

I'm not bitching, Bea. I'm part of this madness. I was glad of the distraction on a Saturday afternoon, and that Frank had taken the boys off my hands and was building suits of armour, and that you were allowed to go up to Carolina and Ulf's and browse through catalogues, and I could let Lynn run around in the garden while I pepped myself up with a glass or two of bubbly, not to mention the totally yummy chocolate mousse.

The kitchen was really lovely. A fantastic flat. I share Vera's dream. Along with countless others. Because it's not a private dream. It's been projected onto our brains. By whom? No idea. Astrid Lindgren? Habitat? *OK* magazine?

There was that photo of Kate Moss's wedding with twenty flower girls between four and fourteen years old, who stood around at her wedding, their tanned limbs showing from under faded yellow dresses.

Somehow, everybody knows what marriage and family should look like to seem laid-back and confident, controlled and free — and Vera and Frank are pretty close. So is the border to envy. It's only natural to assume that I'm looking for the flaw in their perfection, like the fox who says the grapes are too sour.

But there was a gap between Vera's assertion that she was perfectly happy and the way her face seemed to be falling apart. Perhaps it was just the light of the fire, but her features didn't add up to a whole, and if you'd asked me, she was going to burst into tears as soon as the last guest had left.

It's a feeling I know only too well: when you've reached a certain stress level, you need an audience to keep up your façade. Maybe we were only invited for that purpose.

Afterwards at home, I didn't feel very well. The champagne, the chocolate mousse, and the constant supervision — no, *restraint* — of the children didn't go together, after all. In fact, it was precisely the opposite of what we'd wanted. We'd agreed not to become like our parents. We had even agreed on it *with* our parents!

We had wanted to save each other from wising up in the sense of becoming ruthless, grown-up in the sense of being stressed, married in the sense of being trapped, and parents in the sense of being overprotective.

And now?

Scepticism translates into 'being a killjoy' and criticism into 'being a know-it-all'.

I was supposed to keep my mouth shut. It was their business. It was their house: K23.

Woe betide me if I let show that the name alone bugged me with its self-importance, which Ulf and Caroline may have needed for their portfolio, but which soon got out of hand and spread like wildfire, so that no one referred to 'the house' anymore, but only to 'K23', as if it was an institution, like 'Kommune 1'.

Woe betide me if I criticised anything, especially as far as language and names went; first, they wouldn't understand and would accuse me of imagining things, and second, they'd ask me not take that attitude, and third, tell me I was probably just jealous.

It wasn't always like this.

I remember Ulf pointing out to Vera fifteen years ago that she started every other sentence with 'Been there', saying it offended him and he didn't believe her, and that it was probably just a mannerism but irritating for the person she was talking to. And Vera had to admit he was right, which was awful for her, and she became very self-conscious about the way she spoke, went red the next twenty times it slipped out, but then it disappeared, and everybody was grateful to Ulf.

Like me and 'Eh?'. I was weaned off that too, and Ellen was weaned off eating from other people's plates, and Christian weaned off making generalisations that made him sound like his father; except that he didn't target 'shirkers' and 'scroungers', but rather 'short men' and 'only children'.

We did each other a service by pointing out our irritating habits. That's what friends were for.

But not anymore. Now the rule is: no criticism.

Perhaps it'll come back in fashion, but first, the kids have to grow up, and the cement has to really dry, and our friendship has to weather the toddler phase, and the planning application has to be pushed through. How are we supposed to pay attention to finer details with all this stress? We'll have the time and leisure again one day, we tell ourselves. But that's not true, Bea. That day never comes.

Or it comes, but then you still have all those strained, grown-up, salvaged, and cemented relationships, children, houses, and careers that feature unsightly bruises and cracks and strange deformations that have to be bent back into shape, and which aren't any less stressful now than it was to build, design, and raise them.

Didn't we have a different dream? House-squatting rather than home-owning? To live differently? To live together? To live differently together?

I remember Ulf made a vow that he would never, *ever* accept a pfennig from his parents — it was the early 1990s, when money was still marks and pfennigs — because they, in turn, had built their fortune with money from *their* parents, who were Nazis and arms manufacturers, and so it was as brown-tainted as his grandfather's shirt.

K23's façade is light beige. Like delicious vanilla ice cream. The windows are set back into the walls with wooden frames painted in a white glaze that lets the grain shimmer through; in the garden, there are only tender-leafed plants — no evergreens or privets, just birches and lilac trees and bamboo and vines. Not very resistant to constant kicking, and not exactly dirt-repellent: not made to withstand attacks, and if K23 is a castle, then it doesn't look like one from the outside.

'You could have moved in,' Ulf keeps saying.

I don't keep pointing out that he broke his vow. It's not that I want to remind him, but I can't help remembering it myself, and I have to find a place for this memory; and yes, it probably has to do with being older and wiser than the rest. As Winston Churchill said: 'Anybody who's not a socialist by the time they're twenty has no heart. If they are still one at forty, they have no brain.' But I don't want world phenomena, or my friends' odd behaviour, explained to me by birthday cards and Churchill; I'd like to make rhyme and reason of all this myself.

That's another nice phrase about writing right there.

The act of self-empowerment that lies in telling stories is proverbial.

Ulf's mantra goes: 'You could have been a part of this! You could have moved in.' He really seems to think I'm just envious and that if I had everything *he* has, I'd see and feel exactly how he does. And it might even be true, but we'll never find out, because I'm not and I didn't and I probably don't even want to; and this means I'm saying (even if not out loud): 'You didn't *have* to do it, you didn't *have* to build the house, or if you did, you didn't *have* to move in,' and suddenly we're quits, and everything is on the line.

Thirty years ago, when Ulf and I were still together, we really believed there was no difference between us, and that it didn't matter where we came from. There I was, somebody who could only trace their ancestry back to my parents' grandfathers, both of whom they'd known personally; and there he was, somebody whose family tree was bound in a leather book and stood on display in a cabinet at his parents' house. I was the first in my family who had been allowed to take A-levels; his great-grandmother had studied in Heidelberg. It was our mothers' idea not to exclude their families from politics, but to let us children lead the way, even across class boundaries. Which is why I ended up at a *Gymnasium*, and Ulf was not going to attend boarding school on Lake Constance under any circumstances. So we met, and we were equal.

But then there were all these little discrepancies and misunderstandings, molehills that increasingly looked like mountains, and which began to feel painful, and I started asking myself: Am I allowed to mention that? How do I talk about it? How am I meant to find words for something that doesn't officially exist?

February 1989; Stuttgart.

We were seventeen and still living at home. We had made it into the sixth form at school: in two years, we'd be sitting our A-levels.

It was still the 1980s, and the rich still had to pay taxes to build swimming pools for the poor. Our mothers' idea captured the spirit of the age and was also manifested in acts of parliament. So, I knew how to swim, and when the upper grades set off on their annual ski day, I would go with the other upwardly mobile kids to the aqua-fun pool in Sindelfingen and have fun. But then my group of friends — Vera, Friederike, Ulf, Christian, and Ellen, in other words — wanted to spend a weekend skiing at Christian's parents' holiday home in the Bernese highlands of Switzerland.

We were all still living at home, and these homes were differently furnished, but we didn't notice that at all. Christian's parents were the richest by far, and that was just as unimportant as mine being the poorest. The annoying part, though, was that I couldn't ski. I could swim, but we didn't have any skis in our garage. We didn't even have a garage, which I only realised then, and which hadn't bothered me in the least before; quite the opposite, in fact. I didn't like garages. They always stank of petrol, and the whole family had to clear them out once a year, which my friends always complained about. Garages were there to house parents' cars and other junk that didn't interest me, and the door often jammed, or the key was missing, or the automatic opening device didn't work. But along with all the other junk came ski equipment, and with ski equipment came ski holidays and knowing how to ski from an early age, and I lacked all these things, which is why I didn't find the idea of a ski weekend as appealing as the rest of my friends did.

Ulf, who I'd been going out with for nearly two years by then, looked at me pensively and said that skiing was fun, and that he missed it since he'd stopped going away with his parents and spent the holidays with me and the others instead. And that the others felt exactly the same way. And anyway, they weren't that competitive or speed freaks like some, and perhaps I could take a sled, or something to read, or just go for walks during the day until they returned in the evenings. The evenings were the best anyway.

'Okay,' I said, 'then we could just do what we did in the evenings all day long, like we always do.'

But then he said that the evenings were different when you'd done a few hours of exercise — hurtling down slopes, in other words — and I said: 'Yeah, but I can't join in.'

'Yes,' said Ulf sadly. 'I realise that but it's not my fault, and not the others' either.'

Back then, it was already about whose fault it was, I now realise.

In any case, I was at a loss for an answer, and waited to see what they would decide; and then they really did leave without talking to me about it and, at heart, I suppose I couldn't believe it.

I sat at home that weekend and thought about what I would do, meaning the lesson I would learn, as well as the punishment I should mete out.

No one had mobile phones in those days — apart from Christian's dad, who had one in his car, which was parked below their detached house in an underground garage that stank worse than all the others — and that's why I couldn't phone or be phoned, or send a scathing, reproachful, or forgiving text for the next eternal three days. Instead, I argued back and forth with myself in my head.

It was, to put it mildly, awful.

But afterwards, of course, it faded into the background, and life went on and the weekend was over, and I hadn't managed to come to any particularly clever conclusions all alone in my head — certainly nothing about class issues and whether solidarity in such a system can be expected; but something about love instead, with me in the role of Cinderella, whose pride and bravery would shame the prince and even soften him in the end. Not even Cinderella's shoe sprang to mind, or else I might have thought that whatever was too tight or too small for Vera, Friederike, and Ellen, made me, whom it fitted, superior to them. Nothing to do with virginity, though, because we'd all had sex by then.

Afterwards, things just carried on between Ulf and me and the gang: I forgot the whole incident, and no one mentioned it again.

But now the time has come to drag it all out in the open, since 'Everybody knows that' just won't wash. Because that's just the point: I didn't know, and I didn't have any words to describe it. Which meant that I stayed quiet and forgot about it. And it still means that.

Because we are all architects of our own happiness.

I could have gone with the gang and taken my first skiing lessons that weekend. Could have borrowed money from Ulf's parents or stolen it from Christian's dad's wallet. Could have hired equipment in the ski resort or bought it second hand. Okay, not that particular year, because the sales of ski equipment in the primary school gym were always at the start of the season — but if I had really wanted to, I could have caught up, and so, twenty-eight years later, I could have been even with the others.

I could have, but I didn't want to badly enough.

And it's the same with everything else, of course; I could have made better choices, wanted more, worked my way up in steps. First, by making do, and then by cashing in at the right moment.

When the house was in the planning stages, Ingmar spoke to me one morning.

'You know that I've got some money. Some of it is tied up and earmarked for Sissi and Sophie's education. But some of it's free, and I'd like it to be used for the things that money is there for: to create opportunities and give impetus.'

He had intercepted me in front of the school, where I'd just dropped you off, Bea; Kieran in a baby carrier on my back and Jack on the sled. I have no idea why Ingmar turned up like that: Silas was still in childcare back in those days.

I tried to pull the sled although there was barely any snow, but there was no alternative; otherwise I'd have had to carry Jack as well as Kieran, and the sled too. So I dragged it along the pavement, and it made a sound like — well, like grit being pulverised between paving stones and metal runners.

Ingmar pulled up to me in his van that made practically no noise — a hybrid car, already then — with Silas's and Sophie's booster seats in the back. Plush booster seats, the expensive kind. And Ingmar got out and took the baby carrier off my back and got Kieran out, and put him in Sophie's seat. And then he buckled Jack into Silas's seat and stowed the sled in the boot.

'Don't you have to go to work?' I asked.

'Not until nine,' he said with a glance at my baby bump. 'It's really amazing how you manage.'

I thanked him, because I still thought that was a compliment.

Ingmar got out again at the nursery to unbuckle and let out Kieran and Jack, and I went to get out and fetch the sled, but he said he'd wait until I came out and take me home.

When we arrived in front of our flat, I thanked him again, and he smiled and said: 'Of course,' and then he mentioned the thing about money giving impetus, and at first I didn't get it at all, just imagined comic coins with arms and legs and boxing gloves, giving each other impetus and creating opportunities.

Ingmar's smile stayed put, and he said I should talk to Sven — and that he and Friederike would be delighted if we said yes.

That was the first time anybody had offered me so much money: a down payment for a building loan — fifty thousand euros? He didn't name a sum, but it was about being part of K23.

I told Sven who didn't say anything at first.

Then: 'Ingmar must really have a lot of money.'

And I: 'Or must really like us?'

And Sven: 'Friendship and money don't mix.'

And I: 'Perhaps that's exactly what he wants to disprove.'

After that, we didn't know what to do. We couldn't think of anything else to say, and I haven't got a clue what went through Sven's mind over the next few days, but in mine, the words 'fantastic' and 'crazy' alternated: 'fantastic' as in 'wow, this is the big moment,' and 'crazy' as in 'Jesus Christ, there's something not quite right about this.'

During our next conversation, Sven said: 'I honestly think he's a good bloke,' and I said: 'It's easier for a camel to go through the eye of a needle than for a rich man to enter the kingdom of God.'

And Sven said: 'Render unto Caesar the things that are Caesar's.' And I said: 'The wise virgin must always have enough oil in her lamp.'

But that didn't get us much further, and so we thought we should definitely go to a notary and seal the matter with a contract.

Only to realise that there are other kinds of currencies besides euros and cents.

'I don't want to be too closely tied to Ingmar and Friederike,' said Sven in the end, and I said: 'Okay then, let's just leave it.'

Which felt cowardly and petty.

But Ingmar said it was fine.

'I understand,' he said. 'It's a real shame, but I understand.'

How exactly he didn't say, which was a real shame too, because if he had, perhaps I would have understood. Instead, I was depressed by my cowardice, and impressed by Ingmar's generosity — both by his offer and our rejection of it.

He took it in his stride and wasn't insulted in the least.

And I was tense and only had myself to blame and no project.

Vera and Frank thought it was a shame too.

'Then at least take our flat when we move out,' Vera said, and I said: 'Sure, that'd be great,' as Frank served up his quiche Lorraine that we were all addicted to.

'Then at least we'll all be near each other,' I said, and Sven said: 'At least not in Marzahn,' and Frank said: 'To be honest, I'm glad there are still two of us who aren't directly involved.'

'It's still a shame,' said Vera, and prodded the quiche with her fork. 'I mean, it was our idea in the first place!'

And she looked me in the eye and smiled her crooked smile, which I'd already fallen for back at kindergarten: that longing smile, implying something bigger was waiting for us out there, and we hadn't got to the best part yet.

'The idea of a commune, yes,' I said. 'Where we live and work and bring up the children together.'

Vera sighed, and then Leon called from the bedroom, and she stood up.

'Commune?' asked Sven when Vera had left, and Frank shook his head. 'That's not what it is,' and I thought, true, but still — they'll all be living together, and when Vera doesn't come back from the bedroom, which is likely because she always falls asleep next to Leon, then they could all still have breakfast together the next day, which I couldn't do living five blocks away.

And then I was back to brooding over things.

When I add this to the story about the ski trip, Bea, it all gradually makes sense: I was the one who had a problem. Who couldn't just loosen up and come around to the idea. Just like in 1989, when I should have gone to the hut with everybody else. It would have been really great, I'm sure. But no, I had to insist on our differences, dig my heels in, and snub those around me who were trying to find a compromise.

The thing about differences is really tricky.

It's taken me nearly thirty years to tell the story about the ski trip, and even now I'm worried that you or somebody else might think I want to make myself out as the victim. Because that's quite a common accusation aimed at people who point out differences.

Inequality divides us into those with privileges and those without; and for those who want justice, that's a problem, no matter which category they fall into. Ingmar might like being rich as little as I like being poor. Why can't everybody just go skiing, for

Christ's sake? And if this is how things are, can't we at least pretend? So that I don't have to be the loser and Ulf and Ingmar the winners?

There's barely any air in my broom cupboard.

I can't stop smoking, even though it's a pathetic sign of dependence. But I can't air the room either, because then I'd have to stand up and fetch a jacket.

Bea's in the kitchen, making herself a tea. I can hear her walking around, shuffling her feet, clattering the dishes. I bet she wants to talk: after ten at night, she suddenly opens up, or at least doesn't feel like going to bed — she never has.

When she was little, I used to sing to her, one song after the other, because I knew them all by heart. The first survival strategy of a mother with small children: detach your thoughts from whatever is coming out of your mouth. Mum: a pacifying, singing robot.

But that's all over now. I don't want to sing or recite anything else by heart. I want to help my children by helping myself, seventeen-year-old Resi: by asking Ulf, for example, whether he still thinks Resi should have just taken something to read and then everything would have been fine. I want to help the uncertain couple, who shrank back from an opportunity, and ask Ingmar what exactly the opportunity was and for whom: being offered to borrow money, honestly? Or being able to dump money on someone to soothe your conscience?

I don't know where Ingmar got his money from. I haven't known him since we were children, like I have Ulf; he's never made a vow in front of me. I only know that he has always been fascinated with how Sven and I 'manage', how we can bear our atrocious recklessness to bring four children into this world without financial security.

From the very beginning, Ingmar was noticeably interested in my writing and Sven's pictures, especially the production and funding thereof. He always made a big deal about introducing us to people at his parties, explaining to friends and relatives that we were artists and nevertheless — or precisely because of this — the first people in Friederike's circle of friends to become parents.

I was flattered by his curiosity, his reliable presence at readings and exhibition openings, and his attentiveness as a host. I liked listening to how alien our world seemed to him, and I didn't understand that he was serious, or that he was sucking our blood. We were his borrowed plumes. I wasn't aware of the differences in our two worlds, and thought he was exaggerating — and I didn't understand why.

My first inkling came when I was talking to Friederike about Silas starting primary school, and she told me that Ingmar didn't want their school to be the same boring, homogenous sociotype as the building group. That he liked that fact that Silas was friends with kids at childcare who came from underprivileged or immigrant families, who weren't all 'dreadful white upstarts'. It struck me that Ingmar saw poverty as a welcome distinction from himself — when he said things like 'it must be interesting, living so close to the edge' — which seemed utterly absurd.

Only now, six years later, do I understand: Ingmar wanted to lend us to money to have us around, to spice up the building group, so it could be presented to its members and the outside world as a social project. 'Well, we also have low-wage earners on board, you know. Artists …'

If I'd had the merest flicker of class consciousness back then, when Ingmar sat me in his politically correct hybrid car with the plush child seats, I would have laughed at his offer and said: 'Forget it. I'm not playing a part for you. You can't dump your guilt or your money on me. Go and find somebody else, dude.'

But instead, I brooded and fretted, imagining over and over again how things would have turned out if we'd decided to take his money. We might still be friends with Ulf. And definitely with Vera and Frank. Money wouldn't have played a role and we would all still be together, happy, content, and equal—

It's enough to make you weep, Bea.

Because right now, I realise for the first time that I'm in much deeper than I thought.

If I'd had any class consciousness — not just a mere flicker, and the pride of being different and one-upmanship that goes with it, but a real, deep-seated consciousness for how the world works and my position in it — then, of course, I'd have accepted Ingmar's offer. I'd have cold-bloodedly let him dump his money on me and would have played my part without batting an eyelid. Why should I care what purpose I serve him? He would have served my purpose! I'd have been controlling the narrative! And had a flat of my own in the city centre that no one could throw me out of that quickly, whether I was still amusing as their borrowed plume, whether they lost interest, or were even afraid of me.

All of a sudden, I am tired to death.

These things I'm telling you here, child, aren't worth shit.

Controlling the narrative, who am I kidding—

'Mum?' Bea sticks her head around the door. 'Hey, be careful, you're going to suffocate in here.'

'Go to bed, darling.'

'You shouldn't smoke so much.'

'I know. But the main thing is that *you* don't start smoking.'

'No, I definitely won't.'

She stands in the door to my broom cupboard.

'Can you come in a minute?'

'Where to?'

'My room.'

She goes off. Presumes I'm going to get up and follow her—

I'll give myself credit for that today: Bea's faith in my unconditional maternal devotion.

No matter what you do

My alarm clock goes off — gentle, celestial, deceitful sounds, which I swipe away. To the left, so they'll try again in five minutes.

Lynn, though, has been waiting for my alarm to go off and now yanks the door open to ask if she can have a hot chocolate. No, she can't. She tries bravely every morning, and I bravely refuse. Stagger to the loo, bury my head in my hands.

I can't do this yet. I don't want to. I don't know how I'm supposed to wake up.

Not hot chocolate; herbal tea instead.

Herbal tea with brown bread, like in a youth hostel. I take up my position and hold my ground as the youth hostel mother, being hard on myself and all the more so on the others. For their own good, of course. Yes, that's how it is.

And then: snack boxes and PE kits.

I can't do this yet; I don't want to. It's not even properly light outside. When do the clocks go back? Sunday.

From Sunday on, the afternoons will become the problem instead of the mornings. Then it's just gaming and the sofa, because it gets dark right after school and childcare end. What did we use to do as children on autumn afternoons? Made animal figures out of conkers, would you believe.

Kieran wants to put on shorts. Outside it's about eight degrees; on the other hand, boys a hundred years ago used to run around all day in shorts. So, it's just a throwback to his ancestors' values. I tell him he can.

'Teeth!'

I'm hoarse and tired of saying it. What would happen if I never said it again?

Nothing would happen, but nothing happens when I do — nothing, in any case, that amounts to brushing teeth. Toothbrushes hang out of the corners of mouths while hands — 'Just for a second!' — check game scores. Eight clan members were back online at half past midnight; 'Addicts,' criticises Jack. 'And what are you?' says Bea in my tone of voice. Jack farts in reply; Kieran laughs.

'PE kits!'

Jack and Kieran charge out of the door. I hear them in the stairwell jumping down the last steps on each floor. Bea follows them and pulls the door shut.

Now it's just Lynn, sitting in her highchair in pyjamas.

Her legs have outgrown the highchair and her Hello Kitty onesie. Nobody is a baby here anymore—

Suddenly my yearning for them to be old enough to get ready on their own in the mornings flips over into wanting them to stay small forever.

What am I going to do when there's no one to wake up, wash, tell off, and send out of the door?

Sven comes out of the shower.

'Hurry up,' he says to Lynn; but Lynn is incapable of hurrying. She can already do many things that her brothers and sister could only manage when they were at least two years older than she is, but always at her own pace, never on command, and definitely not according to her dad's timetable, which is that he needs to leave now.

She goes into her room and gets dressed.

At least, I hope she does.

Sven eats the boys' half-finished toast and drinks up their tea.

Lynn returns to the kitchen, indeed fully dressed, with her hairbrush in her hand and her hair falling in her face.

'Why do only men go bald?' she asks Sven, who ties her hair into a ponytail, puts on her hat, and holds out her jacket for her to put on while giving a quick summary of sex hormones and their effects.

'So why aren't you?' Lynn asks, and Sven says 'Ciao' to me and 'It has to do with genes too,' to Lynn, and this will probably keep them going until they get to childcare, and I sit here all alone, awake at last but with a lump in my throat; I want to cry for them, put my arms around them all and hug them tightly to my chest, talk to them. Now that they are finally out of the door, I want them close to me and to never let them go, I want to save them—

Woe betide anybody who tries to hurt them out there in the big wide world, doubts their perfection for a second, tries to rival, criticise, or quarrel with them — all the things I do as soon as I'm with them.

Woe betide them!

———

It's quiet in the kitchen: I turn on some music.

Paul Simon is singing that he has to leave. Creep down the alleyway, fly down the highway, before they come to catch him.

Bob Dylan sings that Miss Carefree doesn't know how it feels to live on the edge and out on the street.

Jim Croce sings that he's a fool, but that's exactly why he won't give up his dream; he is and always will be moving down the highway, and his dream will carry him.

The Boss sings that everybody's got a hungry heart.

Mine's thudding and trying to leap out of my chest, but more than that, it doesn't want to be alone. It wants company on a tour bus.

'This is where we part ways.'

When I told Sven, he shrugged.

'They've "made it". Isn't that how they talk? This isn't just where we part ways, it's also the end of theirs.'

'And my hungry heart? What's it going to do without a highway?'

'Sit with a drink in the service area?'

Idea for song lyrics: My hungry heart hitchhikes / my ass is on Sitzstreik / my feet train the moonwalk / my mouth bubbles small talk / my brain is still asleep / my guitar gently weeps.

I don't even have a driver's licence. Have never owned a car, have always been a passenger. Highway songs aren't for me. If anybody, I'm the tramp, jumping on the freight train.

Making music would be so much better. Writing is too close to speaking, and its art gets lost in literacy.

Without music, the lyrics about having a hungry heart seem so trite that I can't sing them out loud.

The last time my father came to visit, Bea, you said: 'I feel so sorry for Grandpa Raimund.' I played it down. 'Why's that? Grandpa's doing just fine,' instead of telling the truth: 'Yes, you're right, Grandpa Raimund's got a hungry heart.'

Everybody does. And the closer you are to somebody, the more their heart touches yours, and then your heart longs to still the hunger of their heart, and because that's not possible, your heart hurts, and you need something to numb the pain.

When you were two, Bea, and Jack was a day old, Sven picked you up from the nursery, and you went to the chemist to get lavender blossom for my sitz bath. Don't worry, dear child, no more torn-perineum stories. At the chemist, you got a packet of gelatine-free gummy bears. Which was an exception, because it was usually a waste of time to make a fuss at the checkout, especially with Sven. But that day, it worked — and why? You remembered when you came home and saw me lying in bed with your baby brother Jack.

You stood there in your much-too-warm quilted jacket and your tiny winter boots and didn't look at us — not at me, not at Jack, just at the gummy bears in your hand. You looked at them, and I looked at you, and saw you were connecting the dots between that packet and how our family had changed. I saw you weighing up the sweets against your bitterness, trying to hold the gummy bears and be pleased. You didn't look up when I said: 'Hi Bea, nice to see you!' but carried on looking at the gummy bears. 'Did you get a packet of gummy bears?' — What a stupid question. You turned on your heel and marched off.

Off down the highway.

Oh, how my heart trembled when I saw your hungry one setting off.

And you feel sorry for Grandpa Raimund, Bea; you see him sitting at our kitchen table drinking coffee and eating cake, and you realise that cake isn't enough to satisfy his hungry heart.

But you're also realistic enough to know that you can't buy happiness, but you can buy cake; that day it was the cheesecake you had made especially for Grandpa. And for a while, it calmed your heart to mix the flour and butter and sugar, stir in the quark, put the cake in the oven and watch it rise. And didn't it turn out well? Grandpa Raimund sliced it up and put a forkful in his mouth. Mmm, how delicious! And it would be some time before his hungry heart needed stilling again, and until then, the cake would gently melt on his tongue.

But unfortunately, the sight of somebody trying to numb their hunger, either with cheesecake or gummy bears, hurts more than anything else, right?

The Boss sings for me. I listen to his comforting diagnosis.

'Hungry heart' sounds better than 'borderline', which is Ingmar's diagnosis for me.

I heard it from Ulf, my conscientious go-between: 'Ingmar said that you probably don't know where you stop and others start.'

'Really?' I said and waited for Ulf to burst out laughing, but he didn't burst: he looked sad and pensive.

'It's not like nobody's trying to understand you.'

Ulf is trying to act as a go-between. He's an architect for

building groups: that requires mediation skills. You don't have to deal with just one homeowner, but five, ten, or twenty. And each one has a hungry heart.

Ingmar could have numbed his six years ago with an act of charity. That didn't work out, so his heart is still pounding and looking for explanations and diagnoses. Diagnoses are so much better than a vague feeling that something's not right!

I understand Ingmar for wanting to tidy up the world for himself and his children according to the DSM.

I understand Ulf for thinking that if we all try to understand each other, then surely we'll be able to see eye to eye, to forgive and forget.

I understand Frank for not wanting to forgive and forget, for wanting to make an utterly unforgiving gesture for once in his life — 'Get out, all of you! I don't give a shit what happens!' — after years of his nerves and boundaries being trampled on by his wife and annoying sons, and his wife's friends and their annoying kids, and God knows who and what else — 'That's enough!' I understand all that.

I am the Queen of Understanding.

Understanding is a highly effective means of numbing hungry, painful hearts; it's much better than anger, because, at some point, anger needs to erupt so that you don't choke on it or burst. And who knows, it might strike the wrong person or be over-the-top in the first place — unjustified even. In any case, it's risky because it's loud and very visible. An angry person is already a victim; an understanding person is in control.

My mother never risked getting angry either.

'I could slit somebody's throat,' she would sometimes say. She would play down the brutal image with a mocking tone, a friendly, calm expression, and restrained posture, all of which erased any suspicion that she would ever slit anybody's throat.

We talked for hours; Renate's right about that.

We discussed hundreds of questions and situations, but the lesson she taught me was to be understanding — as a weapon of defence and evasion, the opposite of justified anger and incisive insight.

Do you think, Bea, that I had the slightest clue what made my mother so angry that she felt like slitting somebody's throat?

She used to tell three stories about her younger days: first, the one about the girls in fourth grade, who gave her the cold shoulder because of a fashion show. Second, about her first boyfriend, who was happy to date but not marry her. And last, about her father, who once beat her with a clothes hanger because he thought it was her fault that her little sister was almost run over by a car.

Stories full of unatoned injustice that were told not to make me take my mother's side and feel angry towards the girls, her boyfriend, or her father, but to make it clear that she too had once been a girl and could empathise with me. Bad things had happened to her, but she'd survived. And she'd done it by figuring everything out and understanding the other side: the girls were probably just jealous, the boyfriend had been too much under his father's thumb, and her father had suffered a nasty shock.

September 1957; Southern Germany.
One day, when Marianne was in the fourth grade of Gomadingen

primary school, her mother told her that Neumaier, the children's outfitter, had asked whether her two daughters would like to take part in an event he was planning that coming Saturday. There was a fair in town, and his shop was going to take part by presenting its new winter collection.

Marianne didn't understand straight away. What was she being asked to do? Who had asked? What was a 'winter correction'?

'A fashion show,' her mother said. 'You'll have to walk down the catwalk and show people what they can buy this winter. And Brigitte too, for the smaller children.'

Marianne thought about it. A fashion show, wow. But unfortunately, only at Neumaier's, not in Paris. It wasn't the same as being booked as a model for a photo shoot, but almost. You had to be pretty to be asked. Did that mean she was pretty? Gerda was the prettiest of all the girls in her class, and Evi, of course. And Ingrid had the best clothes, not from Neumaier, but from Königstraße in Stuttgart. Everybody envied her. But they'd all envy Marianne too, when they heard that she'd been asked to take part in a fashion show. Why didn't Neumaier ask his own children or Gerda or Evi? It's obvious why he didn't ask Ingrid: her mother didn't buy clothes from him.

That evening, Marianne's mother told her father about Neumaier's proposal. And that seemed to put an end to any doubt: Brigitte was excited, her mother chuffed to bits, and her father already planning Saturday: a trip to the beer tent was on the cards, and he hadn't thought about dropping in at Neumaier's, but now that his own daughters would be doing a show, of course he would. There'd be no riches, but fame and glory. His daughters were nothing to be ashamed of, pretty girls, both of them.

Only Marianne wasn't sure. Did she dare walk down the catwalk? Who would be watching? Would she have to put on things she didn't like? Wasn't the whole thing just really embarrassing?

It was the 1950s: Marianne might have thought many things, but she couldn't argue with her parents. Marianne might have felt ambivalent about the proposal, felt that fame was questionable and the whole event suspicious, but she didn't have any framework for what she felt, and even if she had done — there was no way round it. Mum was excited, Dad was excited, Brigitte was excited, and only Marianne had a sense of foreboding that she couldn't pinpoint, and even if she could, she would not have been able to argue. Marianne did what she was told. Full stop.

On Saturday from four o'clock in the afternoon, she modelled winter coats, tweed skirts, and capes on the podium from the shop window in Neumaier's that had been turned into a catwalk. The showroom dummies had to stand in the corner for an hour. On that day there were real girls and music and free nibbles, and it wasn't anything like in Paris, or perhaps it was, because it was all about walking with confidence. Brigitte did it better, that was obvious to Marianne; Brigitte smiled at the crowd, pushed her hands into the pockets of her winter coat and did a twirl. Marianne was glad when the whole thing was over, and she could go home.

Except that it wasn't over.

Disaster struck on Monday morning when Marianne walked into the classroom. None of the girls would talk to her. Why? Ingrid delivered the explanation: 'Because you're vain and think you're better than everybody else.' Marianne looked at Sylvia, her very best friend. *She* knew she wasn't vain: she'd seen how difficult it was for Marianne to model the clothes, because she'd been standing right next to her and had suffered with her. But Sylvia turned away. 'I'm not taking sides. I don't want to get involved.'

Her friends froze her out for a whole fortnight. Marianne kept wondering whether she might have deserved it after all. Arrogance and vanity were deadly sins! Hadn't she been happy for a moment to think she was pretty? Hadn't she basked in the warmth of the attention for a moment? Not in the shop, but at home, and the fact that even Dad had come to watch.

Marianne found proof of her guilt. And *that*, said Ingrid, was precisely the point of the exercise: they had wanted Marianne to take a look at herself. With these words, Ingrid declared an end to Marianne's two-week banishment, and life at school carried on as usual.

I can't begin to explain how angry this story makes me. It doesn't just make me feel like slitting somebody's throat; I feel like blowing up an entire crowd with rocket-propelled grenades. I want to find out where Ingrid and Sylvia live and confront those bitches. But here comes Freud again, telling me that this is mere projection, because it's not about Marianne's pain, it's about mine. And he's right, of course.

Renate and Sigmund are clever and clued-up. I'd like to be too, but I'm not, and if anybody thinks I'm going to calm down, they've got another think coming because that would mean that you, Bea, won't find out what makes your mother so angry.

I'm not going to find excuses for stupid old Sylvia, who really seemed to believe that not saying anything wasn't taking sides.

Not a shred of understanding for poor, rich Ingrid, who was probably just frightened of being victimised herself for wearing fancy, overpriced clothes from Königstraße.

Everybody has a reason; nobody has what they really want.

If my mother had managed to stick up for herself, instead of numbing her pain with excuses and understanding for the others, then as a child I might have understood her.

But she wasn't a victim, God no, she didn't need to stick up for herself: she could keep her emotions out of her stories and take care of other people's needs.

That's wrong, Bea.

Please remind me of that, just like the stewardess reminds her passengers before take-off: in the case of a loss of cabin pressure, please place your own mask over your face first.

September 2013; Prenzlauer Berg, Berlin.
I received a commission. The editor of a magazine who asked me ten years ago to write about the baby boom in our hipster Berlin district remembered me, and asked if I could write about the boom in building groups.

'You weren't going to write for newspapers anymore,' Sven says.

'And our children want to spend the summer holidays by the sea,' I reply.

And it wasn't such a bad commission.

I could turn it into a personal story, the editor said, because that had worked so well with the story I'd written about being a mother ten years ago.

So I wrote two pages about how it felt to be the third from last person in my district *not* to be in a building group; about how it felt to live in a building without a name, how I still sat around on playgrounds instead of in communal gardens, and was envious of lifts, people who got to choose their own tiles, and being able to project onto a project.

On Friday, the article was published in the supplement of a national newspaper.

On Saturday, Carolina hosted a party for her fortieth, and at first, I thought, okay, she's the hostess and has to set priorities, and she can count on my understanding as her friend, that she has more distant relatives to talk to before she can say hello and thank me for my present. However, after four hours had passed, and Vera and Friederike had also ignored me except for a brief hello, but had made a big show of greeting Caro's younger sister and done their best to persuade her to dance with them for the birthday choreography, I knew they were angry with me.

'What's the matter?' I asked Ulf, and he said: 'You could have been a part of it. It's embarrassing how you make yourself out to be the victim.'

That was how it started, Bea, I should have known. First saying nothing and then opening your mouth doesn't work: it has to be either or, you or me, commission or no commission — it shouldn't be about me when it's about them. Getting to grips with your own feelings is a risky business.

———

September 2013; Carolina's fortieth birthday.
'What have I done?'

Ulf opened another bottle of champagne. I offered up my glass, trying to get him to give me a refill, come what may, wanting the others to see that at least Ulf was still talking to me, wasn't giving me the cold shoulder or going to throw me out. The wall of silence from the women might have just been a catfight, a game among fourth-grade girls; they were probably annoyed that my photo had appeared in a magazine and not theirs—

'Is it about the article?'

Ulf said nothing.

'It was a commission!'

Ulf narrowed his eyes at me.

'I was writing about myself!'

'And about us.'

This *us* was a *we* that didn't include me.

Ulf turned away and refilled other people's glasses. Had neither the time nor the inclination to argue with me. It was Carolina's fortieth, and he was not going to let anybody spoil her party, any more than his house, his project, his private or his professional decisions.

The only person who spoke to me at the party was Ulf's father.

'I thought it was funny,' he says.

'Oh, really?'

I was already on my way out, and he was already drunk.

'I liked the thing about the transparent walls that still serve to segregate people. Very well observed, Resi. Hats off.'

'Ulf taught me that. How to reflect on architecture. How to see it as a metaphor as well as something concrete.'

'Now he's offended.' Ulf's father grinned.

I didn't grin back, and he noticed. Looked at me pityingly and almost lovingly.

'He'll get over it,' he said. 'Just you wait.'

And I waited. Avoided the topic and pretended there was nothing wrong. Carried on meeting my friends for coffee — but preferably out in a café rather than in their spacious kitchen-cum-living-rooms, or on their balconies decked with plants, or in the communal garden. Lest we were reminded of that unpleasant subject.

But at the same time, I was always thinking about it. Why was it so terrible to write that the house had created a divide?

'You wrote about yourself,' said Sven.

'Yes, of course! That was what I was asked to do!'

'Perhaps. But you gave yourself that liberty. Why, actually?'

Sven understands more than I do, Bea, you should know that.

Sven realised long ago that this equality thing was a lie. Because as a kid, Sven had not only made it into a *Gymnasium* but even higher, studying the Classics at university, where the people he met had no intention of stooping to his level. They made sure instead that the guinea pig knew where it really belonged: in its pen.

As a kid, I had mixed with people who all agreed that pens, fences, and lines of any kind should be abolished and overcome in the name of freedom. Leftist people, idealists who, even if they were privileged, dreamed of a world that was more just, at least for us children. And that's why they did everything in their power to make us forget the existence of privilege; or, at least, to see it as a nuisance, like an untidy garage with a broken automatic door.

In those circles, people said that money didn't buy happiness, property was a burden, and the rich didn't enter the kingdom of heaven, like Scrooge in *A Christmas Carol*. Evil people like Scrooge were responsible for the misery in what was called the Third World back then. People like that even made pacts with Hitler during the Third Reich, just to keep their revolting privileges. But the rich people we knew were different and were just trying to stop suffering and inequality. And that's why poor, innocent, non-homeowners like us — who were therefore morally superior — weren't allowed to harp on about being poor, honest, and morally superior. No, everybody had to turn over a new leaf *together*. And because at that time, educational establishments had started offering everybody the same access and opportunities, and we had a level playing field — except that term wasn't used at the time, and why should it have been, seeing as we all played fair — it was only natural that things would turn out better for everybody from then on.

It's nice to move in these circles.

Until you realise that something's not right.

That it's necessary to share or even give up privileges instead of merely being ashamed of them or badmouthing them a bit.

That by the time these people become older and wiser than the rest, have children or just with the passing of time, they have become more interested in 'making it' than being able to face their old, idealistic selves in the mirror — the mirror they left behind in their old flat, because it didn't suit the furnishings of their new flat, where even the mirrors are flawlessly fitted.

———

As it happens, the first thing that came to mind when I was writing my article was Ulf's embarrassment when he tried to skip the walk-in wardrobe while showing me around his apartment.

'But why?' I said, opening the door myself. 'These wardrobes are fantastic. I'd love one myself.' Pointing out in my article that I was envious didn't make up for mentioning the wardrobe, along with Ulf's embarrassment.

It was treason. Suddenly everybody knew: Ulf and Carolina had one of those wardrobes, and others, like Sven and me, didn't — and Bea, if you pointed out that everybody knew this beforehand, you'd be completely right. But knowing something and saying it out loud — or even writing about it and publishing it — are two different things.

As soon as the article was in print, it was out in the open: the elephant in the room, the thing you could deduce from the Bible quotations we had picked out for our confirmations.

Idea for a Bible quotation for a confirmation: *making it to higher ground doesn't mean befriending the animals on the ark. It means having your own private cabin and a stake in the mountain.*

It wasn't until the article came out, and all the trouble started, that I realised my parents had, of course, wanted to move up in the world. Not necessarily so they could have a walk-in wardrobe, but so they could decide against it without being suspected of envy. And I realised that Ulf's mother, for her part, longed to get rid of that silly wardrobe and all it stood for. Nobody wanted to feel ashamed of the unfair distribution of wealth anymore; but if it wasn't redistributed or reallocated, the only escape was to focus on being the architect of your own happiness, personal failure, and foolish decisions. Which in my case meant: I could have been a part of it. Studied law. Married an heir. Accepted Ingmar's money. Been proud and happy with little money, carried on doing my own home repairs, and suffered inequality in silence instead of attracting unnecessary attention.

Moving up in the world

The bells in the Gesethmane Church strike midday. I can hear them even through the closed window of my broom cupboard. This is one of Berlin's top locations. The old gaps between buildings caused by bombs and explosions in this Wilhelmine quarter have been filled by discreet blocks of new flats; small boutiques and attractive cafés line the pavement with outdoor seating or ice-cream shops that offer hot chocolate to lure in passers-by in winter. Small children wheel around on balance bikes, big children on skateboards. Teenage wannabe gangsters have a hard time looking threatening, even when they're drunk and playing beer pong in the park — they're too well-dressed and fragile, and you won't catch them rolling around in the dirt or getting blood on their clothes. It's not a test of courage to go to school here. It's very peaceful. Or tastefully subdued, I should say.

You can disparage it. To do so is even in fashion, but not in any way that would actually change something. It's just a ritual to prove your power of discernment and appease the haters. Because there are more takers than flats available here, of course. And no one in their wildest dreams would leave of their own accord.

Living in the city centre is not a human right. In Paris, only wealthy Russians can afford it, and Marzahn, for example, is still totally okay. The layout of East German prefabs is actually better for families than pre-war flats: and anyway, prefab buildings came back in style a long time ago, because you can do them up so wonderfully in 1970s décor.

True, in the lifestyle feature I read, the prefab in question was on Alexanderplatz, which is about as central as it gets, but it's only twenty-five minutes by S-Bahn from Marzahn. With a direct connection! And it's green out there. So nice and green.

The stamp on Frank's letter of notice to the landlord is green too. 'For Your Attention' is emblazoned in aggressive green on the copy of the letter. Because of this stamp, Frank doesn't have to phone me or find the words for a personal note, like 'Hi Resi, take a look at what I've sent the landlord.' The stamp says it all.

The only question I have left is where he got the stamp. It's a lawyer's or clerk's stamp; a freelance management consultant doesn't own such a thing. Frank doesn't have a secretary or a receptionist, and he doesn't usually send documents for attention so he must have borrowed the stamp, or even had it specially made by a stationery shop. How much effort did he go to not to talk to me personally?

I'm an animal, Bea. Unpredictable and dangerous.

People might think I am imprisoned and confined in my broom cupboard, but I am nothing of the sort: it's what I do in here that makes me dangerous to begin with.

Where I'm sitting used to be the space for Vera's washing

machine, and before that, for Frank's. But when Vera moved in with him, she brought her own washing machine, a high-quality Miele, and Frank's old Privileg was dumped on the street.

That wasn't the only violation Frank had to stomach: Vera also ripped up the East German PVC with the geometric pattern against an olive-green background in his kitchen and hallway, even though Frank was against it.

'Help!' he appealed to me. '*You* know it's going to be cool one day.' But I didn't help him: I helped Vera rip it up.

July 2005; me and Vera on our knees in Frank's kitchen.
'You should always change something before you move in with somebody,' said Vera. 'So that it feels like home to both of you!'

We were shoving our paint scrapers underneath the glued-fast PVC.

'But he's attached to it,' I said.

Vera laughed. 'He's attached to the past. To the leftovers of a failed system! To his flat-share life, or to being single!'

We were sweating after ten minutes; it was July, and the sun was blazing through the curtainless windows. Sarah Connor was singing on the radio. It was fun working with Vera — she was full of get-up-and-go, even though she'd been having doubts for the past six months.

'I've lived on my own for too long,' she said. 'I'm bound to ruin it.'

'If you want to have a family, you'll have to get into practice.'

'Do we want a family?'

'You've come off the Pill.'

From under the PVC, floorboards started to show with

centimetre-wide gaps in between. Frank started to tear his hair out.

'The floor can breathe through the gaps!' Vera said. She went to kiss Frank, but he pushed her away.

'Huh?' she said. 'Seriously?'

Frank went back to his office; we went to the DIY store and bought oxblood-coloured paint.

Where the old kitchen stove used to be, the floorboards were missing; it was filled with a slapdash layer of cement. The paintbrush bristled as we painted over it.

'It won't be the last compromise Frank has to make,' said Vera, slightly less buoyant than the morning before.

'He likes his place to be tidy,' I said.

'He's OCD,' said Vera. 'Seriously.'

We carried on painting in silence. I thought it looked okay in the end.

Frank nodded when he dropped in to take another look. 'I thought it would look worse.'

'If you really can't stand it,' I said, 'you can always paint over it in a different colour.'

Frank knows that I remember all of this.

All the stories about this old flat — the transformations of the kitchen floor — and Vera's doubts about their relationship and bringing children into this world.

'What am I supposed to hand down to them? Let alone being an example! Me? Oh please! What a joke!'

And I visited her here after she'd given birth to Willi, and later Leon.

'Look at them! What am I am supposed to do?'

Leon had just been born, and Willi was standing there with a reproachful look: the same look that you'd had too, Bea, the brave, introverted look of the first-born.

'You have to take hold of the reins,' I said to Vera because that was the exact same advice she'd given me when you were three and Jack was one.

November 2006; in our old kitchen in Winsstraße.
Vera was visiting us, but we couldn't have a conversation. Instead, she observed how it was to have children and not manage in the least.

You wouldn't let me feed Jack, and Jack was bawling, but I didn't have the guts to chase you out of the kitchen, or lock you in your room, or assert my authority in any way. It was pathetic, especially as it was clear that you were just testing how far you could go. Did you really have the power to make me starve Jack? You were trying to test my limits, and were suffering most from having me in the palm of your hand. But I still couldn't assert myself — you were stronger than me.

That was when Vera said: 'You can't let this happen, Resi; you have to change something.'

She wasn't able to tell me what or how, of course, but she took a look at the situation, which was complete madness, and repeated several times: 'You have to take hold of the reins, you hear?'

What a strange expression — what reins? But that's why it's so apt and memorable.

I had no idea what reins to take hold of, let alone how, but I knew I had to. I kept that fixed in my mind. Along with Vera's voice, which sounded pretty level-headed in that chaos of churning emotions and soft-boiled carrots. 'You not only have to, but you'll be brilliant at it too,' is what I heard, because if I'd been a lost cause, she wouldn't have said anything.

And I tried to stand by her in exactly the same way in an impossible situation — right here, in this flat — when it was her turn to face the not-coping-and-having-to-anyway part of being a mother.

There was no time for the lengthy talks, plans, and solutions that were part of our past lives, but we had a few short, pithy phrases and sisterly solidarity to fall back on. We were each other's witnesses.

At least, I thought we were.

But, like any criticism, we have witnessed so much that it has become a threat; what used to be a bond is now dynamite. Who knows what else I can remember and, above all, whom I might I tell?

I shut my laptop and go into the kitchen.

For lunch, I usually make myself an instant meal or a packet soup, some kind of unhealthy junk. I bury the packets at the bottom of the bin so that no one finds them, especially Bea on her nightly prowls through the flat when she tries to catch me out. About the fact that I preach water and drink wine — no: preach vitamins and stuff myself with E numbers.

I'm one of those people who likes to hide their hypocrisy.

Frank is worried that the floor might whisper something into my ear. About the day the East German PVC was forced to give way or about the doubts Vera had. About the daily loads of laundry because Willi peed his pants for ages, and about the steps they took to prevent it. How these steps were retracted and reversed, and remedies of a different kind were found. About the day the colour scheme for the new flat's kitchen was chosen. Vera wanted white and Frank green. And who won? It all turned out well in the end, true. I was a witness.

And about a house which, once finished, started to fall apart again: how could the removal men have been so careless?

There were already scratches in the parquet floor and marks on the cupboard doors, and Willi and Leon definitely clashed with the surfaces and the tender-leafed plants in the garden.

But hey, they would just be swapped for new ones at some point. From the reserve funds for refurbishment.

We drank to the kitchen island, the 'couchscape', and the adventure bed. And to Frank, who was still playing with the boys, and still took them swimming every weekend — wow, such stamina, incredible — and to Vera, who looked so tired but managed not to throw anybody out, cry, or let anybody fall asleep alone.

It was enough. It was lovely.

We had fulfilled our dreams, built our façades, and had our kittens and kids. We were queens at deceptive appearances and conjuring up perfect family lives. We were trained and tutored by our mothers, who had turned us into their accomplices. And in the meantime, this role had become second nature, and we took it for granted. We really believed it was enough for us, or at least that we had chosen it ourselves. Which is why we weren't allowed to remember or remind each other of who we used to be.

Autumn 1998.

Vera was listless and depressed, didn't feel like doing anything, left everything lying around. Lay in bed while the biscuit packets and empty yoghurt containers piled up next to her; drank flat, lukewarm Fanta straight from the bottle.

And binge-watched films all day.

Meanwhile, her flat rotted away — in the truest sense of the word, as there was a hole in the kitchen floor. And who cared that the water leaking from the pipe of the washing machine ran all over the place, or that there were little black bugs in the kitchen? Why want anything when it was all shit anyway?

When it was dark, Vera would get out of bed and dress up. She already had cold sores back then, but she just painted over them in bright red lipstick.

Vera was so beautiful and deathly pallid. Oh, to be out on the town for a couple of hours with others who wanted the same vague thing — everything, that is! At least for one night, and forever! In those days she was aimless and inconsistent, far from being older and wiser than the rest.

How Vera swayed back and forth.

Yes, you can only get away with all that when you're young. Because it's disgusting, all that rash, reckless longing. It spills all over the place, and who's going to clean it up? At least when you're young, it doesn't stink as much.

I know that Vera doesn't want to be reminded of this. Not of how she was or what she wanted. These days she just wants everybody to be happy. And for things to be enough, just the way they are!

'Piece of melon?'

Yikes, look at it dripping everywhere.

Vera waves it away with her hand; she'll clean up later. Now it's party time! Vera never lets it show that she's thinking about cleaning up.

But I know.

Because I remember Vera as a child, and her mother thought that if she cleaned up after Vera, they would all live happily ever after. But it didn't work even then. Cleaning up after somebody doesn't make anybody happy. It's tedious, dirty work.

Vera's happiness wasn't enough to leave some spare for her mother; her gratitude wasn't enough to pay for her mother's work. Vera left one day with a mountain of debt on her shoulders which she now has to pay off by cleaning up after Willi and Leon, so that *they're* happy. Tell me it's not true!

But it is. And it's true of me and countless others, because that's the idea someone planted in our brains: who was it, for Christ's sake? Jane Austen? The German economy?

Message to Vera: sorry, sis, but I recognise you in Willi, the way he stands there in a rage, and you stand there, dishcloth in hand — even if you let it drip and congeal for the time being, and Willi is kept in check by Frank in his room. Willi is fighting you, just like you fought your mother: 'She'll never manage to clean all this up!'

I was there. I have been looking into your eyes for as long as I can remember, and you have Willi's eyes. No, other way round — he has yours.

'All I need now are two cats, and I'll be perfectly happy,' Vera said in the back garden on the day of the move, when the group had gathered round the fire pit to celebrate the grand completion of K23.

All the uncertainty and improvisation were over; there the group lived, and there they would stay. They had 'made it', and all I could do was go on about being locked away and empty promises of salvation.

'Where will you get them from?' I asked.

Vera didn't understand.

'The cats?' I asked, and Vera said: 'Why? Who cares?'

So I reminded her of Käthe, the poor cat from my childhood who led the rest of her wild life behind carefully closed windows.

'Okay,' said Vera, 'I get it. I'll go to the animal shelter. I'll save them from an even more miserable life. Will that make it okay?'

And I nodded, and Ingmar added that the cats could use the back garden and it was their fault if they went out, and I said: O-U-T spells OUT, and everybody laughed.

It was a lovely day. I hadn't written anything yet; not my article and certainly not my spiteful book. The sun wasn't shining, but the fire was crackling merrily, and the cats hadn't been rescued yet, so there was no danger of them getting run over. Nobody knew where Frank had got to, whether he was with the kids or had decided to drill in a few screws at the last minute so that everything was done.

Message to Bea: don't wait for better times.

Said Wolf Biermann. No, he wrote those lyrics, and now they've become a cliché. But forty years ago, they were just words to a song he thought up, then played around with until he came up with a tune, which he later sang and recorded and went on tour with.

I think that's good. And now I have some lyrics for you that express my horrible feeling of insecurity: Have we suffered enough yet? Do we have the right to complain yet?

Perhaps if it hadn't been for the article.

Or the next commission from the TV producer who had an idea for a Friday evening show: 'A mother who hides her poverty from her daughter.'

She called and asked me if I could imagine something along those lines, and I said: 'Shouldn't Friday evening shows be light so that people can look forward to the weekend?'

'Of course,' she said, adding: 'Nothing heavy. The premise of the story is a series of funny cover-ups on the mother's part.'

'The mother being poor is supposed to be funny?'

'No, of course not. She shouldn't be so poor that viewers are moved to tears at the sight of her.'

'So, more like: poor but proud, extremely capable and smart?'

'Exactly! I knew you'd get it.'

Sven said: 'I thought you didn't want to write for TV anymore.' And I replied: 'And the kids want presents for Christmas.'

Sorry for always using you kids as an excuse when it comes to jobs, Bea. Parents can't possibly know what kids want. They only know what *they* want — to satisfy their kids' wishes, which is why Christmas exists.

In any case, I sat there and thought about this mother hiding her poverty from her daughter, and I realised it was me. So I wrote a treatment about a woman who goes DIY-crazy so that her daughter can have everything she wants — and it's all very cool, because everything is a one-off as opposed to the lame stuff all the other kids have. But when it comes to making a tablet, the mother hits a wall when she tells her daughter that a sugar-paper lantern is almost the same thing, and the daughter says: 'Well …'

The producer also said 'Well …'; the treatment wasn't quite what she had in mind. She'd prefer the mother to bake cupcakes to raise the cash for the daughter to buy a real tablet. But I didn't think that was realistic because the mother would need a shop to sell the cupcakes and how was she supposed to afford that? And the producer said it didn't matter, people wouldn't care that much about the details on a Friday evening.

That's when I realised how much *I* cared about the fucking details, and that put an end to my collaboration with the producer and the commission, and I started working on my spiteful book.

The ideas have to go somewhere.

No, Bea, that's rubbish. I won't hide behind that. Do you hear me, Ulf? I didn't do it because of the commission: I didn't have to write what I did. Or if I did, I could have just stuck to the fucking cupcakes.

I prepare myself a working-class lunch — tinned ravioli — and eat it in posh style, with freshly grated Parmesan on an Iittala plate.

I'm a wanderer between two worlds, a mother who hides her poverty. Who buries it at the bottom of the bin and has a few tricks to make her seem solidly middle-class. As a child, I learned from my aspiring parents that you can't call ready-grated Parmesan 'cheese', and that Scandinavian design proves you have taste; what I didn't learn was how not to spill tomato sauce. So I prefer not to wear expensive blouses — and off comes my mask. Because real middle-class daughters know how to use serviettes or they have enough money to have stains on their clothes removed.

Not worrying about things, an upright posture from childhood, and the skilful handling of serviettes: these are the kinds of details that indicate the difference.

Take a look at Carolina. True, she has a large open-plan flat with silky-smooth, dark-stained floors and a walk-in wardrobe with motion sensor lights; but I could have had all that too if I'd made an effort and studied the right subjects. If I'd accepted Ingmar's money. Or married Ulf.

What I never could have learned — and never will and therefore can't pass on to you, Bea — is the way Carolina walks into her wardrobe, so naturally and casually, or the way her clothes fall so effortlessly down her upright back, or the way she holds her hair together with just two hairpins. How does she do that? Caro knows how to dress, do her hair and make-up. She knows how to show off her understated femininity to full advantage, order waiters about, delegate to cleaners, and be a role model to interns instead of just giving them tasks.

Ulf doesn't think these qualities are remarkable. His mother and grandmother, sister and cousins all had them too.

Perhaps he just doesn't care.

Perhaps he never noticed I didn't have them when we were together. Or he noticed and was attracted to a vulgar playmate like me — a wild girl who's fun to be with for a while, but whom you eventually have to groom, polish, or dump because she wouldn't be a suitable mother to the children she'd have to teach to walk and behave in the proper way—

Ulf's mother noticed my shortcomings, of that I'm sure. Kept quiet about them, because not saying anything was part of the social project. Ulf's mother *wanted* to stoop to the level of the 'common people' and come into contact with them rather than seal herself off. Ulf's mother opened her door to her children's friends, no matter who they were, where they came from, or what they could do. 'Come in and look! I'll not say anything.' Unlike *her* mother-in-law, who said something straight away.

December 1987; Stuttgart.
In Ulf's family, Christmas was a musical event. His parents sang in a choir, rehearsing Bach's *Oratorio* several times a week; Ulf and his sister were accomplished players of several instruments and could sing carols in harmony.

Before I met Ulf's family, I didn't know that carols could be sung in harmony, but I was invited to his house on the fourth weekend in Advent for coffee, homemade Christmas biscuits, and an afternoon of music. And that's when I heard the different voice parts and met Ulf's grandma for the first time, who I'd imagined would be like mine — old, in other words.

Ulf's mother was seated at the grand piano. Ulf's sister was already warming up, and Ulf's father grinned at me, but then had to come in on the bass line. And Ulf's grandma was definitely old and sang alto.

'What part do you sing?' she asked me before she had even said hello.

I didn't know how to answer. I had no idea what they were doing; it was alien to me, the way they were standing, with very upright postures, in a semi-circle around the grand piano. I offered my hand to Grandma as was expected.

'Hello, I'm Resi.'

'And what do you play?'

I instinctively knew that my two years of learning the recorder in primary school didn't count in this context; that it would be seen as the equivalent of doing a cannonball in the pool.

'Er, nothing,' I said.

Ulf poured me some tea. But then had to rejoin the circle to sing the tenor.

There they stood and sang one carol after another, Grandma propped up with her cane, Daddy hitting an ironic bum note here and there, which earned him a dig in the ribs from his daughter. And I sat at the table, drinking tea and being the audience. I smiled, because at least I could show my teeth after the orthodontic treatment I had been given at the expense of the public health service, into which private patients like Ulf's parents and his grandma had never paid a pfennig, but which nevertheless existed, preventing the insurmountable rift between us that a crooked or, God forbid, toothless smile would cause. It was still the 1980s.

So I smiled and made sure I didn't join in the singing. I recognised the carols from the words and the soprano sung by Ulf and his mother, but I knew that I couldn't for the life of me sing along. Couldn't hit those high notes in a million years.

It's fine. And it was all over a really long time ago.

And those thirty years ago, the concert was eventually over too, although the carols didn't just have four parts but an incredible number of verses on those alien sheets of music.

I didn't suffer that much. Others had it much worse: others weren't let in in the first place or weren't even considered human — speaking of which, Grandma was not only an arms manufacturer but had also grown up in the colonies, but perhaps I imagined that. Ulf wasn't quite sure of the details.

In any case, because I couldn't join in the singing, I bolstered my ego with other things — like the biscuits Ulf's mother had tried to bake, for example. Dry and hard as rocks! I was a thousand times better at baking.

Or with Grandma's age. There she stood, propped up on her stick, with a wrinkly neck and drooping earlobes — I'd outlive her by decades!

Had the earrings dragging down her earlobes been pawned, the money would have covered a hip replacement performed by a chief surgeon, followed by eight weeks of physio in a private hospital room. But I hadn't grasped this yet, nor why Ulf's mother lacked culinary skills: Grandma was the first in the family to have studied, and Ulf's mother, the first not to have a hired kitchen help.

I didn't talk to anybody about this. I can only tell you now, thirty years later, that I wish somebody had warned me.

My mother's second story was about Werner, her first boyfriend, who wanted to sleep with her but not marry her. I always thought it was a strange story and wondered why she told it to me in the first place.

'So what?' I thought, and 'Good riddance to bad rubbish,' and 'Losers weepers.'

I wouldn't for the life of me have realised that this was the story of Marianne's missed opportunity to move up in the world.

The story was very short.

'Werner, oh yes.' Followed by a cheerless smile. 'Dumping me didn't help. He didn't find happiness.'

Unlike Marianne, who married Raimund and had us.

She was happy. Because love is more important than financial security and social standing. Werner didn't get that; he had to learn it through painful experience.

It's not clear to me how my mother knew that Werner never found happiness. And yet this was the moral of the story as I saw it: Werner's unhappiness was the result of kowtowing to social pressure; Marianne's happiness was the transformation of the brief disgrace of being dumped by him.

Exactly how Werner had dumped Marianne and what led up to it, and that she'd lost her virginity to him, along with a few of her dreams that she managed to bury afterwards — not a word was breathed of this.

Perhaps the story was intended as a warning, but if so, its effect was lost on me. It was too short and too abstract, too directed towards the ending, where it became too concrete. I was the result of its fortunate twist: if Werner hadn't dumped my mother, neither I nor my brother and sister would have been born. So I could not identify with my mother because I could only imagine the outcome of the story and not the Marianne of the beginning, who had naively blundered into the wrong social circles.

If she was trying to warn me, she should have told her story differently: 'Okay, darling, go ahead and attend the family carol-singing, but beware. Ulf's parents belong to a different social class than we do and yes, they have invited you, but you don't know the rules and requirements. Do you remember Werner? He was a pastor's son, and I was entirely out of place, no matter how much effort I put into behaving correctly, even though we too said grace before meals in our family. But in Werner's family, there were napkins that you had to spread across your lap, and a serving girl. She always came from the right. How was I supposed to know that? I didn't have a hope in hell, but perhaps the next generation does. Ulf's father is now Werner, you could say, and maybe he had a girlfriend like me too once. Before he married Ulf's mother. Isn't he a lawyer and a member of the SPD? I'm sure he's ashamed of his privileges; in any case, Ulf's mother is always very nice to me. The fact that they're ashamed is to your advantage, but it's quite risky and can change at any moment — if they think you're accusing them, for example. So be careful. Pretend that everything you find strange is second nature to you. Watch how Ulf and his sister behave; but remember you're not one of their children, so don't be cheeky to the parents. Whatever Ulf and his sister are allowed to question, pretend not to notice. Or perhaps stick up for the parents? That's another possibility. To be on the safe side, though, just pretend not to notice. It's best to be quiet. But not too quiet! You have to say something: ask a few questions, but the most important thing is to listen. And to smile. Not in a stupid way, but as if you're really interested. Never turn your back on Grandma. She's thirty years older than Werner, so the same age as his father. And definitely not a member of the SPD. But it doesn't matter, she's not the one who invited you. You've come through Ulf, on his recommendation. He probably chose you just to rile his parents — that was definitely part of Werner's motive I think, even though he might not have realised it— anyway, try to find out what each person wants. What their attitude is towards you. Are they secretly hoping for something better? Find out if they like you. You might rely on Ulf's father's protective instinct, but don't get drawn into flirting with him. If there's anybody you have to win over, it's Ulf's mother. Which side is Grandma from? Hers or his? It's not good if you don't know. Don't turn your back on her! Try to find out how the different family members get on with each other and where you can act as a go-between or scapegoat, and get them to let out their aggression towards each other on you. Sacrifice yourself; it'll pay off in the end. Find out who wants you there and why, and remind them of their social project.. You're just the object, in any case, meaning that you don't decide or want anything. Except in the worst case, to escape very quickly. Before they throw you out, you leave of your own accord, okay?'

I wash up my plate. Hide the ravioli tin right at the bottom of the bin. Crave a cigarette for my digestion. Sorry, Bea, I can't give up smoking, can't be a role model for you. Smoking is an unmistakable sign that you don't believe in your own mortality. That you think you can carry on forever, and keep regenerating each day. I have to believe this. I can't give up; I have no pension plan, you see?

I have to stay young forever — and don't tell me 'smoking has the opposite effect'. I know. But what's important is believing. Hey, are you even listening? I have to *believe* I can carry on like this.

I mustn't play all my aces at once:

I'm young so I don't need a pension plan.

I can cook, bake, sew, hang wallpaper, clean, cut hair, and do all sorts of unpleasant jobs so I can always be of service of others.

I need next to nothing, and can live off tinned ravioli and sliced white bread, so I will have no problem surviving.

I'm not as spoilt and mollycoddled as the others in the group — like Caro and Ulf and their wannabe-democratic building group. But I'm terrified. I am, Bea. I'm terrified of being terrified, and can't imagine anything worse than realising I've failed to move up in the world and will have to see how I get on with my kind out in the sticks, in Marzahn.

Because I'm not one of them either.

That's the awful thing about failing to move up in the world: there's no way back down.

I have inherited Marianne and Raimund's distaste for the hoi polloi but not any money; they placed all their bets on one card — that I'd move up in the world. But as it turns out, it wasn't an ace. And now I'll have to manage on my own.

If only they'd given me karate or pole-dancing lessons instead of the recorder. The recorder! You won't find one in an orchestra, and it's no use in a band. It's just a way of gagging you.

Instead of embarking on that doomed plan to move up, recorder in mouth, to the carefree, silk-clad soprano singers, I should have learned to say 'Fuck you!' in kindergarten. Now I could be voting for populists with a clear conscience and showing the big knobs what's what.

The rest of the time I'd go to the social services office, which I do anyway for top-up benefits and the kids' meals' and activities' allowance, and if I had money to spare, I'd go to the solarium or get my nails done. Nails are almost as much of a giveaway as furniture; I could just get a French manicure, for example, because anything else would be trashy.

After years of hiding my shortcomings, I would have to hide my privileges. And not use the word 'privilege', for starters. Say 'toilet' instead of 'lavatory'. Not say anything anymore. Become invisible.

So that nothing happens to me out there in the big wide world.

The common people's lack of education, you see, makes them stupid, and that makes them dangerous. They don't have a clue about the damage they wreak, or how to control their impulses. They're like wild animals. Have you ever taken the M8 tram towards Ahrensfelde at around five in the afternoon? It's full of overweight people wearing polyester t-shirts with logos, giving their toddlers imitation Red Bull and cuffing them around the ear now and then out of boredom.

I would have to be fast, strong, and fit to stand up to them or run away; but I'm stiff and pampered. I can argue, but I can't hit. Like a reflex, I imagine all the things that would break in my body and theirs, and so I hesitate. I know too much.

I have to hide it somehow. But they would soon notice that I'd lived somewhere else for years: they'd pick up the scent.

Since I was ten, when I went over to Micha Stadler's place and his father, who worked shifts, turned up in Micha's room in his underpants and yelled that we should get the hell out; since seeing Micha's expression, and his mother's panic as she held open the front door for us; since realising outside Micha's house that those two grown-ups were really his parents — in other words, the people he was supposed to love, and, more importantly, the ones who were supposed to love him — and was so horrified that I never went back again, after which I changed to a *Gymnasium* where people like Micha weren't allowed; since then I haven't been in close contact with common people. Just posh ones. They frighten their children too, but in a civilised manner, and while fully clothed.

Christian's dad, for example, the guy with the car telephone and the underground garage. Bought his software company before we did A-levels and then tried out a whole bunch of alternative lifestyle stuff, including self-help methods and healing techniques.

One afternoon we had to do a family constellation according to Bert Hellinger; I was the older sister who had died of cot death aged three months, and Christian was Christian.

And now you'll ask of course why on earth I think these people are less dangerous than the ones on the M8 tram. And you're right, Bea. They're not. Quite the opposite. But I've studied them and all their methods for years, and I feel safe with them. So much so that I even thought they would think I was equal to them and would spare me—

I should have married Ulf. Instead of believing A-levels would impress anybody apart from my parents, who didn't have them.

———

December 1987; at Ulf's house, singing carols.

Resi held fast to the fact that she was younger than Ulf's grandma. She bolstered her ego by comparing her baking skills to those of Ulf's mother. Fancied she was better at French than Ulf, not to mention Maths, German, and Biology too. She had an impeccable school report, so what did she care about music?

Resi smiled.

After they finished singing, the others sat down at the table with Resi.

Grandma asked what her father did.

'He's a draughtsman. He works near our flat, which is in that building on Emil Nolde Street, the grey one opposite the big Fine Fare. Perhaps you know it? There's an orthopaedist on the ground floor.'

'Emil Nolde was one of my husband's protégés,' Grandma said.

Resi thought Grandma was getting all muddled.

None of the other four people at the table felt obliged to say anything: either about Resi's failure to understand what Grandma really meant by 'What does your father do?', or modern-age painters and one's relationship to them.

Bea, you know the painting that hangs next to the balcony door in Ulf and Caro's flat, the one with the church spire and the cow and the wild sky? It's worth about 150,000 euros, but I'm not saying Caro had ulterior motives. Ulf is a good catch even without his inheritance.

The really big
Tupperware containers

We're not poor, Bea. Renate knows that, and she reminded me of it more than once when we were sitting together in the café. Her mother didn't just have twice as many children as me; she didn't own a single book either.

'With your level of education, you can't say you're poor,' Renate said. 'What you can pass on to your children is worth its weight in gold.'

I thought about the autumn holidays, and how some top up their kids' vitamin D and others stock up on lice shampoo.

Renate was right — at least I can see the connections. At the next parent's evening, I could suggest that all those going on trips abroad should kindly cover the expenses their holiday incurs: €12.90 for a bottle of nit lotion, which just about covers one and a half children's heads.

But you've forbidden me from making these kinds of suggestions, Bea, because they seem petty and pathetic. Which I then tried to explain to Renate.

'Being educated but poor turns you into a killjoy. If education is the only thing you have, you have to be right all the time. Because you can't sit back on La Gomera and just chill out!'

Renate has never asked me what we live off. She sees that we somehow manage to have a roof over our heads and decent clothes. And we don't like flying because of the damage to the environment — all that jet fuel blasted into the atmosphere — as well as bringing lice and bed bugs back to northern Europe. So, we set a good example and make sacrifices. Do you hear me, Bea? Better not to travel! It's better to sit at home for two weeks and be bored: idleness is the mother of inspiration, and only boredom can change your thinking because it gives you the necessary leisure. Hardship makes you inventive. Hardship is precious, no matter how contradictory that sounds.

It feels good to be so educated. It's an A-class requirement for hiding your poverty from your children.

'But I don't want to invent anything,' says Bea. 'I want to have plans.'

The children are back from school. Their heads are full of the things their classmates have planned for the autumn holidays.

'What kind of plans are those that others invent for you?'

Bea gives me a hard stare. 'Just because your idea of having fun is sitting in your broom cupboard, and doing DIY, doesn't mean that we have to too.'

Kieran has brought home a brochure from Lidl. When you have stuck in fifty stickers, you get a free Tupperware container: the more you buy, the more you save.

'Have you ever tried it?' I ask Bea. 'Doing absolutely nothing?'

She doesn't react. So I take a look at the Tupperware offer. If I buy a really big container, I save eighty-five per cent!

'Hey Kieran,' I say, 'that's nonsense.'

Now Kieran looks at the offer.

'Don't you get the food inside as well?'

'No, I don't think so.'

'Huh? What do you mean "I don't think so"?' Bea has caught me out.

I take a deep breath.

'Okay. I meant to say: "No, of course not! It's a trick. Tupperware looks boring without food inside, and it's supposed to whet your appetite so that you shop more at Lidl, and collect points and feel like you're saving money. Even though you never wanted the Tupperware to begin with. Why would you if you don't even have the food for it? So, of course, they add it to the photo, and it's the same as flying abroad for the autumn holidays. They don't come with serving suggestions and whoever says differently is lying!"'

I grin at Bea. It's great being so educated.

'If we don't go away, I'll do schoolwork instead,' says Bea. 'At least then I'll be ahead of the others in *some* way.'

She storms out of the room.

It's not nice being this educated. Bea is at the top of her class even though she skipped a year: she can't help it, and suffers from always being right, always being the best.

Her room is also the nicest in the flat. She made it that way, dyeing a bed cover with batik, doing up an old desk, and finding decorating ideas on the internet. Apart from that, she cleans it every week and tidies up every day. She's also the only one who makes her bed.

Now she's sitting at her desk, staring at the shelf on which her files are sorted by colour.

'I'm sorry,' I say.

Next door in his room, Jack yells at the computer. 'Shit! I died, you spaz!' and Bea raises her eyebrows.

I rush over and tell Jack I'm going to take away his computer if the game makes him so aggressive.

When I come back, Bea is sitting there just the same way.

'I wish I didn't care,' she says.

'About what?'

'Everything. What we do. The way things look. Who thinks what, who travels where.'

'I'm sorry.'

I'm helpless. I want to tell her everything, prepare her, explain the facts of life, and give her the right tools. But I haven't got the faintest clue how to help her not care.

'Will you come with me to pick up Lynn?'

'Okay,' says Bea, and stands up.

There's more yelling from next door. I look into the boys' room again.

'Half an hour,' I say to Jack and Kieran. 'And no yelling and no rude words.'

I'm such a twat. Who's supposed to enforce that rule?

Apart from anything, 'twat' is rude too.

———

The childcare centre is hidden in bleak drizzle. The rangy poplars that are supposed to screen the empty lot of the neighbouring building are bare; a plastic bag is tangled in the upper branches.

I carefully slide the child safety lock over the gate. Not once in the past twelve years have I forgotten to do it. Not a single child has been able to slip through the gate and endanger themselves due to my negligence.

'Why are you grinning?' Bea asks.

'Because I'm such a twat — oops, that's the second time today. You can't say "twat".'

'Why not?'

'Because it's an offensive word for women's genitals.'

Lynn's group room is empty: the late shift has started. I prefer picking up Lynn from the garden because then I can imagine she's free — freer at least than the leftover children in the late-shift room lit by neon strips, overseen by whoever happens to be on duty that week.

I confess this to Bea, who shakes her head. 'I always preferred the late-shift room to the garden.'

'But with you, I almost always managed to be on time!'

'Yeah, that was really annoying. The late shift was nice and cosy.'

Another nine months of childcare. Next year, Lynn starts school and then this chapter will be over. Then I'll have slid the safety catch over the gate for fourteen years—

I was less anxious with Lynn than with Bea from the start — or I'd already got used to being anxious. When Lynn was born, Bea had already been at school for two years, and was almost as old as Marianne when the girls gave her the cold shoulder—

Bea hasn't been given the cold shoulder, at least not as far as I know. But I didn't realise either that she liked the late-shift room.

'Have your classmates ever ganged up on you? Have your friends ever stopped talking to you or anything like that?'

We are walking down the corridor that displays the centre's mission statement in quotes by great thinkers on the wall. Copied, and hung with Ikea frames: 'The limits of my language are the limits of my world.'

'I don't have any friends.'

I don't want Bea to say that. Back when she used to go to childcare, I asked her why she didn't get herself a friend — to shore herself up against loneliness, the late shift, and the enforced post-lunch nap; as a compensation for being weaned off her dummy, for the disgusting food and the ban on thumb-sucking. And then I thought she was probably better off without, because having a friend would mean being dependent. The mother of her friend would have probably always arrived punctually before four o'clock, and Bea would have felt twice as abandoned in the late-shift room on the few occasions I had not made it on time. Better not to be a target, better to be independent and practiced in loneliness—

As far as I know, Lynn doesn't have a friend either. But I don't worry about her.

I watch her putting on her jacket. Wrapping her scarf around her neck, slipping on her gloves.

'Whew, it's hot in here,' says Bea. 'I'll wait outside.'

Lynn doesn't just take her time. She almost grinds to a halt, says Bea. I don't mind in Lynn's case.

The three of us go home. Not together: Bea walks several steps ahead of us. Looks into shop windows at her reflection in the glass, straightens her shoulders, pouts.

I pretend not to notice.

Lynn lags behind and collects leaves. Yellow sycamore and withered brown chestnut. In front of the corner shop, there's a sumac tree that she also picks leaves from.

When we get home, Sven's there.

Someone who could have carried out my orders and pulled the boys away from their computers. But Sven doesn't do those kinds of things; he's making supper instead. Grating carrots for a salad. Not all the grated bits land in the bowl, but Sven finishes grating before he mops the floor, and when he mops, he doesn't care about the bits that disappear into the gaps between the floorboards.

If only I could do that.

I already get nervous while I'm grating; and after I've mopped the floor, I have to dig out all the stuff from between the gaps and look at it. I have to take care of everything, even the dirt.

'Leave it,' says Sven, but he doesn't explain how.

The only thing I've managed to learn from him so far is to withdraw, close the door behind me, take a deep breath and: cigarette.

I know it's stupid, Bea. And unhealthy. But I'm addicted. Smoking makes me feel independent when, in fact, I'm totally dependent. But even the addiction is a good feeling. I enjoy doing something bad for me.

Sven understands this. He even openly admits it to you kids.

Of course he doesn't like it when you gawp at the TV and eat junk food, but he doesn't pretend you can just stop, or that he knows how you'll not do it, or that he's any different. Sven owns up that he doesn't know and can't stop either, and I love him for that, even if I sometimes curse him for it too.

'I always have to take care of everything!' I whine, and at the same time, I'm thankful that Sven knows how to stay out of it.

It's not a skill you should despise, Bea: openly admitting things, looking after Number One. You shouldn't confuse it with indifference. Sven waits until he's asked. He doesn't see you or me as his responsibility or property. I know, that's what all fathers and husbands claim, and then prove the opposite by their behaviour.

Ingmar, for example. A modern guy, very nice too. How happy we were when Friederike found him! And don't worry, I won't bitch about him, even though he's the biggest arsehole on earth — but it's partly my fault, as shown by the sentence 'How happy we were when …' Which proves that we were starting to worry that Friederike might be damned to singledom and childlessness for good! *Phew*, we thought, *just in time*.

It's very revealing the way Prince Ingmar's appearance sent us into raptures, how relieved we were. No wonder he doesn't take female autonomy seriously. Instead, he thinks he has to save women, and, if need be, give them orders. In any case, he has to be on constant alert. And if there's no alternative: psychiatric ward.

I used to like him very much. It's easy to like Ingmar, because he's good-looking, and always cocks his head to one side as if he's interested — like Gaby Dohm as Sister Christa in *Die Schwarzwaldklinik*. You won't know that, Bea, you'll have to watch it on YouTube; the opening credits are enough. Gaby Dohm cocks her head to one side three times, and Ingmar does it too, because it means you're listening, taking your time, and showing empathy. A bit over-the-top, yes. I think so too now.

But at the time, I fell for it, didn't notice the parallels to Sister Christa, although Ingmar's eyes are very similar to Gaby Dohm's: big and gentle and hazelnut brown. Add dark-blue sweaters, which make a reliable impression, and lace-up shoes. Men who wear slip-ons are slippery, men who wear lace-ups are solid: it's as simple as it sounds. The worst are men who turn lace-ups into slip-ons by wearing down the backs. I know one of those, but it's not about him now. It's about Ingmar, who always ties his shoes carefully and takes his time.

Friederike met him when she thought nothing good would ever happen in her love life again, and we were all thrilled because Ingmar proved that it would. He was evidence of what we'd been preaching to Friederike for years: 'He'll show up one day!' And he did, at Christian and Ellen's wedding, who were the first in our circle of friends to get married, which is why everybody was still into weddings and thought they were exciting. And then Ingmar came along too, an old friend of an even older friend of Ellen's, new to Berlin and single and a doctor.

Unbelievable! Like in the movies!

Friederike was wearing an outlandish dress, because she wanted to contrast Ellen, as she put it, who was getting hitched, whereas she was mutating straight from schoolgirl to old maid. So her dress was both short and high-necked, with a white round collar that went all the way up to her chin. And against all expectations of where Friederike stood that night, she ended up standing in the corner with her feet turned in, drinking one Caipirinha after another, and it was logical that Ingmar fell for her. He, on the other hand, was so unreal that she flirted with him outrageously and let him get her another drink before slipping her finger into the loop of his belt and pulling him towards her.

It even makes me dizzy now to think of how wonderful it was. A man for Friederike, a good-looking, dependable guy!

He fitted into our circle without a glitch, precisely because he was so nice, confident, and together. He had money, a real job, and wanted kids. And then even more money, and a talent for organisation, and half a doctor's surgery, which quite soon became all his. And that's when we probably should have sat up and asked a few questions, but no one did. We were inexperienced in things like that, and we still are.

I started having doubts on the Sunday we were all supposed to go to the building site together.

March 2013; shortly before K23 was completed.
We were invited to brunch at Frank and Vera's. We, meaning our family — except Lynn, of course, because she wasn't yet born — along with Friederike and Ingmar, Silas and Sophie: a total of six adults and seven children. But it wasn't a problem: there were plenty of pancakes and strawberries and caprese and bubbly. We spread out across the five rooms; you kids were getting on fine, and the new building would soon be finished. The move was imminent, the lawn seeds had been sown, and although Sven and I wouldn't really be part of it, we felt as if the flat we were sitting in having

brunch was already a little bit ours.

Everybody was happy, and there was a good atmosphere.

But Willi didn't want to go.

Brunch had been eaten, it was already half past two, and we'd chatted for long enough. Brunch now had to be digested, and you kids urgently needed some fresh air. And everybody felt like seeing the progress on the building site.

Everybody except Willi.

Willi often has plans of his own, and in this case, he planned to stay at home.

'No, I don't want to,' he said, while the rest of us were putting on our coats.

Vera sighed and tried a weak 'Come on, we're all going,' but for Willi, that never counts as a reason.

Frank tried with: 'Let's see if they've already fitted the sinks!' and then: 'We could get ice cream on the way there!' But Willi stood firm, at which point Silas suddenly said he'd prefer to stay at home too, and Jack said he would too, and the three of them went into Willi's room and closed the door behind them.

We stood about awkwardly in the hallway, and Ingmar said: 'Okay, I'll go and speak to them.' And he went into Willi's room too. Then there were terrible screams.

'Don't touch me!' Willi yelled, and: 'I don't have to listen to you!' and: 'No, I won't look at you!' and: 'Shitty Sunday! Shitty walk! Shitty K23! Shitty Ingmar!'

It sounded like a complete overreaction, especially when we looked through the crack of the door and saw that Ingmar had made an effort to squat down so that he could talk to Willi at eye level. And he definitely hadn't touched him roughly but was gently brushing his arm, like you're supposed to before you speak to children.

Ingmar was very calm, nodding, smiling, and touching Willi, and Willi flipped out.

'Okay, I'll stay here,' said Vera, in that resigned voice she'd acquired because everything was so difficult with that stubborn child.

And Frank shook his head and looked apologetically at me, Friederike, and Sven, and we shrugged to show we understood: but all of a sudden, an unexpected empathy for Willi stirred inside me. Which was odd because I don't particularly like Willi. Because he's so difficult and drives Vera and Frank to the brink of madness. He barely looks at other adults, including me, or if he does, then it's with a wary expression, his chin jutting forward.

But then I realised it was a familiar feeling: one of impotence against the man squatting down and pretending not to fight, even though he is forcing you to do something and trying to wear you down. And to top it all, he hides it with a smile. If he laid a finger on me, I'd kick him in the balls.

Which is exactly what Willi did, and Ingmar's smile vanished. He stood up, sucked in some air between his teeth, and came back out; by the time he reached us, his smile had come back too, and he shook his head and said: 'Okay, no chance.'

And we adults all laughed, and the joke was on stupid Willi, and Vera stayed at home while we went to the building site — except that Jack and Silas trailed a few metres behind us, and I'd have loved to have known what they were talking about.

I didn't say anything, but kept my newfound empathy to myself, along with my first doubts about just how friendly and harmless Ingmar was—

After all, somebody has to keep the show on the road.

Where would we end up if everybody did what they felt like doing?

Ingmar is responsible, good at organising, hardworking, and thoughtful.

He doesn't do whatever he feels like, but what's best for everybody!

What's the first sign of paternalism Bea? Knowing what's best for everybody.

The salad is ready.

I shut my laptop and sit down at the table with my family.

Carrots are good for your eyes because they contain vitamin A, but to absorb it, you need a binding protein. Without these molecules, the vitamin isn't much use to the body. Without these molecules, vitamin A can even lead to toxicity.

I like Sven's reserved nature, his reticence during supper.

Sometimes it's a little oppressive, and I know that Bea is afraid of Sven's mute rejection, and Jack says that his friends think Sven is creepy.

A loud father is nicer. Someone who knows about things and likes to hear the sound of his own voice. Someone who intervenes to keep the order, and who attracts attention. Who and what are we supposed to look at when we're at the table?

'How was school?' I ask, making an honest effort.

'Really good,' says Jack, my ally, my good boy.

The others say nothing.

Kieran stands up to fetch tomato sauce from the fridge.

Tomato sauce on salad: no one says a word.

No one is sure whether it might contain precisely the molecules needed that Kieran might need to absorb who knows what nutrient.

Later I sit in my broom cupboard. Just a bit longer since I didn't get anything worthwhile done all day—

Speaking of which, what is worthwhile? What's an achievement?

I'm used to not worrying even when I'm not sure where the next pay cheque is coming from. Somehow things always work out. In the worst case, I'll write for TV or a newspaper, or do proofreading. Or Sven might get a grant.

I take Frank's letter out of the envelope again and look at the light-green stamp.

Should I have known that Vera would go this far? Why Vera though? This is Frank's doing, and perhaps she doesn't even know about it. Perhaps that's precisely the point: Frank wants to prove for once how he can follow something through, steely and merciless. This is his flat, his contract, and his past, for Christ's sake!

So while Ingmar was browsing the DSM and Vera was writing twee emails, Frank ordered a stamp from a stationary shop and gave notice on his flat. For once, he didn't have to put it to the vote.

I want to comfort him.

'I know you can't help it, Frank. The number of times you had to give in and just take it, rise above it. Like with your lovely East German PVC, for example! Your washing machine, which still worked like a dream. Your jazz records, which Vera couldn't stand. Your penchant for spicy Szechuan. You don't always want to make quiche Lorraine! But the kids don't like anything else. And your wife's friends don't either. Why do you always have to put up with them anyway? And has anybody ever thanked you? I understand, Frank, honestly. I'm happy to be your opportunity to show everybody who wears the trousers.'

That's what sent him completely up the wall in the end: this gooey, emotional understanding. Who am I, and why do I know him so well?

I wasn't there when Vera met him. Unlike Friederike and Ingmar, who we all got to watch, Vera got to know Frank without any witnesses.

'You *what?*' said Friederike when Vera spilled the beans six months later. That she was dating the guy she'd edited a video for, a guy who'd studied art but had retrained since and needed videos for his workshop, just a typical guy, you know? And so, none of anybody's business, right?

'Excuse me,' Friederike said. 'I'm the last one who'll have anything against him.'

'She means it doesn't matter what we think of him,' I said, and Vera: 'Thanks for the translation, darling.'

'And are we going to get a look at him?' Ellen wanted to know, and we got a look at him over the first quiche Lorraine in the old flat share, although it wasn't really a flat share anymore because Frank's flatmate was away teaching in St Gallen half the time.

'Hmmm,' we said with our mouths full while getting a look at Frank.

I don't know. Tell me what you think, Bea. What kind of impression does Frank make?

He's a nice guy. A really nice guy. But I like nearly everybody when I first meet them.

And I had already had you. And Ellen was pregnant and, anyway, it was time to start a family instead of carrying on with plans of shared lives and flats and work — that was too difficult somehow. So we each, in turn, got pregnant, moved in together as couples, tried to resist a little longer, stayed for a few more months in our old flat shares or lived alone until the logistics got too complicated, resistance seemed silly, and the old plans were stashed away — which wasn't possible because they hadn't been concrete enough, and we didn't have any role models.

We tried for a while. After A-levels, we'd moved to Berlin together, into the building Christian's father had bought or repossessed after the fall of the Wall, or however else he came to own it: I couldn't have cared less about the exact details back then.

1993–94; Friedrichshain, Berlin.
We moved into the entire fourth floor of a building in Mühsamstrasse, and in summer we also had use of the attic and rooftop for parties. For a whole summer we sat on the rooftop: Vera, Christian, Ulf, and me. Felt the warmth of the sun-baked bricks of the chimney on our backs, listened to Kurt Cobain on a battery-run Discman, stared down Karl-Marx-Allee at the Berlin TV Tower soaring above the buildings — long before it became ubiquitous as a biscuit cutter or a logo on Babygros.

The other flats were occupied by old tenants who weren't

particularly friendly to us. Now and then, Frau Eisenschmidt knocked on our door at night and asked us to be quiet; she had terrible rings around her eyes that we alone surely couldn't be responsible for. We tried really hard to be quieter because we liked Frau Eisenschmidt.

It was obvious that our idyll could only last one summer and two winters: 'The old dump has to be done up!' we shrieked, aping Christian's dad's voice and feeling as if we were victims as much as the old tenants. Except that our future hadn't yet begun. This was just the start, a warm-up, a foretaste of the real deal of living and working together.

Sounds naïve, doesn't it, Bea? And it was. How else can I describe it?

Vera wrote in her break-up email that she no longer wanted to be stuck in the past, and Ulf said that I'm the only one still interested in the old stories.

And of course, it might be embarrassing to think how we imagined we were like the squatters in Rigaer Straße even though we were the children of the new owner.

And we might be ashamed to remember that we still played BAP and The Police at parties and sang along loudly to Rio Reiser; or that our best artworks were the birthday presents we designed for our parents. But hey! Is the occasion so important?

Yes, probably.

I should have noticed, paid attention to the details. Who had which motives? Who thought what exactly?

———

A comedy of errors, 1991: five twenty-somethings from Stuttgart were gearing up to leave home. Off into the big blue yonder! Out into the Great Wide Open! (I wonder what Tom Petty's estate would want for the rights?) And Berlin was the furthest away we could get.

Resi felt like she was in a film.

Finally, it was real, and she was the one experiencing it.

She sat on a rooftop in the city's former East sector, as if she was in a promo shot of a band. Unfortunately, she didn't play an instrument except for the recorder, but it didn't matter; she got by on irony and picked up some claves. The main thing is that she was herself. No more pretending — Resi *was* the leading role in her own life.

Resi was Paula from *The Legend of Paul and Paula*, Julia from *You Love Me Too*, Tracey from *Manhattan*, Bernd from *Taxi to the Toilet*, Nola from *She's Gotta Have It*, Corky from *Night on Earth*, and Catherine from *Jules et Jim*.

She travelled every day to Kreuzberg and cooked vegetarian lunches for twenty primary school kids in a parent-run after-school centre. Cleaned the place too for twenty marks an hour for those who weren't into the parent-run part. Transcribed interviews with family members of mentally ill patients for a PhD academic. Sewed the teacher a pair of trousers that actually fitted.

Resi found it difficult to fit those scenes into a life where the sky was the limit. On the sun-baked rooftop with Kurt Cobain playing, it was easy. In the supermarket on Reichenberger Straße where she picked up the ingredients for millet risotto, the escalator went down into a neon-lit basement that stank of bananas.

Resi took her camera so that at least she could capture it on film. But there wasn't enough light. And the photos didn't show the smell.

But still. Art was the only way to record and survive the contradictions; to separate references from actual experience, and then to spin it all around again so quickly that you could tell what was what.

And it's still like that, Bea. Or is again.

Even the world of lunchboxes and to-do lists, bank statements and compost buckets, Advent calendars and emails about lice, has to have another side, and I won't stop turning and spinning everything around until it shows up — so that I show up in the only life I have.

Sound overly dramatic? I don't care. I won't let my style be dictated. I can't play the piano; I'll take claves. I owe it to my one and only life not to be intimidated by shame or fear.

I hear Sven putting the kids to bed. I'm ashamed. I'm afraid. I don't know how to tell him.

'Sven, listen. This letter came for me.'

He doesn't look up. He's sitting on the sofa with his laptop on his knees. Or he's outside on the balcony, and the traffic is too loud.

'Sven!'

Now he looks up. Or turns around. I don't know how it goes from here.

When I told Sven about Ingmar's diagnosis of me, he laughed and quoted Michel Foucault. Sven isn't afraid, not of Ingmar, not of being misunderstood or excluded. Sven knows what he knows, and he won't let anybody take it away; all I want is for the letter and everything that led up to it not to exist. I'm willing to give up everything.

I'm too weak for Sven.

I could phone Ulf.

When Ulf told me Ingmar's diagnosis, I laughed and waited for Ulf to join in. But he didn't.

'Okay,' I said, 'as far as I know, I wasn't abused or maltreated as a child; I didn't have to take care of my parents because they couldn't, but of course perhaps I did without noticing. So please tell me, Ulf; you've known me for such a long time.'

He looked sad and reproachful. 'I don't know what's wrong with you.'

'But did you or did you not see Raimund coming out of my room, and me lying bent double on my bed in 1983?'

'Stop that, Resi, it's revolting. Just stop being so revolting.'

As if *I* had thought up this scenario and not Ingmar.

And as a punishment for my revolting thoughts, words, and writing, Frank is sending us to Marzahn, but even that can be interpreted differently.

'He wants to settle things for good.'

'Frank wants to release himself from existing ties.'

'We'll each have to see for ourselves where we go from here — and perhaps one day, we can be reunited.'

This said in a pastor's tone. It's Ulf's voice I hear saying these sentences, Bea, Ulf's effort to act the go-between, Ulf's stooping to my level, like his mother once did, and his great-grandmother in the colonies.

Ulf's favourite song in the book of hymns was 'Jesus my Joy'. We didn't learn it during confirmation lessons, in which the pastor tried to keep us interested with a new set of songs, guitar accompaniment rather than the organ, and the feeling of singing around a campfire.

Ulf preferred the language of the old hymns: Jesus as lamb, God as shepherd, the flock as shelter, and the angels as heavenly hosts.

I didn't find anything comforting in those words, which must have meant that I wasn't living close enough to the edge with my winter jacket, braces, recorder, and library card.

Grandma said I had poor posture.

'Didn't she do ballet?' she asked in Ulf's direction while pinching my back.

I had to giggle. Grandma had a weird way of talking as if I wasn't there. And the way she touched me: like she was testing goods.

I could have married Ulf, back then when I was eighteen. But it didn't occur to me. The status it might have conferred didn't interest me: I was against any kind of status to begin with. Relationships were based on love, and love was only real if it was pure — in other words, free. Untainted by ties, duties, and interests.

'God, the lamb, my faithful man.'

Ulf and I were pure, free, and equal. I liked his voice. I liked it when he sang.

———

January 1986; southern Germany.

Ulf was the captain of the handball team, could shoot the hardest and run the fastest; he was also brilliant at every subject, and the teachers' favourite. But at the same time, he was against everything: against the system. To top it all, he had green eyes and lightly tanned skin even in winter, even at the age of fourteen when all the others were covered in zits—

Ulf was good-looking.

And I wanted to be with him.

Everybody wanted to be with Ulf; when he talked, the others listened, and when he laughed, it was infectious, and when his T-shirt slipped out of his trousers, you only saw smooth, lightly tanned skin. He knew stuff but wasn't arrogant, sang in the choir but wasn't a sissy.

And then it happened! To me! My love of Ulf was requited.

We were sitting in a big group, and he started cracking jokes just for me. All of a sudden, I was in the limelight, and, because Ulf was paying me attention, the other boys started paying me attention too. That had never happened before, and it was the most wonderful day of my life.

I was fourteen.

We set off on the bus, which in itself was a good prospect. Three days away from home on our confirmation trip. Singing and learning and 'finding ourselves' was on the programme, and there was nothing I would have rather been doing. Perhaps not quite in the way that Reverend Löffler and the congregation imagined it, but what *did* they imagine? I was eager and all for it.

The whole setting was so awful and tacky, it was hilarious: a youth hostel in the middle of nowhere with bunk beds, a canteen, and a bowling alley. Pinboards in the classrooms for the collages we were supposedly going to make. The themes were: 'Me & You', 'Trust', 'Hope', 'Forgiveness'. Four groups. We were good at making fun of the tasks; we were fourteen, so we'd already had eight years of doing things we didn't feel like at school all day and still making it entertaining. Failing all else, somebody just fell off their chair.

Reverend Löffler found it quite a challenge. Didn't know how to handle us. Those who refused to join in could be sent home, but we *were* joining in; we could do it all standing on our heads.

In the evening, bowling. No one knew how to; we watched each other. The way we sized up the lane before taking a run-up, the way we giggled, collapsed, waved our hands dismissively. Major beginner's luck, that's for sure. And everything was in flux.

Then later, at the table in the empty canteen. Outside, the middle of nowhere was silent. Where was it again? The Swabian Alps?

Reverend Löffler had long since gone to bed. Why didn't we have a deadline when we had to be back by? Because that word hadn't been invented yet. I wasn't paying attention to what we were talking about. I knew that I wanted things to carry on like this forever; it was half past two and no one wanted to go to bed, and if they did, then not alone. I was powerful. If I stood up to go, Ulf would stand up too. If I sauntered out, he'd follow me. We could have swapped beds — he with Vera or me with Christian, but it didn't have to happen. It was more than enough for me to know that I could. And that I wouldn't get tired. Ulf's attention was like being on speed, and I had Gerald's and Christian's and

Heiko's, because I had Ulf's. I was the greatest. God, it was fucking cool. God, it made me attractive! God, it turned me on. It was like magic.

I had what the others wanted. I *was* what the others wanted.

It was amazing.

It was unfair.

Tough luck

I go to bed. Down the long corridor, all in darkness. The floorboards creak.

The varnish Vera and I applied over ten years ago has been worn away down the centre. It doesn't matter. It's shabby chic. Will the landlord see it that way? What is the exact wording in the contract? Will we have to renovate before we move out? Re-varnish the floor before they sand it anyway? How will Frank find out if he's managed to get rid of us? Will he send somebody round or come himself? What will he say?

Sven is asleep.

I undress and lie down next to him in bed. Protected by the twilight, his closed eyes, and our relationship sealed by four children, I look at his profile. How am I supposed to know what love is? It gives me a lump in my throat to look at him; I'd rather die myself than have somebody lay a finger on him. I'm afraid for him. Of him? It's probably the same thing.

First, I saddled myself with Sven's hungry heart, then with those of our four kids. It's particularly bad when you're all asleep, because then you're all so beautiful it hurts.

Behind Sven's nose, the wardrobe sticks up, and I focus on it: an ugly, half-broken thing. It won't survive another move; Ikea furniture can't be taken apart more than three times. But not having a wardrobe isn't an option either, no more than not having children.

'No one promised you a rose garden!'

Says Renate.

And I say: 'Yes, they did. You planted your hope in us like a seed: hope for a fresh start, a new leaf. It sits there inside us, and speaks to us — and if not of roses, then of what? The promise lies in our existence. No, don't deny it, Renate; I'm sorry that my gripes with your generation always end up at your door. No, I'm not sorry; actually, it's your fault. You're the one who raised the subject in the first place. We could've chatted over tea about unimportant things, but you didn't want to. And why? Because the seed doesn't add up to much, and nothing else adds up either. You need to do more than turn over a fresh leaf all the time. A few tips would be useful, a bit of practical advice. Sometimes it helps to cut notches into hard-coated seeds to help them germinate. Yes, I know, it's an effort, and the knife might slip, but waiting and hoping is not enough. You've been here longer than I have, and you know your way around. Where did you leave the instructions? It's unfair to hand something down but leave out the most crucial part. What are these figures for? What do these squares mean?'

Sven wakes up.

'Resi?'

I've been tossing and turning. I can't sleep.

Sven stretches out a hand and puts it on my neck. Pulls me towards him.

In three or four moves, Sven can take away my feeling of being a victim. I'm not alone and abandoned — quite the opposite. With Sven's help, I have sired a whole gang who will open the door to the bailiffs in slippers, snot hanging from their nostrils, and say: 'Hello? Who have you come to see?'

With the last remnants of my working-class instincts, I did what our sort does best: I bred like a rabbit.

Sex is a form of defiance, I read somewhere, because we do it to defy. Not only because a new person who will preserve the species might be born as a result, but because the act itself is defiant.

Death stands next to us and thinks, 'Damn, they're getting on just fine. I'd better go. Love, desire, and fun? Not my thing. I'm out of here.'

And so death takes off, along with fear, worries about coping, and anger at the injustice of the world: everything disappears, and I end up somewhere entirely different, and I become somebody entirely different, all heartbeat and skin and life.

Okay, for about fifteen minutes. But it amazes me that it still works, even though it's so simple and we've already done it a thousand times.

I know you don't want to hear all this, Bea. No one likes imagining their parents having sex.

———

My mother was very considerate about that.

She managed to tell the story of her lover, who didn't want to marry her, without mentioning sex once.

Werner had a car, as far as I knew. And I also knew that people could have sex in cars, because Raimund liked to recite limericks: 'There once was a couple from Waiblingen / Who used their VW for loving in / It made them quite glad / To be scantily clad / But after the sunroof was jammed right in.'

Resorting to a car because people didn't have their own rooms, or only ones with landladies who didn't let girls come up, or parents who judged the girl as inferior — I didn't know anything about all this. Perhaps my mother mentioned the car because that's where she could have sex with Werner — but for me to understand that, she'd have had to be much more direct.

I knew Marianne loved cars; and that later, when she had one herself, she was reluctant to let anybody else take the wheel.

She didn't have one when she was young. Werner did though, and they went out in it for drives in the country. All the way down to the South of France — where Werner dumped Marianne.

How exactly? What words did he use? And why there?

'His father never liked me. I was a nobody. His parents would have even had to pay for the wedding to do it the way they wanted.'

And then came the part of the story that had nothing to do with Werner, about the wonderful turn of events that occurred because Marianne was dumped by Werner: her wedding to Raimund, which took place in a pizzeria with only the witnesses. It must have cost a hundred marks at most, but money doesn't mean a thing when you really love each other.

But you do have to love each other. And how does love show itself? In sacrifices.

Werner shouldn't have listened to his father. Should've spurned his inheritance, and got married in a pizzeria — no, in a brasserie in the south of France. That would have been cool! But he failed. For that reason alone, I lost interest in Werner: he was a coward, a loser, a walking disaster. A caricature who didn't feature in my life. I didn't know anybody like Werner. I was with Ulf, who back then was never going to accept a pfennig of his grandparents' tainted inheritance—

'A marriage is so much better when you've blown ten thousand euros beforehand.'

Ulf and Caro aren't married.

I don't know where the money for K23 came from. Who paid for Ulf's studies or the Mies van der Rohe cantilever chair in his office. It's indiscreet to ask and unnecessary to think about.

It's spiteful.

Idea for a Christmas series: the architect Ulf is in a tight squeeze. At the age of twenty, in a grand gesture, he spurned his inheritance (black-and-white flashback: forced labourers at the conveyor belt of a German factory, bombs falling on London, Ulf's grandmother steps out of the factory-owner's villa wearing a fur), but now construction has come to a halt on his current building site. The client, a committed NGO manager who builds flats for Syrian war refugees and hires them as workers, has lost his state subsidy. Architect Ulf runs around like a madman to drum up private investment in his project — but in vain. Only his sister Elfie, who accepted her inheritance and is in the process of organising a commemorative exhibition called 'The Dark Years' in the factory owner's modernised villa, offers Ulf help. Researcher Resi, an unsuccessful scriptwriter, who is trying to draw attention to her blog with left-wing radical revelations, posts an article about the involvement of Elfie's firm in arms exports to Syria just when, over champagne, Ulf is pocketing a cheque from his sister at her exhibition opening—

'Resi?' Sven has stopped. He's noticed my mind is elsewhere.

I would like to tell him what I'm thinking. Let myself go and confide in him completely, but how?

Sven barely talks about himself, let alone his past.

A man without a past, an alien from outer space: that's Sven.

He hates hymns.

He doesn't like singing, but he can play the piano: he would have had an answer to Ulf's grandma's question. Sven was talented, ambitious, received a scholarship and piano lessons.

But he wouldn't have told Grandma that he played the piano.

Sven stopped showing his talent very early on; at some point, he kept it to himself instead of peddling it. Tried to avoid using it to open doors at any cost.

'So, you get your foot in the door, and then what? You smell all the nice smells, and the light's so inviting, and you hear laughter — but the gap doesn't get any wider, your foot starts to hurt and goes numb. Eventually your blood circulation is cut off and you faint, and have to be carted off.'

Much earlier than I did, Sven realised that he didn't fit in.

'I'm different,' he thought, looking in the mirror. 'Totally different from the way people are supposed to be.'

That's how he described it to me — unwillingly, because I was determined to find out how he managed not to be afraid of the dark, mustiness, and silence on this side of the door.

'Of course I'm afraid,' he said. 'Very afraid. But I know it's normal. You can't change it. You just have to put up with it — the dark and the mustiness.'

And that's why I don't have the guts to tell him how lonely I am. It doesn't even stop when we're having sex, and so I stop having sex, and death promptly turns up.

'Everything okay?' Sven asks.

I don't have the heart to answer him. It's okay, I'm fine, everything's fine, the dark is fine, and I don't live alone; I have him and four healthy children. We are a long way from living under a bridge — that's rubbish, that's a huge exaggeration. What would real poor or homeless people say? War refugees? AIDS orphans? What we give our children is worth its weight in gold, and anyway, I freely sacrificed all my chances to move up in the world. Who said we deserved to live in the city centre? If I'd wanted it that badly, I should have earned it.

I can't talk to him about how angry I am at my old friends. Because he just thinks they're all twats. And he thinks I'm a twat for getting angry.

And I wanted to stop saying 'twat.'

Why actually?

So that I am correct at all times, and can't be a target. I only have the right to complain about what's wrong if I do everything right.

Too late.

———

146

Speaking of AIDS orphans.

That's why I had children: to use them to hide behind and send them on ahead. Not only to send them to open the door when the bailiffs come, but also to go begging when there's no door left to open. Kids are ten times better at begging than adults because they evoke much more compassion. Kids are normally cut more slack than adults, even when it comes to AIDS — the number one 'O-U-T spells out', 'only yourself to blame' fate. Because unlike their no-good, promiscuous parents, it's probably not the kids' fault.

Speaking of only having yourself to blame for your fate.

Isn't that a paradox?

Sven says: 'Good night, then.'

And me? I lie awake and wonder how it was with Werner. Who Werner was. There's no one to ask. Marianne is dead, and Raimund will squirm his way out of it.

'Hey, Dad. Who was that Werner guy?'

'Which Werner?'

'You know, Werner! The coward who didn't want to marry Mum.'

'No idea. The only son of the esteemed Reverend Eidinger.'

'And what did he look like?'

Raimund looks into the distance. Makes a face that tells me there's no point in going down this path.

'Like Jean-Paul Belmondo.' He grins. 'No, more like Jean-Louis Trintignant.'

147

I imagine Werner to have been like Ulf's father. Trapped in the never-ending expectations of his own father, who didn't let his son become an actor. An actor? Why not just go straight to being a hairdresser?

Ulf's father boasted that he didn't wear a tie. 'The only tieless lawyer south of the River Main!' On the carved colonial tray next to his desk, there was always a bottle of whiskey. When he was drunk, he liked to recite Handke.

I know he told Ulf that he should try other girls besides me, and I didn't hold it against him, seeing as he was trapped and obviously unhappy with his life. No wonder he wanted to ruin what others had. In any case, he needn't have gone to the trouble. Ulf had already 'tried' other girls — we were *Jules et Jim*, after all, and did all those things that Ulf's father watched on late-night TV.

Werner took photos of Marianne. They're stuck at the back of her photo album — her only one — which starts with her parents' wedding photos and has about twenty pictures from her childhood. Then comes a group photo from her trainee days, then Werner — not him, just his portraits of Marianne. She's looking over her shoulder, which brings out her jawline, her small ears, and her cropped hair.

Pictures that were taken in the south of France, the landscape in light grey, white houses on dry hills, Marianne in front of a bar on the *route nationale* in the style of the period with a neck scarf, and a cigarette between her lips. That must have been shortly before it was over — or did they go there more than once? Did Werner give her the photos even though they had split up?

He had a camera and a car: two machines that made him the main character in his own life. Marianne must have been easy prey.

September 1963 (let's say).
Marianne left school and decided to train as a bookseller. The alternatives were the post office, home economics, or household care, and Marianne thought bookselling was the most glamorous, picturing herself among dark-wood, ceiling-high bookshelves in a shop where all kinds of people would stop by, especially clever people looking for something to read.

In summer, her hair was cut in a short pixie style, and the mustard-coloured bouclé sundress she'd made herself was also very short.

So she started her job training in a small-town Swabian bookshop, where the bookshelves were made of light veneer and no higher than two metres fifty. She learned how to index and give advice, and demonstrated a knack for window dressing and calming down irate customers whose orders were late yet again. The boss should have counted himself lucky to have Marianne, and he did.

At some point, Werner came into the shop looking for a road atlas.

A road atlas? Couldn't he have ordered Sartre?

But he would have needed the road atlas to drive to France. In his own — yes, his very own — car, a sky-blue 2CV. Or a Fiat? Not a VW, in any case: too German.

Marianne liked all things foreign. She had never been outside of Germany, still lived at home, had a penchant for the Great Wide

Open and an exotic lifestyle: eating outdoors, dining after ten, brandy snifters, raffia wine bottles and candles, even when it wasn't Christmas.

Werner invited her out for a drink. Chatted cleverly about Hermann Hesse. Ordered Trollinger. Well, it wasn't exactly what Marianne wanted — a quarter-litre carafe with Werner over lamb in a country inn — but at least it was red wine! And the car was really nice! Driving back later, Werner let her take the wheel. Werner filled up the tank. Werner had money, a camera — and no problem seducing Marianne.

When was her last period?

Marianne didn't tell him, just blushed instead—

No, wait:

Werner panted. 'Is it safe now?'

Marianne guessed that he was asking about her menstruation and thought about it for a second. Embraced Werner, who took this to be consent and no longer held back. Then his sperm was in Marianne's vagina, and later in her underwear — instead of being on Werner's clothes or, even worse, his car seats.

Marianne worked in the bookshop. Took Van de Velde's *Ideal Marriage* from the shelf when no one was looking and browsed through it—

No, wait:

They wouldn't have stocked Van de Velde in a small-town Swabian bookshop.

Marianne consulted her best friend who heard from somebody else that it should be safe if she subtracted fourteen from twenty-eight, added two, and subtracted two again to be sure. Or switched to coitus interruptus. Which is bad for car seats.

Oh, what a tricky business!

What would Werner have done if she'd got pregnant? Given Marianne money for an abortion? Why didn't he invest in condoms? Is it even true that Marianne *was* lucky not to have got pregnant? Wouldn't that have been her ticket to move up in the world? Because then, Werner might have married her and 'done the right thing': Werner's parents could have taken comfort in Marianne's pretty ears along with her cooking and needlework skills.

No, hold on:

This isn't Jane Austen. This is September 1963, the eve of the sexual revolution! These were Marianne's formative years in work and in love!

In 1967, Werner dumped her, not while they were in the south of France, but just afterwards. Most relationships end after holidays, but in this case, the main reason was that Marianne wasn't good enough for him. Didn't speak French, had a trainee position for a meagre seventy marks a month, some of which she even had to give to her parents for food and lodging. Happened to be good at sewing and calming down customers, but could neither ski, play tennis, or order waiters about. She was timid; as pretty as the actress Anna Karina, but lacking self-confidence and ballet lessons — that certain something that nobody can pull off except real con artists or those who happen to have been born into a wealthy family. Take a good look! Use a magnifying glass and study those photographs from France!

The scarf that Marianne is wearing is clumsily tied, she's holding her cigarette too far towards the middle, and her knees are turned in. Her expression reveals that she's worried about things that Werner thinks are completely superfluous — like whether the petrol will last all the way to Saintes-Maries-de-la-Mer and whether she should go to the toilet in the bar, or will it just be one of those holes in the ground again? In which case she might as well squat down by the roadside. And that way she'll avoid having to ask '*Où est la toilette, s'il vous plaît?*' (Is that right? Doesn't 'toilette' mean make-up?) And is it okay to leave most of the pastis, or will the barman think that's strange? How come she didn't know that pastis tasted of aniseed?

'Au revoir' were Werner's final words after that holiday.

I'd like to castrate him. Yes, really, for the first time in my life, I want to cut off a man's dick. If Marianne was good enough to be fucked in the back of his 2CV, couldn't he have stuck with her?

No.

You have to see Werner, too, as a victim of the class system, just like Ulf's father, who binge-watched New Wave films on the portable TV in his study with a glass of warm whiskey in his hand.

Werner didn't dump Marianne of his own free will. He was so under his father's thumb that he could only see her through his eyes. It must be awful not to trust your own eyes; first trying to fight somebody's superimposed view, before surrendering and realising your lover is inferior. Poor Werner.

That's how Marianne saw it, but I want nothing to do with that anymore. No change of perspective, no understanding, and no pity. Just Werner's dick.

Arthouse meets horror: Resi, a well-groomed woman in her forties, rings the bell at the gate of a sandstone villa in Frankfurt. The gate buzzes open without anyone asking via intercom who is there. The woman flinches, pushes open the door that bears Werner's name, and crosses the front garden (in full bloom — perhaps hydrangeas?) A housekeeper (without an apron, only identifiable from her tired worker's face and orthopaedic shoes) lets her in. In the study with ceiling-high, dark wooden bookshelves facing the terrace doors to the garden, (next to which hangs a small original Nolde?) sits a well-kempt man in his seventies, flicking though an old road atlas. He turns his friendly, sun-tanned face towards the visitor, raises his wild old gent's eyebrows and smiles affably.

'How can I be of service?'

The visitor does not smile.

'You've never served anybody, so don't say it like you know what you're talking about!'

Her voice sounds hoarse, revealing her overindulgence in cigarettes and alcohol. The old gent's smile becomes strained.

'Do we know each other?'

'No, thank God.'

She looks around.

'So, this is where you live?'

The gent's smile widens again, and his shoulders relax.

'This is my humble abode, yes.'

She walks over to him and grabs him by the neck of his sweater. Pulls him up out of his study chair. Brings her face very close to his.

'You've never been humble either, and if you don't drop that tone straight away, I'll make sure you do—'

She lets him fall back into the swivel chair. Thrusts him, even. The chair creaks dreadfully.

The creaking continues on the soundtrack long after the chair has stopped swivelling and the elderly gent has suffered torture that would have justified screams and groans in the background. But he's not afforded that honour. During the scenes that follow, only the creaking can be heard; it's all filmed in close-up, and even those who are into snuff, and usually hate these kinds of intellectual experiments with their genre, find it pretty interesting. Because there is real loving attention to detail.

Save me

The alarm clock goes off.

Why get up when you have a bed? Shouldn't you stay in it to celebrate that you have one?

The day will come when I don't, at least not my own, and no door to close either — and fear has me up and walking into the kitchen.

It's not happened yet! And I still believe in the importance of being on time for school. As well as the importance of starting the day with breakfast, having a pencil case full of sharpened pencils, getting a kiss on your forehead, and hearing a friendly 'Have a good day!'

I still have the energy to take care of my principles and my children; there's still something between me and my basest physical needs.

Culture. Discipline. And routine.

Jack and Kieran are fighting over the toothpaste.

'Since when have you been so crazy about toothpaste?'

'Okay, then I won't,' says Kieran and chucks his toothbrush into the bathtub.

I fish it out again, get Jack to squeeze some toothpaste on it, sit on the side of the bath and clamp Kieran between my knees. Brush his teeth like I used to when he was two, even singing the song that went along with it: 'This is the way we brush our teeth, brush our teeth, brush our teeth / This is the way we brush our teeth, early in the morning.'

Jack makes an obscene gesture on the way out. Kieran tries to run after him, but I hold onto him.

Then Jack has gone, and Kieran lets all the tension go in his body, so he ends up hanging like a rag doll on the handle of his toothbrush.

'You're really starting to annoy me,' I say and let him go.

Kieran falls on the floor and bumps his elbow. Now I feel like chucking the toothbrush in the bathtub too but just about manage not to.

Just about manage to keep my show on the road. What made me believe I could keep anybody else's show on the road too? I'm the last person who can save anyone. With what? A cheerful toothbrushing song?

October 2010; Mauerpark.
All of a sudden, Vera raised doubts about K23.

'It's a stupid idea. We should be doing it with people we have some distance from.'

We were jogging. Trying to get rid of the flab we'd accumulated during pregnancy. Gasping for breath, we reached Bösebrücke, from where there was a nice view across the zigzagging train tracks.

I didn't answer because I was panting too hard.

'Then again,' Vera carried on, 'we all know what we're letting ourselves in for. We know each other's little quirks.'

'No obligations to capital contributions; I can't take that risk!' she said, mimicking Christian, who, as everybody knew, had the most money, and despite this — or perhaps precisely because of it — was the stingiest of us all.

I laughed and did a few stretches at the railings.

I didn't get the sense Vera was asking me for serious advice. She just needed me to listen to her problems as an outsider, or, as Frank had put it over quiche Lorraine: 'I'm glad there are still two of us who aren't directly involved.'

May 2005; Vera's qualms about moving in with Frank.
'I've lived on my own for too long.'

She was holding you on her lap, Bea, breathing in the smell of your hair, before she placed her chin on your head and looked at me.

'Rubbish,' I said. 'You love him.'

'Yes, that's why. I'm bound to ruin it.'

You reached up and tugged Vera's ear, ruffled her hair. She laughed and pulled away. Stood up and set you on her hip. I had to stop myself from saying how much it suited her.

'If you want to have a family, you'll have to get into practice.'

'Do we want a family?' Vera stared out of the window.

'You've come off the Pill.'

'Well, there is that.' Vera gave you back to me. 'I don't know. I'm not made for it.'

I didn't dare reply. Was I made for it? After all, I was pregnant again. What did Vera think? Did she bitch about me? Did she do an impression of me for Friederike and Ellen to show me pretending to be a mother?

'Frank really wants to,' she said. 'And anyway, it's part of being human, isn't it?

We all fell for it, one after the other. We couldn't have saved anyone. Meanwhile, we can't stand by each other either. Because only those who know how to escape misery can call it by its name, and only those with answers have the right to interfere. Those who live in glass houses shouldn't throw stones. Those who have children should be happy.

Stuttgart; (I don't know exactly when, but I was a child).
Marianne was washing the floor around the toilet bowl, crying. On her knees, without a scrubbing brush. She and Raimund had had an argument, and afterwards, he'd slammed the door to his room. Marianne had no room of her own. She was cleaning the bathroom.

It looked terrible, seeing her kneeling there, crying and wiping those two square metres. I was afraid.

What did it mean? That she was Raimund's cleaning woman? But that wasn't true, she didn't have to do that. That she had no place to go except the bathroom? What about the living room, bedroom, or kitchen?

I would have liked to be her ally, comfort her, help her — but against whom and in what battle exactly?

If this were a novel, it would be the key scene I suppose. Her impotent calls for liberation. But, thank God, the heroine has the chance to save her daughter from a similar fate by daring to tell her the truth: that it is pointless to try and save others from the truth.

To make an omelette, you have to break a few eggs; where people shit, someone needs to clean; where there's love, people get hurt, and there's no point in pretending otherwise.

You need a hammer to forge your own destiny. If you hit things, they change shape. If you have a fire, you can get burnt. And DIY has its limits.

Shortly before Christmas, December 1982; Stuttgart.
Marianne didn't complain that she didn't have her own room. She wanted us kids to have our own rooms — that was important to her. Because she hadn't had one as a child.

The study belonged to Raimund, and he often slept there too, because he snored. Next to the fold-out sofa, there was a desk with drawers of 'documents' — forms, contracts, our children's ID cards. Marianne never sat at that desk. If she wrote letters, she did so in the bookshop, after closing time.

And anyway, she said she wasn't good at writing letters; she preferred Janosch postcards with the message already on the front.

Marianne didn't complain, but I thought it was unfair. And so I decided to give her a room for Christmas.

My favourite chapter in *The Children of Noisy Village* by Astrid Lindgren was the one in which Lisa gets her own room for her seventh birthday. I wanted to re-enact that scene, and so I brought up the old dining table from the cellar, where it had disappeared under a pile of books and suitcases; then I shunted my shelf into the middle of the room as a partition and stuck sheets to the back of it with drawing pins so that you couldn't see through it.

My surprise could have been ruined when I took Marianne's chest of drawers from the living room so that some of her things were already in her new room. But luckily, she didn't notice, because she was so busy at the bookshop in the run-up to Christmas.

I was proud of my idea and played around with the best way to present it to Marianne. Lisa from *Noisy Village* is first led around blindfolded on a wild goose chase before she is guided into her new room. I couldn't do this on Christmas Eve with Marianne. I decided to make her a voucher, something like: 'A room of your own.' 'Your room' — I drew various versions in 3D and joined-up handwriting, and then scorched the edges of the paper to make it look old. While I was drawing, I imagined Marianne's eyes shining.

On Christmas Eve, Marianne opened my envelope. In our family, each person took their time and turn to open a present. I saw amazement in Marianne's eyes when she read what was on the voucher, then she looked at me, and I jumped up and led her by the hand. The others followed a bit reluctantly. I opened the door to my room and presented 'Marianne's room'. But now I saw it through the others' eyes, it didn't look like a room, more like a table behind a shelf, hung with a sheet.

'That's sweet!' said Marianne and hugged me, but by then I'd realised that it was a crazy idea. What was she supposed to do at that table in my room?

I saw my sister's forced Christmas smile and felt ashamed. I had wanted to trump her present with mine, but it hadn't worked at all. Even our brother, who was only five, realised this. If anything, I should have moved into his or my sister's room and made a real sacrifice by giving up my own. But this was just silly—

Marianne politely skirted around this.

At some point around Easter, she suggested clearing out the cellar and while doing that, putting the table back down there. She was discreet and didn't mention my failure. I loved her for that, I really did. Because her silence spared me further shame.

Wrong, Bea. She might have relieved my shame by keeping quiet, but she could have got rid of it altogether. I was probably craving validation, and hadn't carried out my idea radically enough, but what kind of project was it in the first place? The size of our flat couldn't be changed by DIY; it was the flat that Marianne and Raimund could afford, and the fact that every kid had their own room was part of our parents' cover-up, a plan to ensure we didn't feel disadvantaged compared to our schoolmates, who not only had their own rooms but savings accounts too, into which their parents paid the child benefit that they didn't need to spend on a flat big enough for the family.

That Christmas, or that Easter at the latest, Marianne could have started teaching me the facts of life: it wouldn't have discouraged me. I was already discouraged. Discouraged, ashamed, and with only myself to blame. If Marianne had been willing to call her own sacrifice what it was, she might have stopped me feeling guilty, even though the odds were stacked against me.

I know it's painful to admit to your children that the world is unfair. It's more fun to claim that it can be changed by their efforts.

But if their effort only consists of self-denial, eagerness to make sacrifices, and having to be morally perfect, because there are no other means or opportunities, then things get tricky. Then morality becomes a currency.

Afternoon; in 'our' kitchen.
Bea: 'I bumped into Vera and Willi at Lidl.'

I'm cutting celery. Have to make an effort not to show my shock at hearing Vera's name.

It's Tuesday: Jack is at football training and Kieran at judo. Lynn has gone home with Karla, her new friend (perhaps).

Bea has no friends. She's just announced that again.

Is something wrong with her? Is it my fault if there is? Does the fact that I've ruined my friendships have something to do with Bea's lack of friends?

I'm an expert at cutting celery. The perfect cubes fall into the large pot, then sizzle in oil: vegetable soup in the style of my great-grandmother, without a trace of MSG. Bea thinks it's flavourless.

I wipe my hands on my trousers and fetch my laptop from my broom cupboard.

'There you go,' I say. 'Vera's break-up email to me.'

Bea's eyes widen. 'Can I read it?'

For a second, I'm not sure.

'Perhaps you're curious,' I say. 'I would be in your place.'

Bea's eyes flash. There's greed in curiosity and greed is a sin. It's even one of the seven deadly sins—

'You can read it all,' I say. 'It's my laptop, it belongs to me.

Perhaps it's immoral to let you read it, but who invented morality? The rulers did, for the oppressed, to keep them in line. Curiosity is valuable. I learned that at parents' evening at your childcare.'

Dear Resi
I think you already know what's coming, or rather, that this is exactly what you wanted — for me to be the one to end our friendship.

You know I love you, but you're not good for me. Your way of seeing the negative in everything, looking for the hair in the soup, putting salt in the wound … maybe you can't help it, maybe you don't even realise you're doing it and that you leave a trail of destruction in your wake, which others have to clean up for you. But maybe you do, and so let me say it loud and clear: I am no longer at your disposal for this kind of 'friendship'. This is where we part ways. I would like to protect my life and my children's lives from your scathing eye. From now on, you are no longer welcome in my home.

I love you and I will always love you, but I'm no longer prepared to prove it with my eternal understanding. Please keep away from my children and me in future.
Best wishes,
Vera

While Bea is reading, I've strained off the soup and begun

washing up. No one can accuse me of not cleaning up after myself!

When Bea has finished, she takes a tea towel and starts drying up. She already knows that busy hands can calm a spinning head—

'And?' I ask.

'I thought it'd be much worse.'

Really? Was it too mild? Not enough MSG?

'And what about the part with the evil eye?'

'She didn't say "evil". She said "scathing".'

'That's even worse.'

Bea dries up. I wait. I sense that something else is coming, and then it comes.

'Does that mean we won't be able to go to Laueli anymore?'

So that's what she's worried about: Christian's holiday home in Switzerland. The cursed place of my youth, back when it was still Christian's parents' holiday home. But for Bea, it's magical. We were there together six years ago, all fifteen of us, with tents on the meadow into which goats poked their noses in the morning; chopping wood, and making fondue, and Carolina showing Bea how to press flowers.

'Yes, you can, with Ulf and Carolina or with Christian and Ellen, or everybody together. Just not with me.'

'Then I don't want to go either.'

She puts away the dishes.

'You don't have to take my side.'

'But I'm on your side. I think they're all annoying too, with their K23 and their garden, and their kids in striped sweaters and Fjällräven backpacks.'

'Would you like a Fjällräven backpack?'

'No!' she says, a bit too quickly.

My heart contracts. Bea twists the tea towel into a whip.

'And what if I did?' she adds.

'Don't criticise those who have one.'

I take the tea towel from her and hang it up. Bea stands there with empty hands.

'I'll buy you one,' I say.

'What?'

'A Fjällräven backpack. So that you realise it won't make you happy.'

We need fables about how to bear unhappiness. Stories about hungry hearts, which you can tell without breaking your own: the fox who thinks the grapes he can't reach are too sour. Or the stork who serves soup to the fox in a vase — serves him right! Or the gentle, innocent deer, lying under a fir tree and listening to the shindig going on in the hunting lodge. The whole place shimmies, and everybody's grooving at the hunter's ball. 'Trash music,' says the deer, flattens its ears, and tucks its four legs under its belly.

I'll put on a mask, Bea, so that no one recognises me. I'll put you kids in costumes, fluffy onesies, so that you look like animals. Even better, I'll squeeze you into outfits, two in each, to make four-legged animals. Then it'll look real; I'll throw a brown blanket over you, and — Bob's your uncle. Then I'll be free to do whatever I like. Why didn't I think of it before?

———

The dishes have been washed; the table is set.

Everybody is at home, and so real that it hurts.

Next week it's the autumn holidays.

Kieran announces that he's not doing the school holiday program. Jack says, 'You have to. When I was eight, I had to as well.' Bea repeats that everybody in her class has something nice planned — everybody, except her.

Me (not thinking): 'Really? Like what?'

Bea: 'Sicily, Barcelona, Mallorca. Karl is even flying to LA with his dad.'

Me (after a short pause in which I luckily remember last summer): 'But you hate family holidays.'

Bea: 'Amelie and Ronja are going to Ronja's sister in Cologne.'

Me: 'You could go and stay with Aunt Gitti in Munich.'

Bea: 'What am I supposed to do there?'

Me: 'I don't know. What are Amelie and Ronja going to do in Cologne?'

Bea: 'Have fun?'

Me: 'Okay, I—' (desperately trying to come up with anybody I know under forty in a different city).

Bea: 'We never do anything! You go to work, and I have to stay at home and put up with my stupid brothers.'

Me: 'Kieran's doing the holiday program.'

Kieran: 'No, I'm not.'

Me: 'Yes, of course you are.'

Kieran (angrily): 'And Jack gets to stay at home and play computer games all day!'

Me: 'Jack has to make his own lunch and tidy up and do

homework. It's not as great as you think.'

Jack: 'Yeah, exactly.'

Bea: 'Don't pretend. Of course you play computer games all day.'

Jack: 'Shut up.'

Bea (to me): 'See? I can't stand it.'

Kieran: 'I'm not doing the holiday program.'

Me: 'Okay, then. Stay at home. Everybody can stay at home. I don't care.'

Lynn: 'Can I stay too?'

Me: 'Sure!'

Bea: 'Seriously?'

Me: 'What? You can go and visit Gitti in Munich. You're the only one who can actually do what she wants.'

Jack (gloating): 'Yeah, exactly Bea.'

Bea lunges at Jack and spits in his face.

Me: 'Seriously, Bea? Are you nuts?'

Jack starts crying and wipes his nose with the sleeve of his sweater.

Bea has gone red in the face, but her voice is calm.

'That's what I can do.' She disappears into her room.

You can't dance on four legs.

I'm terrible at knowing where the boundaries are between Bea and me. You could say that I *am* her. I'd love to go to Cologne with a friend! Or at least to her grandparents' house in the countryside. It's better than these never-ending days, these last grey three months of the year. What are we supposed to do with all this grey? All this dragging time?

Oh yes, and when the year's over, we won't have a flat anymore either.

Yes, my dear, I could say, then there'll be some action around here! Don't tempt fate! Soon you'll long for the days when nothing worse happened than a fight over screen-time and the washing-up. You'll miss your brothers' gentle features when the Marzahn mob has disfigured them beyond recognition.

I so wish everybody was happy.

How can I force them?

I pull up in our estate car. No, it's no longer big enough. We need a seven-seater, a Renault Espace with safety locks that bolt all the doors in case we have to drive through the inner city at night. And we will, because we have a long way to drive and the days are short.

It's the last day of school before the autumn holidays, and I packed everything this morning: the Renault is loaded up, and Lynn is already sitting in her velvet-covered child seat. Sven is in front next to me. We park in front of the school and wait. 'Yes!' Here they come, striding over, her big sisters and brothers. 'Hello!' Then they say goodbye to their friends at the gate and, 'Off we go!' to the grandparents in the countryside.

We sing cheerfully because their tablets are off limits in the holidays. 'Take Me Home, Country Roads' by John Denver and other songs. It's autumn, and the Renault roars on towards Magdeburg, straight on down the highway.

Sven says that's the nice thing about Niedersachsen: it never looks like anything in particular.

There are heathland potatoes for sale by the roadside.

When it gets dark, we drive through the area around the railway station in Lehrte. I activate the automatic locking device, and the little nubs on the doors drop down with a clack. They're called 'Pinökel' in Niedersachsen, I tell the kids. They laugh.

At Sven's parents' in the countryside, the lights are on. Grandma is standing at the door in an apron, waving. Grandpa has a pipe in his mouth.

No, wait: Grandma is smoking — because Grandpa isn't allowed to anymore. He's indoors with an oxygen mask over his mouth. Grandma stands alone in front of the house and doesn't notice us, throws her cigarette into the rainwater collector, and is wearing baggy tracksuit pants and Crocs, not an apron. She lights another cigarette so that it's been worth coming out. We watch her from the car.

'Should I honk?' I ask Sven.

'You'll scare her to death,' he replies.

The children wait.

I've turned off the headlamps to see better. The rhododendron has grown tall, hiding the view through the panorama window, behind which my father-in-law is lying in the living room. There's nothing to see now that my mother-in-law has disappeared into the house.

'What are they doing?'

Sven doesn't reply. As soon as he gets close to his parents' house, his imagination fails him.

He turns his head away, and I say: 'Shall I drive on?'

He nods.

'Let's go to *my* parents'!' I shout because that's the great thing:

there's always an alternative — a second, hopeful possibility.

I steer the Renault south.

We have stopped singing. Sven has turned on the radio; it's now night-time. The traffic warnings on the radio regularly announce new things lying on the motorway ahead: car parts, branches, dead animals.

'Perhaps it's a code,' Sven says.

The kids have fallen asleep.

We daren't take a break because they might wake up. The Renault has a large petrol tank.

The further south we get, the more my hope dwindles. My imagination fails me too, such as how we're all supposed to fit into my dad's one-room flat. We could sleep next to my mother at the cemetery.

Sven decodes the traffic warnings: they're telling us to forget the whole idea.

I realise that I don't have a driver's licence. Let alone a Renault Espace.

I so wish everybody was happy. At least in the autumn holidays!

I must be a megalomaniac to think I could start a mega-big family without mega-grandparents and a mega-car and mega-incomes. It was rash. It was anti-social.

Now my progeny has started attacking one another. I don't have control over them anymore. I can't provide for them; they will have to fend for themselves, and we all know where that leads.

Bea will become another statistic in the teenage pregnancy figures.

Jack will become an assassin, as befits his name.

Kieran will kill himself because he won't be up to living the ghetto life.

And Lynn might be fortunate enough to be taken in by a foster family at the age of twelve; to have a father like Ingmar, who likes to take on responsibility for injured souls, an adoptive father like Woody Allen.

Whose fault is all this?

Clearly mine.

I could have spared them the burden of life by not giving birth to them. I'm not so blind that I can't see a simple truth: how you plan the autumn holidays separates those who have the right to reproduce from those who don't.

The truth

'Ate way too much again.' This is the only sentence written in the diary my mother left behind when she died. She didn't have a lot of personal things, because she was used to not having her own room. At the end of her life, she had one: my brothers and sister and I had given her space. There, in the first room she'd had to herself, we sorted through her things and thought about who would like what to remember her by. I took her diary, a thick notebook with lined pages and a plasticised apple-green cover, in which she had written this one sentence in red felt-tip. Perhaps she was going to use it as a diet book?

Marianne had always been on diets. If only she could be as slim as she had been before she'd had children, then ... I've no idea what. She never told me; her diary doesn't reveal anything either. No notes of secret desires or dreams, just this one sentence hinting at what constantly preoccupied her. She counted calories all the time. In hospital, she was happy to have lost weight. 'Hello Death, just look at how slim I am now I'm about to die!' And then Death screwed her on the spot.

———

I also go on diets. Secretly. Not that I'm overweight, but there's always room to be thinner. Thinner, more beautiful, more in control. Less influenced by looks from strangers who notice: 'There goes a woman who's let herself go! She thinks she can satisfy her hunger by feeding it all the time. What a twat! It'll only get bigger, along with her BMI.'

I want to know what Marianne hungered for.

Want to dig her up and shake her so that she'll tell me. And if not her, then Renate. 'Tell me!'

Renate gives me a look. 'If you knew how it was back then, you'd understand what it was that we achieved.'

She doesn't want anybody to destroy her life's work.

'Oh, really?' I say. 'Why don't I know how it was? Why do I only know that Marianne would have liked to be thinner?'

Renate doesn't say anything else. She keeps her mouth shut. She's thin.

Wednesday, early in the morning. Three more days of school. Bea doesn't want to go because her hair is greasy.

'Then wash it,' I say.

'It won't dry in time.'

'Then use the hairdryer!'

'It's not good for your hair.'

'Then cut it off.'

I could strangle her. Hasn't she got any real problems?

Oh yes.

She tells me them, and I feel helpless. No one should have to go to a place like ninth grade, governed by such strict but random rules, and enormous peer pressure to fit in and still prove you're an individual.

'Try not to concentrate on what the others think about you,' I say. 'When you feel them looking at your hair, think about decimal equations. If you notice you're holding in your stomach, remember that in other cultures, it would give you prestige. I'll buy you a Fjällräven backpack later today.'

Bea washes her hair angrily. I begin to blow it dry for her. She hisses that the hairdryer's too hot. I shove it into her hand and leave the bathroom. Now she's crying hysterically. I push Jack and Kieran out of the door while my thoughts club each other over the head.

She should sort it out herself — *no, I have to support her.*

It's useless — of course it is; *but who's supposed to help, if not me?*

I understand her — *great, that's never helped anybody.*

What doesn't kill you makes you stronger — *my poor little baby.*

Lynn looks at me. Lynn's expression is hard to fathom. What does Lynn expect me to do?

'Do you think I should go in and comfort her?'

Lynn nods.

'But maybe she'll scream and throw the hairdryer at me?'

At that moment, the hairdryer goes on again. We both listen for more sounds coming from the bathroom.

'She's doing it herself,' says Lynn. 'You can go back to bed.'

'Don't you want me to read you something?'

'You just get some sleep,' says Lynn in a sympathetic tone. And as always, that's what finishes me off: when one of my kids is compassionate and selfless.

Sven is lying in bed with his eyes open. I can't remember the last time I saw him do that.

'Everything okay with you?' I ask anxiously.

He nods.

'Did we wake you up?

He shakes his head.

'Are you worried?'

He doesn't react, just stares in front of him. I shed my slippers and lie down next to him. Hear Bea's steps, hear Bea talking to Lynn, hear the front door clack — thank God. Everything else that happens will be just like always: bad, but we'll survive. I just shouldn't think about it too hard.

What is Lynn doing on her own in the kitchen? Won't she be lonely?

'Oh God, these mornings,' I say.

'Only one more day, then it's the autumn holidays,' Sven replies.

Is that supposed to be a joke? I laugh. He gets up.

Sven will sort it out. I can let him take care of things and go to sleep.

When I fall asleep in the morning, I always have the same dreams. There's a train on the platform, and the ticket machine won't accept my money; or the connecting train is coming, but I don't know where it's arriving. I wander, lost and breathless, through the underpass and can't decide what to wear, even though I'm in a hurry. I'm back in ninth grade, and there's a geography test, and

I haven't studied. Can't even remember the subjects we're being tested on, so I'm definitely up shit creek. Oh, and speaking of shit, there are only dirty toilets in my dreams. I desperately try to hold it all in. Why can't I relax? Why am I so afraid of things being dirty?

Bea gets all that from me.

Her fears of having greasy hair, a fat stomach, and unsuitable clothes. Her fear of smelling bad, taking up too much room, being thought of as slutty. I passed this all down to her through genes, example, or upbringing.

I have to work against all this: I should swear, stink, stuff myself with food, and fuck. I should talk much more often about sex organs because soon it'll be too late. How opportune that we'll soon be living under a bridge! Then she can see about her hair! Washing it in the canal water, rubbing it dry with newspaper—

When Bea was about ten, we saw a woman at Friedrichstraße underground station, squatting next to the lift with her trousers down. You could see everything — her arsehole, vulva, the lot. People walked past her, or stood right next to her, waiting for the lift, or came up from the lower floor and saw her when they got out. The way she squatted there. Peeing. She seemed alert, not drunk at all, just very dirty and fat, with several plastic bags filled to bursting next to her. She just let it all out, peed right in the middle of the underground station as if it were the most normal thing in the world.

'Uh-oh, look at that,' Bea said.

'Uh-oh' was the phrase that kindergarten teachers used to

express displeasure. 'Uh-oh' was not used to mean 'Oops, how clumsy!' but: 'You know very well you can't do that.'

That day in the underground station, Bea reclaimed the phrase 'Uh-oh.' Hers was a combination of uneasiness, indignation, and sympathy. Instead of distinguishing the difference between normality and abnormality, it expressed the boundary itself.

'Yes, I can see,' I said and carried on walking. As if nothing was happening. But in fact, a lot was happening. It was a revelation. I still see that woman very clearly in front of me, and I'm still looking for words to describe that boundary myself.

Jack was with us too and wanted to go back to the lift and have a longer and better look. I pulled him away roughly, fearfully.

'Mum-my!'

Lynn is standing by my bed in her jacket, hat, and scarf. She proffers her pursed lips for me to kiss goodbye. I kiss them.

Sven comes in again. I feel a stab of guilt in my chest, as always when I'm visibly doing nothing and he's busy. I imagine an accusation just because he's come in — 'Why do I have to go to childcare and not you?' — Although I know he'd deny it. 'Stay in bed!' he'd tell me if I actually said it out loud, but even that would sound like an accusation to my ears. I want to get rid of these ears. Sven wasn't the one who gave me them.

Sven bends down and kisses me. I am unwashed and ashamed — of my hair, my bad breath, my idleness. I want to become the woman next to the lift. How did she manage to be so free?

I may have given birth to our children in front of Sven, but even that was dictated to me by the fashion of our times. If it hadn't been for the extreme circumstances and adrenalin, I would have felt ashamed then too: of my appearance, my lack of control, and for everything that came out of my body alongside the baby.

I want to masturbate in front of him. I've never done it before in case it repulsed him. Or bored him! I'd rather ride along in the slipstream of his arousal, and do my thing in secret. Don't attract attention, don't disturb, just oblige and disappear.

'How pathetic,' Bea would say, a word she's started to use often recently.

Did I teach her that word?

'To be pathetic is to sink even lower than poverty,' I write in my broom cupboard after getting washed and dressed. What is the opposite of pathetic? Admirable? Feisty? Doesn't pathos come from suffering, and so isn't even related to the idea of uselessness? I flick through the etymological dictionary. 'Stirring, arousing pity, so miserable as to be ridiculous.' From the Greek, *pathos*.

Outside in the backyard, a child is crying. She sobs with heart-rending, throaty, gurgling noises — not the contrived crying used for blackmail, but real suffering. Now she even manages to articulate what the problem is, faltering and choking on her own tears: 'Mummy — don't want to. Mummy. Don't want to. Mummy, don't want to. Go childcare.' And then she takes a deep breath and carries on crying. The sound is so bleak and full of suffering, it could make the skies fall. I try not to pay any more attention, but the noise carries on, and on, and on. How come no one is helping her? I lean forward so I can see out onto the back yard. She's standing there in a green raincoat, two and a half, perhaps three years old. Her mother is standing in the passageway, looking at her smartphone. Is she waiting for her daughter to stop crying by herself? Or does she really need to check her emails?

I tidy up the kitchen. Soak the encrusted muesli bowls, sweep oats and breadcrumbs into the gaps between the floorboards. I really have to hoover, but the bag is full, and our supply has run out. I pick up dirty clothes. If I do the washing today, then there'll be fewer drying racks in the way at the weekend. But it's stupid to waste working hours doing the laundry.

Even this endless deliberation over what's the most efficient way of doing things is inefficient. How come I didn't set up a routine long ago?

I should just quickly do the washing.

I should drive over to a housing agency, find out about offers, and apply for a flat.

I should give up looking for a flat.

On the website of a housing association, my search for a flat in zone A or B returns no listings.

I have to call Ulf to find out whether he knows about Frank's letter of notice.

I have to call Ulf, Bea's godfather, and ask him whether he knows that the autumn holidays are around the corner and that Bea is the only one in her class who has nothing planned—

I have to go to the store and buy vacuum-cleaner bags.

It's good to be outside and walking around among strangers. They look pretty much like me, don't seem any more efficient, and all still have a roof over their heads. They dither from A to B, hover around the make-up section of the store and can't decide. Mobile phones ring in their handbags and pockets, and they take calls while paying or even serving at the cash register, and nobody looks unhappy.

I add some peppermints to the vacuum-cleaner bags on the conveyor belt.

'Receipt?' asks the cashier.

'Don't need it, thanks,' I reply.

I don't ask her where she lives, who she loves, who loves her, and how long she's been doing this job. Whether it's just a temporary thing or her real job, what school qualifications or dreams she has.

The so-called common people have long been discovered as main characters; the only strange part is when they open their mouths without being asked, thinking they're important enough to add their own perspective. Did anybody say they could?

There are way too many people. They have to be sorted.

Where would we be if everybody just talked about themselves? One at a time, please.

Seen from this angle, I was lucky to find out anything at all about my mother.

Three stories, all about how she was humiliated. How she should have felt ashamed, and on no account think that she was something special, let alone better, and therefore the next in line.

Ulf: 'Hello?'

'Hello, it's Resi.'

'Hi! This is a surprise!'

'Yes, I thought I'd give you a call.'

I didn't want to say 'I thought' anymore. It sounds much too much like an excuse or apology.

Ulf: 'Lovely! How are you?'

Does he really mean it? Does that mean he doesn't know anything?

'Well — um, I'm not sure. You?'

'I'm fine. Very busy. Time just flies by.'

A pause. And now? It's my turn because I called.

'I just thought I'd give you a call.'

I've already said that. And 'I thought' for the second time. If I don't spit it out quickly—

What do I expect from him? What's he supposed to do, and what do I want to talk about?

I'm ashamed. I'm afraid of exposing myself, afraid that Ulf will give me a bollocking at the first wrong move:

'Yes, of course you thought that. It's your guilty conscience. You know what you've done, and now you think everybody's going to behave the way you would — by being petty and cold-hearted. You weren't generous. You were self-righteous, and thought you could tell others off instead of solving the problems in your own backyard. And now you're afraid of being exposed? Well.'

Well.

A short, handy synonym for 'Everybody knows that.' A word like a slap across the face — no, like an electric shock. Leaves no visible traces, is inconspicuous and casual.

I was never hit as a child. I was slapped a couple of times, more by Marianne than by Raimund, and always in a moment of high emotion, never as a means of punishment. But that doesn't mean I don't know how violence feels, Bea.

The world is full of it.

Questioning your experience is another good way of making you feel small and silencing you, Bea. Yet again, you're not worth listening to, and yet again, others take the spotlight — those who have already been beaten to death.

Let's hold a minute of silence for them.

Would those who have suffered less kindly back off. Be still now, please shut your mouths. Violence is what they do over there; what we do here is called keeping peace and order.

Marianne was thrashed by her father with a clothes hanger. That's the third story; and if I could, I would leave out the clothes hanger. Just like I made up the nibbles for the fashion show and the pastis bar in the south of France, I'd like to spare you the exact kind of punishment and replace it with something else — like her pocket money was stopped, or she was grounded. But that's nonsense. Marianne didn't get pocket money and being grounded hadn't been invented yet. Children were thrashed and — boom! — the story already becomes irrelevant. Placed in the world of the 1950s; over and done with and obsolete.

September 1955; a rented flat in Gomadingen.
It was still the summer holidays, and the farmers' children had a lot to do, like bringing in the harvest. The other children didn't: they drifted around for hours on the streets in packs. 'Hanging', as they called it in Gomadingen.

The big kids had the younger ones in tow; the bigger you were, the more responsibility you had. Marianne had to look after her sister Brigitte; it was her contribution to the household.

And Brigitte ran across the road without looking. Her father happened to be standing at the window and saw it, but Marianne was nowhere to be seen. Luckily, Brigitte was unhurt, but Marianne wasn't let off the hook — quite the opposite. Her punishment would remind her how lucky she was and how little she had earned it.

'Just – count – your – lucky – stars,' groaned her father in time with his thrashes, 'that – nothing – worse – happened!'

With her arms covering her head, Marianne could feel just how lucky she was.

'Put your arms down!' yelled her father, and in the end, he thrashed her bottom.

Marianne couldn't put her arms down. She instinctively protected her head. The paranoid child. As if her father would have aimed at her head. What did she take him for?

I hate this father. I hate him, but I don't recognise him. Is he supposed to be my grandfather? That toothless old man who Grandma cut sandwiches into small pieces for? No, it can't be him; he was completely harmless.

To recognise him, I'll have to look at myself — the person who grabs you by the arm, Bea, who takes Jack's tablet away, shoves Kieran onto the bed, and forces Lynn to look her in the eye. Always for your own good, so that you realise how lucky you are.

This burning desire for it to be someone else.

For it to be the others instead; preferably the evil father in the

1950s, or even better, in the 1930s — in any case, long ago, lost in the mists of time, when people still wore galoshes and thrashed their children with clothes hangers.

It's nicer to tell stories about these people, isn't that right, Ingmar? That's what you wanted to imply when you confessed to being a book lover, somebody who reads real literature — whereas borderline Resi tried to remove the line between what she writes and what Goethe wrote, between her and her violent grandfather, between a modern man like Ingmar who is always concerned with everybody's wellbeing, and, let's say, Gauleiter Franz.

Idea for a real novel: the main character is Gauleiter Franz. A giant of a man, bull-necked, who hobbled and had a cleft lip. Never had much, was always poor, grew up in cramped conditions with eight brothers and sisters, and was the butt of his classmates' jokes, but still worked his way up and made a career for himself. In the Party, in fact, at which point this simple locksmith from Rhön-Grabfeld became Gauleiter of Unterfranken.

First, it takes hard work and months of research to understand this man's background and portray him credibly and conscientiously. The details are important; they make the reader able to see this monster as a man.

Shortly after the Nazis seize power, at the wedding of a Party member, Franz gets to know a woman who has been 'left on the shelf' — that's what they used to call unmarried women over the age of twenty-five back then — and a year later, they move into an Aryanised flat in Aschaffenburg. It's nice there. Fully furnished, with polished cabinet fronts.

Franz's wife becomes pregnant, she bears him a son, Adi, and then a daughter. A proper family at last! The family grows proudly and steadily like the Third Reich, but it also perishes with the Reich — because something built on such wrongdoing cannot last.

Franz's habit of striking the same tone at the dinner table as in the Party office is the first thing to make the attentive reader sit up and take notice. His wife doesn't reply; she simply sends the children out into the street. The mood worsens with every battle lost; Franz has trouble standing his ground against the scathing gossip of the neighbours, who by now all tune into the enemy broadcasts—

When Franz is called up to the Volkssturm despite his gammy leg, even the inattentive reader knows that things are going to get tricky for Franz's children—

At least there should be order at home! But then young Adi refuses to go for a Sunday walk.

Real literature has staff. People who sacrifice themselves for the story — and in doing so, spare you from having to tell your own story.

They're like housekeepers or handymen; and here I am, trying to do everything myself yet again. Not just wanting to be the main character in my life but also the centre of my thoughts.

You can get used to staff: while the nouveau riche still tidy up before their cleaners come, and are embarrassed in front of their au pairs, the aristocracy regard butlers as an extension of themselves.

Perhaps that's the difference?

On one side, there's the freedom not to need art. Because it doesn't offer anything to aspire to, achieve, or understand. At most, perhaps, it's after-work entertainment, something to enjoy over a glass of wine—

On the other side, there's hard work, collecting, sifting through ideas, weighing things up, observing: to understand, grow, and survive. And to prevent winter laying you low with all the other little mice—

I am naïve. Yes, of course I am.

I wasn't aware of this divide. Wanted to serve without being summoned. Why summoned, I thought, when it's me I serve? Who, if not us? Why say am I 'serving myself'? I'm serving everybody!

'Hello Ulf, it's Resi.'

Silence.

'Hey, I'm calling because I wanted to ask you what's going on.'

More silence.

'Back then, the article … To be honest, I still don't understand. What was so bad about it?'

'You mocked us. The façade. You said it looked delicious, like vanilla ice cream.'

'Don't you understand what I was trying to do?'

'Yes, I do. Very well. I understood it as an attack. I worked on that compromise for weeks, and you know how hard it is with ten people who have a stake — and you know them all, and why it turned out that way.'

I don't say anything.

'You used that against us. To make us look foolish.'

'This is it, boys, this is war.'

'What?'

'It's Nena. "99 Red Balloons." You know!'

'Listen, there's no point. Why are you calling me anyway?'

'Because I think it's weird that we don't speak the same language anymore. And don't even share the same past.'

'You're the one who said you were different.'

'I still like Nena. And everything that makes her different too.'

Summer 2010; Laueli.

The K23 planning and building committee put aside its plans and planning application for two weeks to go on a group holiday in Switzerland: to the lovely Bernese highlands and Christian's parents' house, which by then belonged to Christian and his brother, Bernd, who luckily lived in Bavaria, meaning that their summer holidays didn't clash. Bernd and his wife were pretty stuffy, and incredibly fussy when it came to the house and furniture. They talked a lot about 'overbooking', and how not everybody had the right to spend their holidays in the house, just because they happened to be old friends with somebody in the family. Christian ignored all that. He invited whomever he wanted, although in practice, 'invite' meant that you arrived and put up your own tent. The house had a high turnover of guests and whoever mowed the lawn, chopped wood, and chipped in with the running costs — everybody showered and cooked in the house — was always more than welcome.

It was wonderful there. A lively motley crew, with kids from zero to twelve, in a place where everybody constantly took photos.

'Everybody together on the hill! And … "Cheese"!'

A foretaste of how life would be when K23 was finished; then, the freedom they felt on holiday would never stop, and all the solidarity, adventure, purpose, and community that went along with it—

Ellen organised a cooking and washing-up plan, and it worked out really well. We all pulled our weight.

Vera and Frank slept in their VW van. They had bought it just before the holiday, having wanted one for a long time. They were independent, and on the second day, when it rained, they drove down to Lausanne, where the weather was better, with Willi and Leon, so that the kids could top up their vitamin D.

Sven and I borrowed two igloo tents from friends, and Vera and Frank let us pack them in their van, together with our camping mats and sleeping bags — there was always so little space for luggage on the night train. But then there was some misunderstanding: we were supposed to know that Vera and Frank would stop over in Stuttgart to see the grandparents on the way. So we spent the first night in the hotel in Adelboden; a bit of a pain, but Sven preferred that to hearing the word 'overbooking' again. When it was generous enough that we were all allowed to stay, and it wasn't Christian, but his brother who was the stickler.

Ulf and Carolina were allowed to stay in the room with the antique beds.

'Much too soft,' said Ulf, clutching his lower back in the morning. 'Want to swap?' Sven asked. Ulf waved his suggestion away.

Carolina showed Bea and Charlotte how to press flowers.

Sven chopped wood and mowed the lawn.

I shunted Kieran in his buggy up the mountain, over the gravel path, so that he took a nap after lunch. The wheels were too small, and I envied Vera's baby jogger, but Leon didn't like it when other children used his pram.

'He's like his old man and the van — his precious wheels!' Vera mocked, and it was true that Frank didn't like lending anybody his VW.

But Sven preferred taking the post van to do the shopping anyway; and if you went to the smaller shops a few more times, the grocery bill didn't come as such a shock.

The share was smaller.

And we all shared.

Everybody had to take their turn.

Everybody acted according to their best knowledge and beliefs, and if something bothered you, you had to say so; otherwise, the others couldn't be expected to know.

It was a lovely holiday.

I don't want to spoil anybody's memories — neither yours nor mine — because I really do love being in the mountains.

I love the scent of evergreens in the sun, the incredible variety of flowers, the cheerful sound of cow bells and goat bells; the punctuality of Swiss trains and post vans, the cleanliness of public toilets that don't even cost anything, and those delicious *Gipfeli* that cost the same as an entire loaf of bread. Were we supposed to bring one back for everybody? Fifteen of them? Or eat one secretly on the way home? Or were we to justify it, like: 'In some matters, my nuclear family is dearer to me than my chosen one,' or 'I'd like my kids to try one of these *Gipfeli* and the other parents have other life goals,' or 'Christian's children won't appreciate them anyway,' or 'If I could buy fifteen, I would'?

All that was undignified: I didn't want to think it, let alone say it, when we were all sitting together in the evenings.

The evenings were short anyway, after all that exercise during the day.

If we talked at all, it was about trivialities; Vera was never there because she had to help one of the boys fall asleep in the van. Christian tried to google what the mountain he'd always climbed as a child was called, and failing that, called his brother, having to leave the room as soon as Bernd picked up so that he wouldn't hear that there were seven adults in a living room designed for four.

Sven was standing outside, surveying his pile of freshly chopped wood and smoking. I went out and joined him.

'Don't you think you've contributed enough now?'

'It'll collapse,' said Sven, 'if I don't finish it.'

'That's impossible,' I said. 'Then you'd never be able to take a piece for firewood.'

Sven pulled a surly face. He wanted to saw, chop, and stack; he wanted to have something that belonged to him and him alone, even if it was work. I went back inside to join the others. I enjoyed the company.

On the ninth day, there was an almighty clash.

Vera and Frank weren't there. They had headed south in the van with Willi and Leon. The rest of us had been sitting in the house for three days — a genuine overbooking — because of the non-stop rain; Laueli, being up in the clouds, was misty and cold.

At lunchtime, I forced Kieran into rain gear and the buggy, and myself out of the door and up the gravel path. I borrowed an umbrella from the house's supply but closed it again after a few metres: I needed both hands to push the buggy up the mountain. I could feel the rain coming through at my shoulder seams. Never mind; it smelled wonderful in the woods. Those who can shoulder adversity shall be rewarded with the unexpected! Kieran fell asleep, I turned back, parked the buggy under the awning, and laid my wet jacket over his legs as a blanket. An hour's break perhaps, if I was lucky …

The living room was strangely silent. There was nobody there except for Sven and Jack, who were sitting playing Malefiz.

'Where are the others?'

Sven said: 'There was an argument.'

Jack said: 'We're playing it like Ludo, so if you get a six, you get another go.'

'That's good,' I said. 'Then it doesn't take ages.'

I went into the kitchen to make myself a tea. There was no one in the kitchen either.

'Have they all left?'

'Bea drove to Adelboden with Ulf and Carolina. And the others, if I got it right, have driven off to some thermal baths. A fun pool. Spa thing. I dunno, I was outside.'

'And you?' I looked at Jack. He loved swimming and diving. He was friends with Silas, and Ingmar and Friederike would have had room in their car.

Jack shrugged and looked at the board. 'You have to get all your men back home, so it still takes ages.'

'What was the argument about?'

Sven sighed. 'I yelled at Charlotte.'

'You did what?' I said, feeling sick. I quickly took a sip of my tea.

'He said she should stop saying dumb things.' Jack looked at me and grinned.

My chest tightened. 'Okay. And then?'

'Dunno,' said Sven. 'Emergency plan. Was about time anyway. This place needed some air.'

'Did you say sorry?'

'Nah. I went out for a smoke.'

'They already think you're short-tempered and hard to understand.'

Sven seemed unbothered by this.

'She really got on my bloody nerves.'

'She can't help it.'

'Oh, really?'

'She just does it automatically.'

'Yeah, so do I.' Sven scraped back his chair.

'Where are you going?' Jack asked.

'For a quick smoke.'

'Don't wake up Kieran,' I said.

Jack went into the kitchen to look for lollies. With fifteen people, there was never much left over, and the only thing he found was rusks.

'Use a plate,' I said.

I had a feeling of dread. Couldn't it have been somebody else instead of Sven?

I went to stand outside with him.

'Did everybody see what happened?'

'No, just the kids.'

'And how come they all took off?'

'No idea. They all just left suddenly.'

'And Jack?'

'He said he didn't want to go.'

'Did they ask him?'

Sven's eyes were narrowed against the smoke.

'Don't worry, Resi, Jack's a bright kid. He knows how things work.'

'Don't be too relaxed about that!'

Sven snorted. 'Relax? As if! I've been playing Malefiz for seven hours!'

The less people talk, the more difficult it is to find definitions: the difference between 'violence' and 'drawing boundaries', or what was 'legitimate' or 'objectionable', hadn't been clear between us for a long time.

I thought Sven's behaviour was authentic; Ellen thought he was brutal. Whereas I thought Ingmar was brutal beneath all his tolerance — driving his fast car to the thermal baths and cutting corners at high speed to keep the balance.

I didn't know where you were, Bea, but I hoped you were having a nice time with Ulf and Carolina, and that, as our child, nothing Sven or I did would be blamed on you.

Having said that, though, I blamed Charlotte's parents for her irritating behaviour. They gave detailed answers to even her dumbest questions, praised her every fart, and simply shrugged if she was mean. 'Love' is what they called it. I called it 'fear of conflict' — then panicked at the idea of our conflict if I told them how I saw things. I loved Sven's courage. And was afraid it would risk our place in the group.

Do you see how we couldn't say even the tiniest thing anymore?

There were fifteen of us, fifteen egos between zero and forty, all desperately trying to take hold of the reins.

I could have used that as a reference, but Vera would've had to be there, and *she* was trying to take hold of the reins by driving to Lausanne. Which wasn't a problem, don't get me wrong.

You see, Bea? That's how it starts all over again.

Once again, just to be sure: it was absolutely no problem. I would've done the same in Vera's shoes.

And then?

Things would have turned out the same. Unfortunately.

It makes no difference whether I'm envious or happy for the others. When tempers clashed in Laueli, Vera wasn't there; she was sitting in the sun in Lausanne. And I wasn't there either; I was in the woods. And then thankfully, the sun came out again, and not a word was spoken about the incident — at least none that reached my ears.

We didn't talk about it, and I'm sick of hearing that I should've said something and that if only I had, things would have been okay.

Speak, don't write. Whether in our confirmation lessons, at school, in Laueli, before Carolina's fortieth birthday, at Vera and Frank's housewarming party.

Just to say out loud for once: 'That vanilla façade — seriously? It's a pathetic, shoddy compromise.'

But I didn't need to say it. Everybody knew. They got what they deserved: the façade, the house, the children, the money.

This is the awful realisation that everybody is running away from, me more than anybody: there is nothing to talk about, let alone discuss. It was all fated. It was as it was. It was true.

The misery contest

Bea comes home first as usual. She finishes school at four o' clock, like Jack and Kieran, but doesn't hang around at school, or pop into Lidl on the way home to buy 99-cent biscuits. You can set your watch by Bea: at four-oh-nine, her key is in the lock.

'Hello, darling.'

'Hi.'

'And? How was your day?'

No answer. A bad-mood cloud hangs over her; I have exactly the daughter I deserve, exactly the girl she is: tongue-tied with a hungry heart.

And what do I have to offer? Empty hands? The only thing I can think of is to put her misery in words.

'It doesn't bother her to talk about these things in public. She can barely distinguish between personal and public interest, which is a further indication of a borderline disorder. She lacks all shame, which would prevent a normal person from exposing herself and others.'

Ingmar has invited everyone to dinner; I'm no longer part of the group, but I can imagine what they're saying, because I know how they talk.

Vera: 'I don't think it's fair to caricature us to that extent, as if we're narrow-minded.'

Friederike: 'It was supposed to be funny. But it wasn't.'

Ingmar: 'I don't think she can help it. It's how she expresses herself.'

Christian: 'As a writer.'

Friederike: 'If she were really a writer, she'd have a bit of imagination. Then she wouldn't need to expose other people's lives.'

Ulf sits there and ponders where to begin. He'd like to defend me — perhaps by saying that the writer is dead and the reader is now the real writer, a text is a text, and a perspective is always tied to the point of view — but he realises that they have no patience for such finer details. It will only take one word for him to end up on my side instead of theirs.

So, Ulf says: 'She went too far, that's for sure.' And he stares at his hands, crumbling the baguette that is served with the soup.

A delicious Asian fish soup, one of Ingmar's specialities — he really knows how to cook.

Ingmar's fish soup, Frank's quiche Lorraine, Vera's raspberry dessert with homemade caramel brittle, Ulf's lovingly made sandwiches with mustard and cress, Carolina's vinaigrette with garlic and sour cream, Friederike's yeast waffles from her grandmother's family recipe — I've cast all this to the wind, and now I crave it.

Kieran really has been to Lidl: a twelve-pack of milk rolls, a real alternative to haute cuisine. They taste of preservatives, but when you bite into them, they're lovely and soft. I could scoff the whole packet, but Kieran only gives me half.

'So unhealthy,' I say in revenge. 'Where have you had these before?'

'Anselm always brings them to school.'

Ah, must be a white-trash kid. Wouldn't have thought so with a name like that. And in this neighbourhood too. Perhaps he won't be here for much longer, because his parents will have to move to the sticks as well, and he could help Kieran make a new start at the rough school we'll have to send him to.

'I'm going to pick up Lynn,' I say. 'And when I come back, I want your screens to be off. Half an hour, like we agreed.'

'Okay,' says Kieran.

'Jack?'

He's not listening to me.

At the entrance to the childcare centre, I hold the door open for a mother with an empty double stroller and a baby strapped around her waist. It's been a long time since I was so hampered and weighed down! The only child of mine I ever took out of her pram and carried in a sling was Bea, when she cried on our way somewhere; the others just had to lie there and accept their fate. This mother does it differently, and wants to give her second kid the pleasure of changing its fate. Perhaps she's trying to be fair in all ways or hasn't got used to the screaming yet. I'd say that Jack didn't cry, not like Bea. But even if he had, it wasn't fair, of course. He was only quiet because he sensed there was no point in complaining. Because, as a baby, he already spared me.

'There's no such thing as fair,' Sven says regularly, and doesn't get his message through — to any of us.

In the coat area, a grandparent couple is in full action: he's watching her trying to get their grandson to put his shoes on; she's singing a song that I remember from my nursery days and haven't heard since then: 'One two, buckle my shoe / Three, four, knock at the door / Five, six, pick up sticks / Seven, eight, lay them straight / Nine, ten, big fat hen / Eleven, twelve, dig and delve.'

I look at the grandfather's expression and try to fathom what he's thinking, but I only see myself and what I'm thinking.

Lynn comes around the corner scuffing her feet: the sound of slippers on sandy linoleum.

'Say goodbye,' I tell her, like always, and Lynn swerves sharply left to shake hands with her teacher, who is busy with some kind of file.

'Bye bye, big girl,' she says, and even to me, Lynn seems really big today, and I wonder whether I should have put her in school already. What exactly is it that we're letting her enjoy a bit longer?

She dillydallies. She's overtaken three times, by three kids whose parents arrived after me.

I have taken off my coat and am sitting down. I look at the collages made of autumn leaves pinned on the wall above the coat hooks. Due to privacy concerns, the kids' names are no longer written on them. I found that out at the parents' evening. The kids are protected from the parents' compulsion to compare: the most creative children can no longer be determined at a glance. Unlike who is the slowest at putting on their shoes.

I receive pitying looks.

I want to say, 'Don't worry! I think my kids are the best anyway!' The trick is not to focus on what is expected of them, but to focus on the kids themselves. In no time at all, they become heroes shining with individuality. Just look at Lynn's composure: the way she nonchalantly drags her scarf behind her is enough to make any 1920s silent-movie diva be overcome with jealousy.

Even back at the flat where, of course, all the screens are still on, I manage to stick to my well-disposed view of things. In evolutionary terms, the kids are only doing what's wise, after all. Those who listen to warnings won't develop any new attitudes. Resistance is the order of the day, especially against the rules of elders. And anyway, it's not proven that gaming softens the brain. Parental fear of the unknown dictates the rules. So, break them! Outsmart me.

Jack has that innocent expression he puts on when faced with a parent, or any other adult authorised to give discipline or orders. Kieran, on the other hand, is frowning and thrusting his chin forward, which means he's going to resist to the death.

Even Bea has her mobile phone two inches from her face; she's lying on her stomach on her made bed, watching make-up tips from a YouTuber. I remember another piece of advice from the parents' evening: I'm supposed to act according to the 'five-star principle' when I talk to my kids about school. Don't lay down the law, just give tips and emphasise the positive.

Bea's YouTube Mum: 'Hi guys! Today I'm going to show you how to say goodbye to fear and constant anxiety. It's awesome if you manage to look and behave like everybody else because then you stand out less. Except in the ways where you *want* to be different, because they're really cool and make you stand out positively. Five-star things, like singing, or your decolletage. And if there's something you really don't like about yourself, just try not to think about it. Letting little inadequacies seem important by thinking about them is a mistake. Positive thinking is the be-all and end-all. For example, people with beautiful hands often don't pay attention to them, but they're a five-star feature. As a tip, I'd say: prop up your face with them, highlight your hands. Knit, or use them to gesticulate. Everyone thinks Italian girls are beautiful, but in fact they just wave their hands about a lot. It's good to be cheerful. If everything is totally shit — I mean, less than five-star — then just remember, chin up! Fashions are always changing. For example, in the past, bushy eyebrows were a real no-go. And today? Everybody's envious of them. So my tip is: the thing that bothers you most today might be totally in tomorrow. Perhaps the girl who calls the shots in your class will break a leg, or everybody will succumb to a pandemic and will have to stay at home for weeks. In that time, you can patch together a new fear-free, resistant, and really, really gorgeous you. Please like my page, and then we'll meet again for my next episode of Bea's mum *Five-Star Tips* when I'll be talking about teeny boobs and padded bras.'

Bea comes into the kitchen.

'What's for dinner?'

I don't answer. Sometimes it's good to swap roles.

Bea sits down and watches me cutting onions. It works: she starts talking without prompting.

'I argued with Lola again today.'

'What about?' Go very carefully. Casual, disinterested tone.

'She said she's going to Mallorca to learn Spanish.'

I laugh. And cry too. Because of the onions.

'Perhaps it depends where you go in Mallorca,' I say, and throw the onions in the pan. They sizzle, and I can't hear Bea anymore. 'What did you say?'

'I said her grandma lives there and that's why she's really going!'

'Ah. Then she probably won't learn Spanish. Everybody will speak German.'

'Lola said that wasn't true, and that she'd been there before and I hadn't, and anyway, she said it was just a joke but that's not true, and she only said that because everybody laughed, but she'd meant it when she first said it and wasn't being sarcastic.'

'Jeez,' I say.

'Everything is shit,' says Bea 'and I'm the idiot.'

'Why are you the idiot?'

'Because I said to her, admit it, you were serious. And she was like, I'm not admitting anything. And I always look like I'm being mean, and want to be right the whole time. But she's the one who wants to be right!'

'Just let her. She probably knows you're right anyway.'

'But she talks so much rubbish.'

'Then don't listen to her.'

'How are we supposed to be friends if I don't listen to her?'

Hmmm. Good question.

'I don't want to be like this. But I keep noticing all these things she says, like "twat", and you say you can't say "twat". So I say, why do you say "twat" all the time, I thought you were a feminist? And she says what has that got to do with it? So I say "twat" is a word for a woman's you-know-what. And she says no, that's crap. And I say it's true. And she says no if it was, I'd know. So I say, well, what does it mean then? She says I don't give a shit. I say exactly. She says, exactly what? I say you don't give a shit, you're not interested, and you don't know what you're talking about. And she says, yeah, that's right, but at least I'm not a total twat.'

'Oh, God, darling. I'm really sorry.'

'I don't want to be this way,' says Bea, 'but I can't help it.'

> Dear Vera,
> I can imagine that I am a burden to you and that you want to get rid of me and my tedious way of remembering everything and being a know-it-all. But please, what do the children have to do with it? You know that they're mixed up in it and tied to me, and that handing in the notice on the flat affects them too. I can already hear you softly saying 'you only have yourself to blame,' but you can't mean that, Vera — you're not like that. Are you? Is Frank like that? Yes, maybe. And you're tied to him. So forget what I've said, because I'm not going to send this letter anyway.

I want to tell Bea to drop it, that she shouldn't care, and should just concentrate on herself, her goals, and her schoolwork instead.

By the end of those two weeks in Laueli, the woodpile that Sven stacked was as high as my shoulder, and Sven had welts on the inside of his right hand and scabs on the knuckles of both.

By the time I'd finished my book, it had about two hundred manuscript pages, and I rewrote many times the scene where the main character cuts her friend's kid's hair and accidentally cuts his ear — before I decided to leave it out.

What if we'd built K23 together?

We could have been a part of it. Taken up Ingmar's offer — either the money or the idea to move into the ground-floor flat that he financed with the money he couldn't dump on us. Because no one else wanted that flat, but you can't build a house without a ground floor. So, after a great deal of back and forth, he called the ground floor an investment, even though he was against the idea of owning but not living in a property. And we would have been a good compromise because although we're not Ingmar, we're like family, and so in a way, him, and nice and colourful too, and we add spice to the mix.

Ingmar: 'It's outrageous that there are empty flats in the city centre. In these times! In this global situation!'

Frank: 'Put an ad on Immoscout, and you'll have thirty requests by tomorrow.'

Ingmar: 'But I don't want to live with just anybody. Some Immoscout user.'

Frank: 'What have you got against Immoscout?'

Ingmar: 'Nothing. I'd just like somebody I know and like. Who suits us.'

Vera: 'Then wait a bit. Perhaps somebody will turn up.'

Ellen: 'My cousin might be moving to Berlin next year.'

Ingmar: 'When next year?'

Ellen: 'Although … would she take the ground floor?'

Friederike: 'Is she the one with the fair-trade clothes?'

Ellen: 'Yes, that's her. "Port Coton."'

Friederike: 'Cool. Get her over here.'

Ellen: 'She said she *might* be moving. But to be honest …'

Friederike: 'Aren't we good enough for her?'

Ellen: 'Of course! She'd love it. But on the ground floor? Without kids? I wouldn't.'

Ingmar: 'I'd like somebody with kids, who needs a flat, who'd appreciate it. Preferably somebody normal and uncomplicated—'

Vera: 'Jana's always looking for private flats for refugees.'

Friederike: 'Uncomplicated?'

Vera: 'Somebody who needs it and would appreciate it.'

Christian: 'Don't fall for that. Some refugees have really high expectations. Whoever manages to get over here comes from money. And they have pretty big ideas. Just like your fair-trade cousin.'

Ellen: 'Her name's Britta. And you didn't want to live on the ground floor either.'

Christian: 'I'm not saying I did. I like high expectations.'

Ingmar: 'You make it sound like the flat is a cesspit — and not all refugees are the same. The ones who have lived in the shelter long enough with their families—'

Christian: 'I'd be careful. It turns them into animals. A friend of my dad's in Stuttgart owns a block of flats that are being renovated especially for refugees, and six weeks after they moved in, they had to start all over again. They cooked on the floor, didn't clean the toilets—'

Vera: 'They were unaccompanied children. Boys.'

Friederike: 'They're the ones who need housing the most.'

Frank: 'And are you going to look after them?'

Friederike: 'No, why? They have counsellors from Youth Welfare and some sort of voluntary helpers.'

Christian: 'And the rent is always paid on time by social services.'

Ingmar: 'It's not about the rent.'

Ellen: 'Are you serious? A bunch of young machos living on the ground floor? Our girls aren't that little anymore—'

No one said anything of the sort. And even if they had, it wasn't meant that way. And anyway, anybody else would have done the same! An agreement had to be reached somehow.

January 2014; the K23 common room.

Every K23 resident was given three sticky dots — three votes, in other words. Votes could be accumulated or split.

There was a brief discussion about whether the children should be allowed to vote, and if so, from what age, and whether they could have only one vote. Christian managed to assert himself with the argument that some life experience was required to make such an important decision.

Frank brought a flipchart from work.

On it, Friederike noted the options in her lovely handwriting, and then everybody stuck on their dots.

'Stop, stop, stop!' Ingmar cried. 'Please take into account the different criteria.'

What were they again?

Friederike flipped over the paper with the options and noted on a new piece of paper:

Poverty
Nice personality
Threat to the house community
Usefulness for the house community
Threatened in their country of origin
Culture (macho, good at music, language barriers, religion)
~~Rent~~
Suits us
New horizons

as people shouted these suggestions out.

Everybody memorised the criteria. Then Friederike flipped the paper back to the first page, and everybody stuck their dots.

Ingmar: 'What we're doing here is nobody's business. If you ask me, Resi has been planning this for a long time. She could've moved in, but didn't because she wanted to see what we would do with the empty flat. Just so she could provoke exactly this scene and capitalise on it.'

Friederike: 'Exactly like in her article. She always hated our house.'

Vera: 'And I loved her. I still love her.'

Dear Vera,
Perhaps the first thing you should do is to stop loving me.

True, we have known each other since we were three years old, and we've been through a lot together, and you know and understand me in a way that hardly anybody else does. But you don't have to love me because of that. No one has to.

Your instinct is yours alone, and the commandment about loving thy neighbour is probably the biggest bunch of codswallop in the Bible and an excellent reason to leave the Church. It's also a reason to refuse the role model of girl/wife/mother, seventy-eight per cent or so of which is about being loving.

Let's just say 'fuck it'. Let's hate each other and then maybe we'll find out if we like each other — when and why and what for.

All the best,

Resi

I could send this letter, but I should probably wait until tomorrow and read it through again. It's always better to sleep on it first, and that's why letters are better than emails, and books are better than letters, and the afterlife is better than Lidl on the corner.

I've been creeping around Sven all evening as if I'm ashamed of something. Well, some might say I'm partly to blame for our imminent homelessness. And even though I know that Sven doesn't think like that, I'm not sure this time. I avoid him precisely because he doesn't believe I'm to blame, but I can't talk about anything else except the fact that I am. And that's another thing I'm sure of: Sven doesn't want to talk about something he doesn't believe in. He never wants to think the thoughts of other people; if anybody's, then probably mine if I ask him straight out. But then they definitely have to be mine, and not what I think other people's thoughts are. And at this stage, I can't guarantee that. Come to think of it, I never can. So I'm silent. And lonely. Stuck in other people's thoughts.

I pick up my mobile and press Ulf's number.

'Hello, it's Resi.'

'Hi,' he says. And then nothing.

I know him; his silence speaks to me. He knows about the notice on the flat, and he knows that this phone call is to confront him.

'So?' I say.

He sighs.

'Listen,' he says, 'I did my best, and I have to say that it didn't help much.'

'So this is a punishment?'

'If you want to put it like that.'

'That means everybody knows?'

He says nothing, so yes.

'And that's okay, is it?'

He sighs. 'It's Frank's business.'

'Can I now say I'm a victim, or am I still not allowed?'

'What?'

'Well, you said I shouldn't make myself out to be the victim.'

'Listen, I don't want to talk about this on the phone. We can meet up, but this is just too confronting. Sorry.'

'What are you sorry about?'

'That it's come to this. No one's happy about it. Everybody has to figure out for themselves how they're going to deal with it.'

'Really.'

'But there's still a difference. You acted; Frank reacted.'

'That's a fact now?'

'Yes; the way I see it, it is.'

September 1955; Gomadingen.

Father called Marianne into the living room from where he had just seen a car nearly run Brigitte over. Father grabbed Marianne and started thrashing her with the clothes hanger, and Marianne shouted: 'Stop! It wasn't me! *She* was the one who ran across the road without looking!' And Father yelled: 'Exactly, she's still little, and you're supposed to look after her!' And Marianne said: 'But I don't want to look after her! I want to play and do what I want!' And Father yelled: 'I want doesn't get!' which meant that what Marianne wanted wasn't important. The only important thing was what Father wanted.

And to drum this into her, he beat Marianne.

Marianne had it drummed into her, and from then on, she was able to stand Brigitte even less than before. Thirty years later, she defended her father with the argument that he had probably suffered a huge shock; thirty years later she had her own children, whom she always worried about, and because of that, or because she was an adult herself by then, she still felt she had too much responsibility and too little freedom, and was never able to do what she wanted. And perhaps her father felt the same way, although he tried for a while to pass responsibility for Brigitte to Marianne, just so he could have a nap in peace for once. But that doesn't work, you can never pass it on: your child ends up dead, and then it all falls back on you, because you didn't manage to teach her sister how to take on responsibility. And want doesn't get.

In 1955 it was completely normal to give an eight-year-old responsibility for a five-year-old. An eight-year-old knows that cars are dangerous and that you can't just run across the road. A five-year-old doesn't know that yet, and that's why she's free to do so. All fingers were pointing at Marianne. If anything, she should have refused the responsibility in the first place: 'No Daddy, I can't look after Brigitte. I'd rather play on my own.' To say this later was not okay. It was Marianne's fault, and whoever says that Brigitte was her father's child and not Marianne's might just as well say that Marianne was also her father's child, and that's why she was already in his debt. That wouldn't have been strange for Father to think and so the only question left was how and whether Marianne could have refused responsibility from the get-go. If not, then she didn't stand a chance. She was unlucky: to be a girl, to be the oldest, to be born into a family with many children, and no money or staff. And to be upset all the time about being unlucky and the unfavourable circumstances of your birth isn't healthy. It's good that Marianne stopped that as an adult, forgave her father in retrospect, and understood why he did what he did; otherwise she would have been unhappy for the rest of her life. Worrying gives you wrinkles, and anyway, Marianne wanted to have her cake and eat it, and that's exactly what I want to do too, and so I'm not making myself out to be the victim, but the perpetrator.

The story starts with me. I made the decision of my own free will; the sheet of paper was blank when I first held it in my hand, or rather opened it in Word on my feeble old laptop. I could have easily written something else on it.

Go. Fuck. Yourselves. You. Pathetic. Arseholes.

Love

What time can it be? Ten?

Probably later, because most of the windows facing the road are already dark. All the bedrooms face the back except for Ulf and Carolina's, which is a loft, and so it's impossible to tell what's the bedroom and what's not.

Whatever I'm looking for here, the façade facing the road isn't giving anything away.

To get into their courtyard, I have to go through the gate of the next-door house, which is almost always open, and then I have to climb up on the wall of the next-door house, which is not a problem because the rubbish bins stand next to it. What is a problem: it's night-time, and I'm not a kid. Especially since I have to hitch up my skirt to even clamber up on the recycling bins.

So what.

Go fuck yourselves, you neighbours, fellow parents, guardians of public morals, homeowners, landlords, and prigs. Go and mind your own bloody business.

I am the woman by the lift. No one can tell me what to do and what not to do, where I am allowed to stand, and where not. I am part of this community and am going to get the best view of it I can. The lid of the bin gives a little. In the K23 courtyard, there are lights on in some of the windows, but just soft night ones or the blue flickering of television screens. No one is outside on the balconies. Why would they be? No one smokes anymore, and it's much too cold to sit out there. And yet, the building is saying something to me. Something about wealth and warmth, security and seriousness. There is no clutter lying around except for a few empty flowerpots on Friederike's balcony. Friederike goes to the garden show every year, repots her purchases in balcony boxes, and plans to grow new plants in the empty pots. Well, next year perhaps. It's okay; it doesn't mean she's not serious. The façade hums comfortingly. The façade is holding the building together and preventing me and all the other outsiders from getting inside. That's okay. That's what façades are for.

Come out, you cowards! Fuck you!

I have nothing to throw. Perhaps I could take a shit on the lawn. Because lying below me, in nocturnal peace and autumnal decay, is the garden. But first of all, I don't need to go, and second, no one would notice. It would even be welcome, as fucking fertiliser.

My heart hammers as I walk home. I don't want to be alone: I want to see the others, and I want them to see me. The road is all mine, but it's no use to me: I want company, not a motorway.

Marianne was more like our grandfathers in that respect. She didn't bake cakes or surround herself with people, but she got her driver's licence as soon as she could afford it, and a car as well.

The main reason she dated Werner was probably his car. He let her drive. Ecological concerns, which I raised many times when German forests began dying in the early 1980s, just bounced off her. She even drove the shortest of distances. Never had a cassette recorder or CD player in the car because she didn't need any other incentive or entertainment.

Perhaps I should just try it out, Bea. On the road, down the highway. After all, I don't know what I'm missing. Maybe it's so addictive that I'd have kept on going if I'd had a car.

I could have driven instead of writing books. Eyes fixed on the road instead of on people's faces; escaping from Laueli, you kids strapped safely in the back. Instead of having to climb aboard Ingmar's plan, I wouldn't have had to climb aboard or join in anything, let alone be grateful or relieved.

And even if everything had turned out the same way, at least we could have crawled into the car and slept in the Lidl carpark.

Thursday, early in the morning. Two more days of school.
No doubt about it — I'm writing for my life, like a woman possessed.

What's the difference between baking cakes and driving cars? Does being creative help a hungry heart more than being destructive? What role do speed, sugar, and dizziness play?

While in the shower, I sketch connecting lines and transitions in my mind. Later, in my broom cupboard, I won't use any of it. I hear voices and listen out for the ones I don't hear.

There's a quarrel going on outside. Sven is yelling at someone in the hallway.

Kieran has lost his jacket, and Sven can't understand how.

'Weren't you cold, for Christ's sake?'

I don't want Sven to scold Kieran — but what else is he supposed to do? I would do the same.

But when I do it, it's not the same. And why? Because I love Kieran. I don't care about his jacket.

I let the water run over my head and face.

Oh, to be under this shower and its warm, soothing jet forever.

List for Bea: be careful not to become addicted.

To motorways, sugar, or cigarettes, and certainly not to wanting to be understood or any other kind of attention.

You can lose it all at any moment.

Practise karate. Do pole dancing. Keep fit.

Make your body supple but sturdy, hard but flexible. Practise holding your breath every day. Take cold showers.

Train your soul. Be aware that things are never entirely black and white. Everything has at least two sides. Love is security and dependency at the same time, dependency is connection and impotence, impotence is helplessness as well as freedom, and then it starts all over again.

Nothing is solid. Everything's always in motion. Don't lean on things, whatever you do. Treat all certainties like the partition doors in our flat: at first glance, stately and solid, but when you lean against them, they give way and swing open, because the lock is broken.

Idea for a dance-theatre piece: empty stage, except for doors. Dancers reel about, trying to rest by leaning against them and — whoops — the doors fly open, they have no time to take a breather, and have to dance away again. Probably for ever. Until the audience decides to leave.

Vera loves me.

I love her too.

I was never envious of her, not even as a child, although her parents had a house with an enormous garden, a massive fridge that was always well stocked with food, which we were allowed to help ourselves to. The garage was the size of a small house and full of clutter — including skis, of course — and in the cellar, there was a deep freezer with popsicles.

It doesn't sound like anything special to you, Bea, because everybody has them these days. But back then, you could only buy popsicles in a shop or at the petrol station. It wasn't something you had at home. But Vera did. Vera had it all and more, but that was okay. She wasn't mean; she shared. And most of all, with me, her soulmate and friend.

1981; Stuttgart.

Vera and I were special. Our friendship went deeper than anyone else's, and we were going to accomplish things no one had before. Our future was a shining beacon, our strength was infinite.

When people asked us what we wanted to be, we would say: 'Chancellor of Germany.' Because we were sure that no other girl would say something like that. We hadn't a clue what chancellors did, but we knew they had power. And that a woman had never been chancellor, so we would be the first, like in so many other things.

We bragged and we were bold. We painted our faces and played pirates. Pretended that the world belonged to us. And it did.

We bellowed songs on the tram until old people stepped in, then we outdid each other in impertinent replies to their scolding. Those people had no idea of all the other things we could do.

We were strong. We were equal.

Our family homes looked different because our families were different. Vera's mother was more laid back than mine about eating salami without bread. At Vera's, we could eat and do as we pleased. And we didn't have to clean up after ourselves. We were supposed to play and feel at home. I felt at home.

1984; Stuttgart.

We both wore berets: Vera's was pink, mine was turquoise. We never took them off, ever, especially when we were asked to.

'Ladies may keep on their hats in enclosed quarters,' Vera said, in reply to her English teacher's request to take hers off. She should know, after all — just look at the Queen.

We giggled.

'Does your hat have a religious meaning?' my sports teacher asked, and I was briefly tempted to say it did, but I didn't want to lie, and so I said: 'Well, kind of. To me it does.' Which the teacher let pass, because she liked me, and so I was allowed to keep it on.

We talked to each other about our battles in the afternoons and at weekends, because we now went to separate schools. I didn't know why that was, just that Marianne was upset about it. I didn't mind. Vera and I fought for freedom and justice at our separate outposts, and then counted our successes afterwards. And we were very successful; in our reports to each other perhaps more than in reality. But mostly, we couldn't wait to see what life would be like in the glorious time after school was over. Like famous female pirates Anne Bonny and Mary Read, we'd hoist the flag and sail away, and nothing and no one would be able to stop us.

Marianne didn't explain to me why she was upset. She didn't want the parents' differences to cast a cloud on the girls' friendship. And anyway, perhaps she was wrong: perhaps sending your child to a private school wasn't a decision based on principles, but just a concession to the grandparents' wishes. And so, not a rejection of the joint social project that was supposed to change everything. Marianne didn't dare explain all this. Or her hope was greater.

1991; Stuttgart.
School was out for ever, and we were ready to start the new phase of our lives. No matter what our A-level certificates said, it was going to consist of art, sex, agriculture, and house-squatting; of brightly painted rooms, sofas in the kitchen, shooting films, making masks and puppets, doing street theatre, and singing as we drove through southern Europe in converted vans. Starting bands, or at least having sex with musicians in converted vans. And, of course, goats wandering among old barns.

Where did it all come from? Our imaginations or the vans? Old barns or musicians?

We wondered that too. And we soon realised we had to reconsider, study for some kind of career and learn instruments, find allies or sponsors, and suitable places or possibilities to set them up so that our ideas could become a reality.

Vera's father wanted Vera to get a degree. Especially because she was a woman.

'What's that supposed to mean?' we asked, outraged. And we really didn't know.

But in the end, Vera accepted his money and went to a private design school. In the end, she was the best paid of all of us for a while because she could use Photoshop and edit digital videos before anybody else could. I didn't take computers seriously. I wanted something tangible. I applied for art school and got rejected. I didn't care — those who failed there would end up as teachers anyway.

1993–94; Berlin.
At last! A taste of the life we'd always wanted. One and a half years in Mühsamstraße in the house Christian's father bought or repossessed or came by in whichever way — we didn't care; Christian found it and told us, and we arrived and set off, pointing our Super-8 camera at it all.

Kurt Cobain sang that Sunday morning was every day, for all he cared. His voice patched together the contradictions, shaded over the parts where the ideas didn't quite meet reality. The sun shone down on us.

I cleaned and cooked and proofread. The others went to university twice a week and got money from their parents. The main thing was to be authentic, and leading a double life was just the thing for people who couldn't get enough, like us.

Kurt sang that he liked it and wasn't gonna crack.

Kurt put a bullet through his brain.

We had to leave Mühsamstraße.

Ulf grieved for Kurt as if he knew him personally. I knitted him an olive-green mohair cardigan, like the one Kurt was wearing on *MTV Unplugged*.

Ulf split up with me. He started applying himself seriously to his architecture studies.

1995; Berlin.

Vera edited music videos. Soon got to know real bands, Berlin musicians, and the clubs they played in; I didn't want to go with her just to stand around. I still couldn't sing, but maybe I could write pretty well.

I wrote lyrics, and Vera sang them. We shot a video.

We dreamed about becoming famous like — yeah, like who actually? Simon and Garfunkel? George Michael and Andrew Ridgeley? Annie Lennox and Dave Stewart?

A guy from Friedrichshain wanted to be our manager. He sent out our demo tapes but didn't know the right people in the end. Or didn't know them well enough. Vera shagged him but not because of that. We were after love, not a career. Or preferably both, like — yeah, like who actually? Kurt and Courtney?

Kurt was dead, and Courtney had managed to have his baby just in time, thank God.

And Marianne was so looking forward to having grandchildren.

Vera's mother, too; she didn't think it was *ever* going to happen.

Not to mention Friederike's mum. She was already worried that Friederike might be — but no. Everything turned out fine.

We weren't like our mothers.

We had our wild times, after all, fulfilled our dreams, got to know more than one penis, watched our waistlines only secretly, if at all, and our husbands knew how to use the washing machine.

Vera and I stayed close. We knew everything there was to know about each other, knew precisely what made the other tick, witnessed who we had been and who we had become. We belonged together. We were family, we had a maternal love for each other. Selfless and self-righteous at the same time. We were understanding about our lack of understanding. There was no hassle. No envy.

'Just help yourself,' we said unhesitatingly. 'You can have the last, biggest, tastiest piece — because if you're happy, I'm happy too. And anyway, I'm stronger than you. I can resist. I don't have to keep stuffing myself—'

Maternal love is poisonous. It pretends not to demand anything, and in truth, it wants everything. It says: 'I am because you are, and you only exist because I am. Because I take care of you! But don't worry about me.' When in truth, every step you make and every breath you take is about me.

Some stories might have warned us, stories about seduction, traps, and disguises; about the poison of maternal love, the other side of the coin when you indulge somebody's every whim, and a mother's fear of no longer being needed. Fairy tales.

In the Brothers' Grimm, they've all been censored and turned into stepmothers. Did you know that, Bea? I didn't.

Free will

'Why didn't you want to marry me?'

It seems like a good idea to start with an abstract, over-and-done-with accusation instead of a concrete, still-smouldering one.

Ulf has ordered a bottle of beer for himself, and wine for me. Ulf is emphasising his willingness to take the side of the working class, whereas I still don't know the difference between Cabernet and Bordeaux and Pinot noir. I could have taught myself by now, but I bluff instead, pretending to think for a moment before ordering.

'I don't know,' says Ulf. 'No one wanted to get married. Did you? That's news to me.'

'No,' I say, 'I didn't.'

I clear my throat.

'But that's my point,' I continue. 'I didn't want to move into K23 either. So, where does that leave will? So-called free will?'

Ulf's expression is sad. He looks good: he's slim, well-toned, has an upright posture from yoga, and still has all his hair, which he'll always keep if he hasn't lost it by now, as I know from my hairdresser. His sad expression reveals his age, and will scare off potential candidates for an affair, unless they're into psychological problems, misery, and arguments. If you look closely, you'll see that the sadness weighs down his well-toned shoulders too.

'We don't have to beat around the bush,' says Ulf.

'Exactly,' I say. 'So what's at the bottom of all this?'

'To muck out the past?' says Ulf. 'You're not the only one who gets to do that.'

'What do you mean?'

'You broke away from us. With your article. And definitely with your book.'

'Well, I think I used you as examples too often. *Seeing* you as examples, that was the problem.'

'The problem was you going it alone. You were underhand. Clearly you think everything we do is stupid. Well, then. Suit yourself.'

'Do you remember the skiing holiday?'

'What skiing holiday?'

'In twelfth grade, when you all went to Laueli, and I didn't.'

'Dimly, yes.'

'You mean the memories are dim, or we were dim?'

'Stop it, Resi. I'm not going to walk into your trap.'

He gets up to swap his empty beer bottle for a full one. I rub the corners of my mouth in case spit or red wine has collected in the cracks.

When Ulf comes back, I ask: 'Should I have accepted Ingmar's money?'

Ulf looks tortured. I suddenly remember that when he split up with me, back when we were twenty, his reason was very similar to

224

Vera's. He said that, as my partner, he saw the world through my eyes, and although it had been a very inspiring experience, he was curious to see the world through his own eyes.

It had seemed a lovely, understandable reason to split up with somebody, and I loved him for that, even though at the time, he had implied that only a gentler, funnier way of seeing things than mine would be bearable in the long term. However, that was just speculation, and back then, criticism wasn't criticised as much as it is now, but was desirable and inspiring, as Ulf said. At least, I only felt a brief twinge of shame, as if he'd said he'd like to try a girl with bigger breasts, because who knows, perhaps it would be a kick. 'To be a kick' was an expression we used back then.

I ask: 'Do you think it would have been a kick?'

Ulf doesn't react. Perhaps he really has forgotten everything. How it was when we were together, and the reason he split up with me, and the plans we had, like having cats and kids, goats and street theatre, sex and house squatting. Like the expression 'It'd be a kick.'

I decide to go for broke because none of this matters anymore.

'I think we had extremely different starting points in life, which we ignored at all costs, and I think it's still the case, or even more the case, and it's being ignored more than ever — or worse, it's being glossed over with neoliberal rubbish about opportunities of moving up in the world and "Everybody knows that", and I hate to say it, because you've joined in with that horrible mantra that I'm making myself out to be a victim, but while I'm sure I'm partly to blame, and others have suffered because of me, I still think it's right to think and talk about what's at the bottom of all this, because it's just too easy to make me a scapegoat and declare me insane. And effectively evicting us from the flat is totally outrageous, and can't be justified at all, especially not with "Everybody knows that", "You only have yourself to blame", and "Well, it was just a reaction". Okay, maybe Frank has decided to muck out the past, but the muck he's cleaning out is still breathing!'

Now I'm out of breath.

Ulf's handsome face, shaven early this morning, is now a silvery, elegantly stubbled mask. I know that he was against the vanilla-coloured façade. He wanted grey with a sparkly mica finish, so that the house would glitter when it caught the sunlight, but would otherwise look modest. I know he thought about pushing his choice through, against the majority, and stepping forward as the architect rather than an equal member of the building group. But he decided against it in the end, because the exterior wasn't that important to him: being accepted by the group was more valuable than recognition in his professional circle. I sense how difficult it was for him, because he has always been ahead of the times in aesthetics. He knows that he knew better, had proved it a thousand times, and yet, decided to sacrifice himself for the sake of the others.

'You only think of yourself, that's your problem,' he says, while almost at the same time, I say: 'I'm openly selfish, that's your problem.'

We don't laugh. We don't say 'Jinx', like the kids do, and anyway, we didn't quite say the same thing; but we *are* jinxed somehow, and I understand this phrase for the first time.

Ulf doesn't have any children, and I don't feel like explaining it to him. I want him to explain something to me. I want to force him.

'How's Willi?' I ask.

For the first time, I realise that Willi is called Willi and lives with Vera and Frank.

'He's famed for his selfishness too,' I say, 'famous for having a will of his own, and that's why the adults can't stand him.'

Ulf looks at me blankly. He's sticking to the etiquette of not talking about people in their absence. This is another rule I break. 'But he's tormented and pushed around and never gets what he wants in the end. Which is for everybody to admit that they're lying. That they wish they were somewhere else and had some peace and quiet. Do you think Frank really wants to take his boys to the swimming pool every weekend? No. But it's the only place left where he can keep them under control. The last resort. All these holidays, parties, the whole eternal show. Being. A. Family. Isn't. *Nice*. It's exhausting and gruelling, and just one long bickering session. You get cold, you get athlete's foot, and end up with soggy biscuits on the changing-room floor. And it's fucking convenient to put the blame on one person, especially if it's someone who doesn't realise what's going on and can't defend themselves, because they're small, or weak, or a little rebel. And it's fucking convenient to dump your guilt on somebody while making out it's just your way of helping, disciplining, or restraining them, and to use self-defence as a justification for tougher measures — not of your own free will, of course, but because you were forced, and it was just a reaction.'

'Are you talking about yourself now, or Willi?'

'You were there, for fuck's sake! At that awful christening. You saw the way Frank dragged out Willi with his hand over his mouth. It was brutal!'

Ulf says nothing.

I close my eyes. Ulf must have seen it; we were standing right next to each other. He didn't say anything at the time, obviously, and neither did I. Nobody said anything, as far as I know. It was Willi's fault, because he'd provoked Frank and wouldn't behave in church, and Frank didn't know what to do and was probably in shock, like my grandfather when he saw Brigitte running across the road without looking. You have to keep your kids under control; otherwise things happen, and that's why these measures are always for their own good. I'm the last one who wants them to die, and I understand Frank, and I understand why he dragged Willi out and held his mouth, and the silence afterwards. What was there to say? But it's true that the clothes hanger broke, and that Willi's shin hit the church pew on the way out. A mistake, a consequence, unintentional, but a fact, nevertheless.

Ulf isn't listening to me. Ulf says nothing. Here in the bar, we are not speaking the same language. But you, Bea, you have to listen to me, because I'm the one who taught you how to speak.

September 2014.

You remember, don't you?

You were there too, Bea, at the huge christening party for Fritz, the son of Vera's friend Nele, for whom Frank was the sperm donor.

You kids didn't think it was anything special. Fritz was just a chubby baby with two mums. A father is necessary, but he doesn't have to be the dad.

Frank donated sperm so that Nele and Tina could have a child, and it was Vera's idea to have the post-christening party in K23, because there was plenty of room, and the right atmosphere, and we were one big happy family, and Fritz was part of this colourful chosen family and its gene pool.

Of course, there were a few pensive frowns here and there; somebody standing next to the tall grasses by the rubbish containers with a glass of beer wondered what he should make of this whole *queer family* business — some old uncle from Bavaria who immediately got a top-up from one of the mothers in a strappy dress. She had been standing at the font earlier; in fact, there was a real crowd up there, what with the mothers, the biological father, his wife, and three godparents. The uncle wondered who was who again, and who you-know-whatted whom? But that was precisely what this was all about: uncles like these were no longer in charge but had to stand and be quiet next to tall grasses by the rubbish bins and drink their beer. And the rest of the people at the party were happy that Fritz had been born and would have a good life, with his two mothers and two half-brothers, and the donor father who was throwing a frisbee around in the back garden, while his wife and her friends passed the cute baby around, in a house whose garden was such a wonderful place to celebrate in.

I realise I sound ironic, Bea. Even though it's all true.

It was a fantastic party, there were piles of food, and everybody looked terrific. You had those plaits, do you remember? And that red velvet skirt. Tina already fitted back into her black jeans, although Fritz was only four months old, and Nele was wearing a dress that Vera had bought for herself from Oxfam years ago and never wore, but which Nele looked great in; she's one of those women who can really wear 1950s dresses. The atmosphere was fantastic. The weather played along.

The only person who didn't want to play along — surprise, surprise — was Willi.

'That's not my brother! I don't know him!' he yelled in the church. So loudly and angrily that everybody heard him.

Do you remember?

You were supposed to go up to the altar, all you children, and make a circle for Fritz. The pastor was an old friend of the family's, one of the '68 generation, progressive and well-meaning. He'd come up with a plan to stop the kids being bored and include them in the ritual. You were all called up to the front to make a circle for Fritz — to welcome him into the community together. 'As your friend and brother!' said the pastor, and you were supposed to raise your arms and cry out 'Welcome, Fritz!'

Which you all did, you big kids slightly hesitantly. You threw me a look, then joined in.

Only Willi refused. 'He's not my brother!' he yelled and tried to run away.

Frank bounded over to him in two strides and grabbed him by the arm.

'Let go!' Willi yelled. 'You can't make me! He's not my brother and never will be!'

And Frank covered his mouth with one hand and dragged him out.

Not that I didn't understand Frank's reaction; Willi, of all people, Fritz's real half-brother. It was embarrassing, especially as Willi hadn't properly understood. The pastor had meant 'brother' in the sense of 'fellow believer' or 'comrade', hadn't he? Not as a reference to Frank's sperm donation. But why couldn't Frank accept Willi's refusal to take part? Why did he react so harshly?

It was a delightful party, but one where nothing was supposed to disturb the planning — a family gathering where you had to keep your mouth shut and play along, like at any family party. Sure, the circumstances were different, and other people had to shut up — the Bavarian uncle instead of Berlin butches — but it wasn't liberal and carefree either, let's not kid ourselves.

But we did.

Because we weren't going to let our display of a colourful, progressive get-together be ruined any more than others would their patriarchal hierarchy or happy family. Not by a snotty-nosed brat like Willi, and certainly not by a hallucinating witch like me, who only sees the worst in everything.

I open my eyes again. Ulf, who is drinking quite quickly, has already finished his second bottle of beer, and I ask: 'Do you want another?'

He shakes his head.

'What do you think you're going to change?' he asks. 'Why didn't you step in straight away if it was such a big deal for you?'

'Because I was afraid. *Perhaps it wasn't as bad as I thought. Perhaps it just comes with the territory. Perhaps it would go away if I ignored it.* There's always something going on, and always somebody who ends up crying, and on the whole, it was really nice.'

'You obviously didn't think so.'

'But I wanted it to be. I wanted everything to be nice — you, your house, our friendship, the past, the future, the children, the parties. Why do you think I didn't want it to be nice?'

'Because you don't act like it.'

'No! Willi wants it to be nice too. Everybody does. BUT – IT – ISN'T – NICE!'

Ulf glances to one side where a group of young women is sitting. They're still radiant and fresh, so clearly they're not mothers, and they don't seem bothered by me screaming my head off. The couple to our right, the same age as us and quiet, probably *are* bothered; perhaps they're thinking that Ulf and I are a couple having an argument, and Ulf would do better with one of the bubbly twenty-somethings to our left instead of putting up with the hysterical old lady.

I drain my glass and slam it down on the table. 'Embarrassing, isn't it? To get upset and scream in public. And to do it in front of an entire christening party as well. Willi dared, but I didn't. What if I'd misunderstood something? Or I was the only one who felt the way I did? What if no one stuck up for me? Then I'd rather bail on Willi, even though I knew he was right. "Brother?" What a load of crap. "I don't know him!" *Exactly*. But you need guts to be that honest.'

I imagine jumping into the aisle between the two pews and pulling Willi from Frank's arms. And that's where the problems start, because Frank is obviously stronger than I am. But the element of surprise would be to my advantage — Frank would let go of Willi, and Willi would run away, and me after him. Frank wouldn't. He'd sit down at the back near the hymn books, take deep breaths, and try to calm down.

Ulf pays for his beer. Pays for my wine too, puts his jacket on, wraps his scarf around his neck.

That's what I like about him: he just leaves and doesn't need to make a big speech about it.

We trudge alongside each other through the neighbourhood on this dark, wet autumn night.

In the place where the homeless sat for years outside the supermarket, there's now a huge hole. There's no sign saying who is going to build here. Ulf will know, but I don't ask him. The tarpaulin covering the hole flaps in the wind. Drizzle shows in the light from the streetlamps. My face is wet too, but I don't mind. I like walking around here with Ulf.

Willi and me. Outside the church.

There are some low shrubs planted, and Willi disappears into the thicket. I wouldn't normally dream of going into such a place because of the dog shit, but perhaps around a church, it's okay. So I follow Willi into the bushes. He's sitting there, cowering under a conifer. Huddled in a hedge. His legs and arms are crossed, and he's holding himself tight.

'Hey,' I say. He doesn't look up.

I copy his posture: huddle down too, and hold myself tightly. It doesn't feel bad, but it's pretty tiring at my age. But I'm no longer my age, I'm like Willi now: I have the courage to yell my head off, make a fool of myself, stop something happening, and be wrong.

'What was so awful?' I ask.

He doesn't answer. I wonder if I know the answer.

'The pastor had a stupid voice. But he was taught to speak like that. At his pastor's training, when he learned how to speak in God's name in front of so many people.'

Willi still doesn't say anything. I can only see his hair, which is

233

covering his face. His head is bowed down, and he's silent. His hair is matted and tangled: he doesn't like having it combed. I pull out my hairband and try letting my hair dangle in my face too. And in between my teeth.

'Fucking idiot,' I say. 'I don't care what they taught him, the stupid fucker.'

I let myself fall over. Lie there with my hair in my face and my cheek in the earth among the shrubs with their hard needles and leathery leaves. It smells mouldy and unpleasantly pungent. There's no dog shit, but there's bird poo and bugs.

'Maybe the pastor pissed in here?'

I can hear Willi breathing. Otherwise he doesn't make a sound, just sits very still. He won't look at me, ever, because he knows I'm not on his side. Saving him once is not enough, and maybe he would have managed to get away on his own. Would be sitting here anyway, without me.

'I didn't do it for you,' I say. 'I did it for me. Singing songs together and chanting is all very well, but not if you don't feel like it. And it's twice as annoying when you have to do it for the sake of others. They can make their circle, keep their new baby, and have their party without me. I don't want to be told where to sit. It's all so silly and predictable. So rehearsed, even the improvised parts. They don't even know how to improvise.'

'What did you say?' Ulf has stopped walking.

I hug him, pull his head towards mine. He acquiesces, and we kiss; we can still do this, even though we haven't for decades. Ulf's lips are familiar, incomparable, warm. I want to unbutton his jacket, but he's already doing it. We learned together how sex works, and it took a long time, and wasn't made any easier by our terrible lack of confidence. 'Whatever turns you on,' was the saying when we were growing up — the mantra of the sexual revolution and the biggest lie of all. Because shame was still doled out in massive portions. I'm full of it, up to here, and can't move for fear that it'll spill over. And now Ulf realises what we're up to, and doesn't want to, and shakes himself free and walks away. I stay where I am: I can't and mustn't be the pissing woman next to the lift. And I certainly can't fuck Ulf standing up outside on the pavement, even if it's the only meaningful thing for us to do. Instead, I watch him put his key into the lock of the glazed, white solid-wood door, which he commissioned a carpenter friend to make, and I turn back to the other door, whose key I have to hand in soon. Speaking of which, how many keys do we have? How many did Frank give us? Fucking sloppy of me, yet again. I'm a fucking slut, which is obvious from the moment you set eyes on me.

Shame

Friday morning, the last day of school before the holidays.

Bea going away with Ulf now seems like a distant dream. Not that he's tarring us all with the same brush, but how's he supposed to ask her without me getting in the way, or at least being in the picture? How is Bea supposed to ask him without me knowing; I'm her shadow, just like Frank and Co. are Ulf's. What did he say yesterday? 'To muck out the past?' Did he really say that?

I steady myself by holding onto the worktop. There are three lunchboxes to be filled; Lynn doesn't need one because the parents take turns in buying snacks for childcare. Everything goes black in front of my eyes, but that's my circulation and low blood pressure. A glass of champagne for breakfast is supposed to help. Perhaps it would help *too* much, though, and lead to misunderstandings — a weed-smoking father, an alcoholic mother? Let's muck them out, sweep them away, disinfect their place, gas it.

Stop it, Resi, that's not what he meant. He just chose his words awkwardly. But why am I saying that of Ulf, of all people, the eloquent mediator? Why should I protect him, a self-appointed defender, from his own words? So that he takes Bea off my hands for the holidays? Perhaps I'll never let him see Bea again.

Dear Ulf,

I'm pretty appalled by what you told me last night.

Things have taken a direction that I wasn't aware they would. I assumed we might have different attitudes and opinions, but that we would, of course, agree on fundamental human rights — together. Now I realise that none of you even see my family or me as people anymore, but as muck to be gotten rid of. And that makes any argument impossible and this letter I'm writing to you absurd: muck can't write, and it doesn't need to forbid you to see its daughter, because that daughter isn't a person either, but is also muck, which the piece of muck has somehow managed to produce because people couldn't muck out, mop, and disinfect the place it lives in fast enough; Ulf, my dear, what's that I see? Are *you* still clean?

You dirty old Nazi, stay away from my daughter.

No best wishes,

Resi

I just about make it into the bathroom, which is luckily empty. Bea is still asleep, and the boys never wash. I throw up in the toilet bowl. It hurts, but it's also good. The last time I vomited was five and a half years ago, while giving birth to Lynn; at every birth, just before the final contractions, everything I had in me came out.

There's something nice about being so close to the edge, not being in control of whether the baby comes or you throw up.

Disgusting, acidic red-wine puke swims in the toilet: I flush it away, rinse my mouth out, drink water from the toothbrush mug with Miffy on the front, a rabbit without a mouth. If you don't have a mouth, you always look surprised and cute. What an excellent idea to draw Miffy without a mouth and just give her a cross instead, whatever that's supposed to be — a muzzle, whiskers? I imagine it's the secret of Bruna's success.

'Mum?' Jack is outside the door.

'I'm coming.'

I make endless sandwiches; cut apples into slices; soak oats.

Pull yourself together, Resi. Hide your fangs, stitch up your mouth with a cross — that's what it is! A stitch! A cross-stitch! Anyway, you literally took something Ulf said the wrong way. It wasn't his intention — and it's out now.

I stand at the living-room window and watch my kids walking off to school. Feeding them has set off those pacifying phrases in my head, and I sing the Miffy song for Lynn: 'Miffy, Miffy, we love you / you always know just what to do / two long ears and button eyes / and just my size / Miffy, Miffy, oh so true / we do love you.'

Sven gets up, and I take his side of the bed; try to fall back to sleep. I had a late night last night, and it was surreal. I don't even *know* what it was.

I want to fall asleep, keep my mouth shut, and be loyal, like Miffy: I'm a decent person, I know what's expected and how to behave.

Sometimes I might want sex to defy death and loneliness, or

because I can do it myself and it doesn't cost anything. But this will be a well-kept secret. I won't share any emotions anymore, and I won't wash my dirty laundry in public. I will wash silently, be respectful, provide for my children, and feel shame.

Like my mother. My grandmother. My great-grandmother.

None of us are worthy enough to give ourselves airs. Normal, modest, and ashamed, private parts hidden. We keep ourselves covered and have no obvious needs, let alone ones we can write down.

'Ate way too much again.' That's all, and it's already more than enough.

I hear Sven in the hallway with Lynn, then the front door shuts.

I want to know how my parents divided up the jobs in the morning. Who made the breakfast and who did the lunchboxes?

But there weren't any lunchboxes: my brothers and sisters and I never had them. There was no real breakfast either. When Raimund got up, he brought us rusks in bed, two on a saucer, which he waved in our faces; a bit like at the zoo, I now think, but at the time, I thought it was completely normal. I was able to stay in bed a bit longer, nibble my rusks, and reach for the bottle of fizzy water next to my bed. We all had bottles of fizzy water next to the bed, and no one drank from glasses. I later found out that friends of mine thought it was strange: no breakfast in the morning, no snacks, us all drinking from bottles, and a mother who slept in.

I wonder if it gave her a guilty conscience?

I breathe on the mirror so that I don't have to see myself in it anymore.

———

Sometimes, in the middle of the week, Marianne got up before anybody else and went to the baker and laid the table for breakfast. No one had the time or energy to sit down and enjoy it, but on those days, I had a sandwich for recess. Better still, I had a fresh bread roll.

I'm sure that's how she pacified her conscience. Defended herself in front of an invisible jury against the charge of being lazy. I thought it was normal that my mother slept in. Who likes getting up at half past six?

But that's not acceptable behaviour, as I now know; and Marianne must have known it back then.

She took liberties and flouted the rules.

Only to be regularly shocked, feel ashamed, and try to correct her self-image in a fit of maternal care.

'Ate way too much again.'

She claimed it was our fault that she was fat. She divided her appearance in two: 'before the children' and 'after the children'. I didn't mind or try to get to the bottom of this ploy, even though other mothers I knew didn't have a spare tyre after giving birth. In fact, this was the case with nearly all other mothers, at least later on at school. But what did I know? They also wore make-up, did exercise, and some had even had 'work' done. Or they were better at sticking to diets than Marianne.

I didn't know anything. I still don't know anything, and Raimund can't remember — he just shrugs when I ask. He doesn't even remember giving us rusks for breakfast.

Classifying your own social background still seems forbidden: we weren't poor, we weren't victims. If anything, it was our own fault — see how brilliantly neoliberal brainwashing still works? Even now, I can't admit that Marianne belonged to a different social class than Ulf's or Friederike's mothers: a class in which mothers get fat and watch TV, and lug Lidl bags home instead of doing ski-conditioning workouts.

It's not the way I want to see Marianne — she was clever!

Listen, Bea, because this is important: having children doesn't automatically make you fat. You'll put on weight during pregnancy, and you'll put on a lot of weight if you've always starved yourself before to look the way you thought you should. You'll be told to make sure you lose it all afterwards; you'll be told that breastfeeding helps. You'll see models in underwear four weeks after giving birth as if it was nothing, but it's all just propaganda. Exercise. Torture. C-section in the eighth month. Perhaps you'll never look like you did before, and you might think it's a shame, or very beautiful, or unimportant. Perhaps you won't be fatter after having children but thinner than ever instead; however, that shouldn't be a reason to get pregnant, though, just as you shouldn't get cancer to lose weight like your grandma did. Perhaps you'll get really fat for the first time after having children, and perhaps having children will be to blame, or more likely, being a mother. Because suddenly you're at home a lot, bored, and all you do is shop, cook, eat, and crave things. And eating makes you fatter, especially the kind of eating you do when you're bored and crave things. So, you might get fat from having children just because you lead a life you think you have to because you have children, and you can't come up with any ideas of your own or another kind of life, and this isn't your fault, and certainly not your children's fault. Ask yourself who stands to gain from this situation, Bea; it's essential, especially in this case.

Most importantly, ask yourself where these ideas come from. And where the ideas of other people — who aren't full of craving and boredom — come from. Is there something that makes it easier for them to have ideas? Or helps them try their ideas out?

Most importantly, don't starve yourself. Ask who stands to gain if you punish and deny yourself the last bit of fun: food. Or you might not deny yourself food, but feel ashamed after you eat. You might feel ashamed of your behaviour, eating habits, appearance, big thighs, fat hips, wobbly upper arms, and stomach. And of your vulva — yes, another terrible word, I know. You're ashamed of your vulva, its name, and everything that comes out of it. I know, it's just really awful.

But shame makes you small and dumb, a mouthless Miffy. So please, Bea, ask why. And then try as hard as you can to resist.

I have to stop being afraid of the autumn holidays and of my own children.

I'm being hysterical. What can happen? My picture of a successful family life might not be fulfilled? And where does this picture come from, for fuck's sake? I'm worse than all of K23. I'm terrified of admitting I'm not in control and might make a mistake.

I rush into my broom cupboard and turn on my laptop. It takes a while to boot so that I can finally write down what feels like a revelation.

242

1. It's not wrong to have children. What's wrong is to believe that certain things have to follow. For example, we established long ago that parents don't have to marry just because they're having a baby. We could equally think it's fine not to invite friends over to play Pass the Parcel on our kid's birthday.

2. I can't bear parents who act like animal trainers, getting their kids to behave in a certain way by using a carrot and a stick. As if their kids were unpredictable, wild animals. In the same vein, I should stop being afraid that my kids will 'be spoilt', 'flip out', 'waste away', or 'be failures' as soon as my back is turned. That's disrespectful to them as people and a sign of my own inflated self-esteem.

3. Over the past week, I've decided that people can definitely hear the truth. So, I don't have to hide away in my broom cupboard anymore. I want to teach my kids the facts of life without sparing them, and immunise them with stories. And I should be grateful for this opportunity to be with them!

At last, I have time to explain to my kids the background of their upbringing. Even though they've experienced it firsthand.

Bea: 'What are we doing at half-term?'

Resi: 'Nothing. Holidays are to ensure that the school system doesn't collapse, the teachers don't resign, and the schoolchildren don't revolt. Holidays aren't for families to do special things together.'

Bea: 'But everybody's doing something special. Everybody's going away except us.'

Resi: 'Then they're deluded. Travelling isn't special. It's bad for the environment. And for us, it's too expensive, and for couples like Sven and me, too risky. The divorce rate rises significantly after holidays. And I no longer have any friends you could go away with or visit. I wouldn't count on your grandparents either. If they'd wanted to build a relationship, they'd come here or would invite you to stay with them. But they don't, so they're obviously too busy or not interested.'

Bea: 'But when you were a child, you did such great things.'

Resi: 'That's wrong. I said I did because, like everybody, I was still taken in by the myth of childhood, and wanted to say I'd been really happy at one time in my life. But it's not true. My childhood was just as boring and dull as yours.'

Bea: 'But the others—'

Resi: 'Do you really believe that? Are you inside their heads? Do you go on holiday with them?'

Bea: 'They post photos on Instagram!'

Resi: 'Exactly. And you believe their photos? You're fourteen years old, but you still haven't figured out that the photos are carefully curated? Two dimensional? Maybe staged? Photoshopped? Posted to impress, brag, or affirm? To make you feel inferior, outdo you, impress you with something that doesn't exist? Down with holidays! Down with childhood! Stop Instagram! Destroy your mobile phones! Open your eyes and see the truth behind the autumn holidays!'

I'm happy. I feel liberated.

The next two weeks will be lovely as long as I'm completely myself and accept the others as they are.

Misery

Okay, Resi. Keep calm.

Saturday doesn't count. It would be the weekend anyway, even if Monday and the following two weeks weren't free.

So I shouldn't feel depressed when I send Kieran off at nine on Saturday to buy bread rolls — 'Go and buy something nice for breakfast, here's five euros — no, take ten instead' — and while he's doing that, lay the table and arrange a plate of fruit, and make coffee for Sven, all with that wonderful feeling of being in control and that my life is going well, that it's Saturday and no one has to go anywhere, and we'll all have breakfast together, and then see what the day has in store. Sure, we'll have to go shopping, perhaps clean the bathroom, and most definitely do some washing. I'm wearing my last pair of knickers for the second day in a row, and don't want to think about how long Jack has had *his* on. Oh, perhaps it'd be a good idea to go shopping for some basics.

And it shouldn't surprise me that I feel annoyed when Kieran comes back, stands in front of the fridge, digs a finger into one of the rolls, and squirts ketchup into it, before disappearing into the boys' room, where Jack is already awake and gaming, despite the rule of no computers before ten o'clock. And, to stop myself getting even angrier, I stick my head around the door of our bedroom and say to Sven: 'Would you like to get up and have breakfast, darling?', not in a demanding way, but just as information, and I don't bother Bea, because I know she's not mad about rolls for breakfast.

It shouldn't make me stop and think when I realise that I'm not mad about rolls for breakfast either, and that I can't remember one single family breakfast I've enjoyed, if I'm honest — not with my own parents, brother, and sister, or with Sven and the children. Sven sits there in silence, stubbornly drinking his coffee; Kieran spreads crumbs everywhere, even if he's sitting at the table; Bea complains that Jack chomps; Jack chomps, and Lynn is too big for her toddler chair and gets her hair in the Nutella. Bea asks why we buy Nutella in the first place, seeing as it's only made of sugar and palm oil, and I have to assume that she gets this ghastly know-it-all attitude from me, and quickly snap: 'Let me worry about that.'

My exposure of the Family Holiday Lie doesn't necessarily mean I won't fall for the Weekend Lie the next day: the one that says it's nice to have breakfast together on Saturdays when nobody has to go anywhere, when we can eat fresh rolls with smiling faces, and there's Nutella, love, and fruit.

But it *is* a bit strange that I've blocked out the fact that I don't like eating before half past eleven, or feel like talking to anyone, especially to people who don't feel like talking to me — about what, anyway? And that I think it's even worse to sit next to each other in annoyed silence, which always prompts me to make plans that consist of my own three points if I'm honest: 'We have to clean, and do the washing, and then go shopping for new clothes.'

But I understand the problem: The Weekend Lie is persuasive.

It operates with a brutal causality: 'If I don't like sitting together with you, then it means that I don't like you.'

It operates using simple opposites: weekdays are stressful, and now everything is lovely for a change.

It operates cruelly and tenaciously, every five days, all year long, come rain or shine.

The fact that I can't rebel against the Weekend Lie doesn't mean that I have to fall for the Family Holiday Lie. I stick to my plan: to stick it out without a plan. To build on the fact that we're all responsible for keeping our own show on the road, including me.

Sunday.
The boys' room stinks.

I know it'll get worse the older they get. Now, it only smells of farts, hot plastic, and metal casing, rotting fruit cores and Jack's dental brace, which is lying among the half-chewed apples.

'Get some fresh air in here,' I say and receive a growl as a reply. Which could mean anything, including 'yes', so I close the door again.

I ask Lynn if she wants to play Halma.

'Do I have to?'

'No, but I thought you might like to.'

I ask Bea what she's up to. She's sitting at her desk.

'Nothing. Why?'

She covers up whatever she's doing.

'A secret? A present for me?'

She groans and rolls her eyes.

'Sorry. I was only joking.'

None of the kids needs me. I can do what I want!

What do I want?

Bake a cake. Tidy up the flat. Freeze the present moment, extend it into infinity, so that I can be truly free.

I could sleep. Get some rest. It is Sunday, after all!

Sven is sitting in the bedroom, looking at his computer screen.

'What are you doing?' I ask.

'Writing emails.'

'Will you go for a walk with me?'

'A Sunday stroll?'

It's raining. I stare out of the window.

'I can't relax.'

'Why not?' he says.

'Because the flat's a mess again.'

Sven laughs.

'What's funny about that?'

'Nothing.' Sven looks serious. 'I thought you'd got used to it. You gave a speech yesterday about how cleaning was a Sisyphean task. You quoted Camus.'

'That was just waffle. I was showing off in front of the kids.'

'Come here, I'll make you feel better.'

'I don't want to stop you from working. I'm going to make a cake.'

Sven doesn't stop me.

I bake a cake. I have absolute freedom to do whatever I want — and I bake a cake.

Will I at least manage to leave all the utensils, bowls, spoons, spatula, and baking tin unwashed in the sink? The flour on the worktop and the crumbs in the gaps between the floorboards?

No. I clean it all up. I wipe the mixer with a damp cloth. I hang up fresh tea towels.

What I manage *not* to do is to lay the table and call out to anybody who's listening that it's time for coffee and cake.

As evening draws on, the screams from the boys' room get louder. When a chair falls over, I allow myself to knock on the door. 'Everything okay in there?' And hear: 'Go fuck yourself, you fucking motherfucker, fuck you!'

The door opens, and Kieran comes out with that zoned-out expression of his and sweaty hair.

'I need to kill something,' he says.

'I beg your pardon?'

He gives me a nasty look. A very, very nasty look.

'An animal,' he says. 'A small animal I can kill.'

Bea comes out of her room.

'You do know, don't you,' she says, 'that last summer, Kieran peed on a butterfly until it died. He drowned it.'

'Yeah,' says Kieran, 'and I enjoyed it.'

He goes back into his room and picks up his tablet.

Jack says to him, 'Just *stop*.'

Kieran does something on his tablet then starts howling again. No words this time, just animal sounds.

Jack raises his hands. 'I warned you.'

Kieran thwacks the table and hurts himself as he does. Yells again.

Jack says in a put-on voice: 'Dude, don't scream like that,' and holds his head as if he's getting a migraine.

Kieran throws his tablet at him.

Now Jack is crying. The corner of the tablet has caught his face.

I don't know how bad it is, if Jack still has two eyes, if the tablet still works, whether Kieran might be crazy — a real animal torturer, a sadist. Or an animal himself. Or whether they're all just pretending.

I think of the twenty episodes of *Supernanny* that I watched years ago, which were always filmed in households with too little money, too many children, too little space, and too many cuddly toys. Those are the kind of people who need help and want to be on TV, who aren't ashamed to expose themselves, and are connected by walkie-talkie to Jo Frost, who says encouragingly and assertively: 'Don't get pulled into this argument. You're the adult. Check if anybody is hurt, but sort out later what actually happened. Well done. I'm proud of you.'

I see Jo Frost standing on the balcony next to Sven, who's smoking a joint. She's standing very close to him, because it's still raining and the two of them are trying to shelter underneath the balcony above. 'Yes, Sven, I understand the theory of learning to be effective yourself, and I understand that you don't want to police your kids.' I wait for her to add that they have been plugged into their devices since this morning, or since lunchtime yesterday, if we're honest, and have eaten nothing but sweets all day. But no, not even an insinuated 'Everybody knows that' passes Jo Frost's lips. Instead, she puckers them and takes Sven's joint.

I want to stand between them up and shout 'Seriously?' like the boys, but then I hear Jo's voice again in my ear, saying I shouldn't get involved and to only intervene if somebody is seriously hurt — and 'seriously hurt' in daytime trash TV means blood and bullet wounds, not disappointed emotions and dented utopias. It's just a couple of people smoking a joint!

I sit down on the sofa.

It stinks here too, even though I cleaned earlier on.

Sven's mobile is lying on the arm of the sofa and bleeps at regular intervals, crying out for electricity. I have to stop myself from throwing it on the floor and jumping all over it.

I have to find a way to concentrate on myself and to get in touch with my feelings. Where have my needs gone? I can't go into my broom cupboard now; there's no peace and quiet, no analysing things, no writing about myself, no floating above myself, no turning myself into a character, or moving myself around a playing board.

Thank God Jo's voice is still guiding me, up from the sofa and out to Sven on the balcony, where I become her. I stand next to Sven and smell the rain, the wet city, Sven's smoke, and the smell of baking in my hair and clothes. I sway a little, gingerly half-sit on the windowsill, and lean the back of my head against the pane. That's good. I take a deep breath.

Sven rolls me a cigarette.

I smoke.

Sven and I smoke and suffer together in silence.

Monday, Tuesday, Wednesday.
No broom cupboard.

No words.

No opportunity to transform.

I practise existing. I think of meals, of the ingredients for them and whether I should buy them in Lidl or go all the way over to Aldi. I'm glad I have enough money to go shopping. I remind myself that none of us has to starve. I tell myself that none of the kids is hurt in the strict sense of the word — or will be just by hanging around, watching YouTube videos and eating chocolate.

I constantly tidy up but stop myself throwing away cuddly toys or other things that don't belong to me.

I keep moving and force myself not to be annoyed that I'm always active while others are lying in bed.

I force myself to cook meals just for myself that I eat alone. I only force the others to put their encrusted muesli bowls into the dishwasher.

I keep going.

I force myself to accept that we barely talk to each other.

I practise being silent.

I force myself to accept that my desire is ebbing away.

I practise abstinence.

I fight back wishes and ideas until I no longer know what I want; I practise being disoriented, wander about in a room, forget what I wanted to do there, go on the balcony and smoke.

I am totally exhausted.

I go to bed at the same time as Lynn.

Something in me becomes calmer.

Something in me completely stops working.

I feel like gambling. I play dice games with Lynn and Kieran for hours.

I get addicted to *Candy Crush*, *Farm Heroes*, and *2048*. I ask Jack to download them on my phone. I like the fact that Jack can do this and the way he looks when he does.

Every single one of my children seems more confident than me.

Lynn lies on her back, practising sucking in her stomach and then ballooning it out as far as she can. Kieran builds a tower made of Lego taller than he is.

Bea says: 'If I manage *not* to imagine something, because the image is probably a lie and unattainable anyway, and it only puts me under pressure — like cool holidays, beauty, or a happy life, all that — then how do I know that "living in the moment" isn't just another construct too? Another way of pressuring me and making me feel small? Huh?'

The leap

I've been awarded a prize. A whole bunch of people like the book I've written. My publisher calls and says they're going to print a second edition. A journalist calls and asks for an interview, if we can find a quiet place to meet.

I say: 'It's the half-term holidays.'

And she says: 'Tell me about it.'

She no longer has a desk since her department was merged with another; I think of the clerk at the housing-benefit office who said, with pursed lips, that she was in the same boat, as she too lived in an incalculable shared household and didn't get a cent because of it.

I say: 'Okay, then, let's meet on the quietest possible street corner.'

The journalist laughs, and although I think it's wrong to joke about these things, I realise that I'm able to joke again, draw parallels, and remember stuff.

The journalist really does look like me. We meet in an almost empty money-laundering café in Mitte, where there's no music playing, and the staff are mostly making private calls. When I arrive, the journalist is on the phone to her daughter, who's not doing the school holiday programme, but is alone at home.

'I'm turning my mobile off now!' she says decisively and slips off her rain jacket, which doesn't go with her skirt, because waterproof jackets always look too sporty. At least the ones in our price range.

'So,' she says, stealing a look at her mobile, then at the questions she's prepared.

'As a mother of four, how do you do manage to write successful novels?'

I stare at her. She smiles back, but she's serious about her question; at least she doesn't slap her thigh or laugh out loud over her great joke. My chest tightens. What am I supposed to do now? She must know how it is! She's in the same boat!

My thoughts race. I could just stop the interview. Sven would: and everything else is patronising. She's an adult woman, and I have to presume that she means what she says. And therefore has to take the consequences.

But I can't. Instead, I think up excuses for her: it's the autumn holidays, so she couldn't prepare herself. She's confusing herself with me, just like I'm confusing myself with her. She didn't formulate the question properly, and of course she knows the difference between production and reception, market forces and artistic criteria, and anyway, she didn't necessarily want to talk about my situation as a mother but was told to write a profile, not a review. And that's why she wanted to meet me; otherwise, it would have been enough to read the book. She has to find out what kind of jacket I wear, who I am.

And I'm vain: a missionary. If I explain to her how life works, we'll change things together! 'Yes, we can!'

'I don't manage,' I say. 'It's impossible to manage. "How do you manage?" isn't a question; it's a way of creating distance, it's phony praise. Just think of Obama and Merkel and Bob the Builder, and "Yes, we can!" That should make us wary of "managing". None of us is managing. Who told us to anyway? Who are "we"? Who's carrying whose load? Who stands to gain from it?'

'Erm, I meant: you write successful novels.'

'What's that supposed to mean? "I write successful novels?" Are there people who write unsuccessful novels?'

'Yes, of course!'

'No! They write novels that aren't successful, but they don't sit down and write an unsuccessful novel!'

She looks at me. She doesn't understand what I'm trying to say. I don't know how else to say it, so I say what I didn't want to say:

'My book was rejected by twenty publishers.'

But it doesn't help. Why did I think she'd understand me? Because she has the same rain jacket as me? Because she's a journalist without a desk? A mother who can't assert herself? A woman with a brain?

And still, I can't give up. I don't want to: not on her, nor the hope that I'll manage. I want to manage.

'Oh, really?' she says. 'Well, they're really going to kick themselves now.'

'How was it?' Sven asks.

'You would have left.'

'No one ever wants to meet me.'

'Because they're afraid of you. You don't walk into traps, and you don't need understanding at all costs. Now she thinks we understand each other. Because I didn't walk away!'

'Keep it in mind for next time.'

'But I already had it in mind — I realised it after her first question! I don't have the guts to walk away. I can't just accept things.'

'You believe in understanding.'

'And what's needed is resistance. Now *I'm* the example that it's possible to manage!' I laugh manically.

The newspaper sends a photographer over.

I can't put on make-up. I've never learned how to and have to ask Bea, who learned from YouTube videos, but can't do it either because the videos are sale pitches, and Bea doesn't order the product at the end. Bea is frugal and saves her money rather than buying brushes, eye shadow, and eyelash curlers. That's a good thing — and a bad thing. I have terrible posture and a face that looks completely different in the mirror from how it feels on the inside. Unlike Bea's, which doesn't need make-up, but like my mother's when she went to the drugstore at the age of fifty to buy something for age spots and rings under her eyes, and showed me her concealer the next time I saw her, saying: 'It cost 29.95, and I look like a clown!' 'Mum, that's because you're doing one step instead of three!'

The photographer says I should smile.

I can't smile without looking dopey, and I'm putting up resistance, so I don't smile.

'You look scared,' the photographer says. 'I'm not going to do anything bad to you.'

'I'm no good at smiling.'

'Yes, you are. I can see you are — there you go!'

She's outwitted me. I should tell her to delete the photo: it's up to me. She's the pro, and she should know that looking dopey is no better than looking scared: but it's her photo.

I don't want to come across as pretentious or difficult. Who am I, after all, the Princess of Windsor? It doesn't matter what I look like. Why am I here in front of the camera in the first place? Because the interview needs a photo. And I need the interview for publicity; being noticed is the first requirement to telling the truth, and I won't let you stop me, not in this case either. I'm going to show you.

And to be honest, I look in real life exactly like I do in the photo: amateurly made up, not able to manage but not resisting either, hiding my terror with fake dopiness, looking stiffly unpretentious, and old.

The photographer sticks her head around the door of my broom cupboard when we're done.

'This is where you write?'

I nod. 'People normally put a washing machine in here.'

She nods too. 'I've set up a darkroom in my broom cupboard.'

'Isn't it too cramped?'

'No, no. It's just for decoration these days anyway.'

'You need plasterboard screws.' I knock on my wooden board.

'Yes, that's right. It's all a bloody balancing act.'

Ulf calls to congratulate me on my prize.

'I read about it in the newspaper.'

'Oh. Really?'

'Well, congratulations.'

'Thank you.'

Silence.

'I think it's quite something,' Ulf says. 'A huge leap.'

I still don't know what to say.

'It still feels unreal for you,' says Ulf. 'Just like it was for us. Just one commendation by the German Architectural Prize, and we had ten times as many commissions.'

I don't reply.

'Are you going to do a reading tour?'

'Well, I have a few dates.'

'You make it sound like you don't want to.'

'No, no! It's wonderful. I like talking about my book. I've been getting plenty of positive feedback.'

Now it's his turn to be silent.

'I don't know what to say. You're the one who phoned.'

'Ahh, yeah, of course. I didn't want to pretend that I hadn't heard.'

'That's nice of you.'

'Sorry?'

'Really, Ulf. The prize doesn't mean that much. Well, better to win a prize than no prize, of course. But it's just the fucking literary business. It's a trap to pay it too much attention. You can't let the value of your work be determined by the public.'

I almost say: 'Everybody knows that.'

'But if you want to live off writing, then you have to,' says Ulf.

'You're talking about money.'

'I'm talking about opportunities to work. To publish. Or in my case, to build.'

'Yes, of course. But it's what you build or publish that matters.'

'I don't understand. You want to be a writer, don't you?'

'Yes, of course. But some prize won't turn me into one.'

'Did I say it did?'

'Sort of, yes. Up to now, my writing was seen as a problem.'

'What you wrote, yes.'

'That's exactly what I'm talking about! It's the same thing.'

'I don't know what you mean.'

I can tell. And I don't want to come across as arrogant, don't want to make myself out to be a victim, and don't want to fall into any of the usual traps. So, what should I do? There's not a trace of a connection between us: we belong to two different systems, and we'd have to start from scratch to find a common language and, from there, a common view on what we're talking about — and then talk about it.

Am I prepared to do that?

First, I have to answer that question myself, and then, if I decide I want to, ask Ulf the same question.

'I have to go now.'

I don't know what to wear. It has to be smart, because I'm receiving a prize, but at the same time, it's taking place in the morning, so evening dress isn't appropriate. No brown shoes after six pm, no bare shoulders before four pm, and blue and green should never be seen, and artists can do what the hell they like anyway, and that's why they have to do something and not end up looking like company reps. I wish I'd gone for a particular style fifteen years ago, like all in black, or an oversized suit, and that way I'd already have a look.

'It's okay,' says Sven when I come out of the bedroom in a skirt with red tights.

'You look like my French teacher,' says Bea, and I turn around to put on the blue trousers after all.

'The shoes are the most important part,' says Sven when I come out again.

'The brown ones are the only ones that go with the blue trousers.'

'That why I preferred the skirt,' says Sven.

'I like my French teacher!' says Bea.

Why did I involve her in the first place? I'm on my own, anyway. It's a fight, I'm Rambo, no one can help me, and asking somebody to give me cover is nonsense if I don't know where the enemy lines are.

A 'huge leap' is what Ulf called it. And what I'm leaping over is the threshold of the most established literary venue in Berlin.

Coffee has already been made in the director's office, where there's a meeting to talk about what will happen at the event. I lay my rain jacket over the photocopier, because it won't look good on stage. I should have worn the blue trousers after all.

The person presenting the award is Olli, who studied with me at university. He's wearing a suit and looks good.

'I'm happy for you, Resi,' he says. 'Enormously happy.'

I watch how he does everything — where he puts his bag, how

he drinks his coffee. He takes milk and sugar. His coat is lying over the photocopier too.

The event will run in the usual way, and we go through it quickly. I'll be the fourth on stage, and then there'll be a photo session.

Olli says he thought my novel was 'really big'.

Paradoxically, 'really big' is bigger than 'major'. 'Really big' was a phrase rarely used during our studies, and we had to think carefully about contradicting whoever used it, because they wouldn't back down easily.

'Thank you,' I say once.

'Thank you,' I say again on the stage, when it's my official turn to say thank you. 'I'm happy that my book has found such a huge resonance.'

And then I move from resonances to sounds, to the timbres of the world, and words to express anger, and the audience is mostly made up of people over sixty, in fact probably closer to eighty, with white hair and grey pullovers, and they listen indulgently. The leap that Ulf mentioned is the leap into their indulgence. And I see Sven at the end of the first row, wearing a suit like Olli, but without a belly; and it's not that I have anything against bellies, Bea, not at all, but a suit can't be worn like a hipster if you have a belly. I want to say that it's easier without a belly, just like red tights suggest 'rebellion' and not 'French teacher' when they're on girlish, slim legs instead of sturdy maternal ones. I want to say that words to express anger in an established literary venue will inevitably be indulged — and how couldn't they be? That's the reason it was built.

Sven says afterwards, 'Well done, babe,' and disappears for a smoke, then disappears completely.

'He's looking after the kids,' I say when asked why, and it's true. It's Sunday and the kids are at home. I have to go to the photo session alone, drink bubbly on my own, and attend the lunch afterwards on my own. I think about 'Well done,' and whether I should order a steak, the most expensive thing on the menu. If not now, then when?

I'm sitting across from Olli.

'Is it true that you've got four kids?' he asks.

'No,' I say, 'that's rubbish. How would I manage?'

Olli tells me that he and his boyfriend have two dogs, and that's more than enough.

'What breed?' I ask, and the topic spreads around the table. The director of the literary venue also has dogs, the publisher would like one, and the young intern says that having dogs in the city is cruel to animals. Everybody turns to her.

It's good when people speak their minds. Especially when they're young and still finding their way and have something to lose. Like, having their contract renewed after an unpaid internship, or getting a publishing contract or a dog-sitting job to tide them over.

Then she says she comes from a farm in Holstein where the dogs are regularly taken out on hunts so they get enough exercise. I ask her what breed they are, and my publisher is curious to know since when I've cared so much about dogs, and I say: 'Since I was hounded out of my home.'

It just slips out; I'm not trying to make myself out to be a victim, and I don't want to draw attention to myself. I was already the centre of attention during the event. But then, of course, I have to explain what I meant, so I say: 'Well, the usual: the city centre is out of my price range.'

Olli nods. The publisher nods too, as does the intern, and the director of the literary venue. This general remark takes me out of the spotlight again; they can all relate to it, they are or know somebody in the same boat, if not here, then in Paris or London, or in that film at the Berlin Film Festival. Which nevertheless had a happy ending.

'When one door closes, another opens,' I say, and, 'Setting off for new shores means having the courage to leap into the unknown, out onto the open sea.'

'Freedom's just another word for nothing left to lose,' cites Olli, and my publisher says: 'How does it feel?', and I say to the intern that I think it's good that she's concerned about how animals live, because that's often the first step to being concerned about how people live. 'Isn't that right, Miss Carefree?' I add, then realise I should be careful what I say in my tipsiness and in this circle, and that I've just won fifteen thousand euros, so what the hell do I care — and wonder whether I'll have to declare it on my tax return, and whether the kids will lose their school meals' and activities' allowance as a result.

Yes, probably. But luckily, they don't exist.

I order another beer.

The director of the literary house says goodbye. He pays up at the bar; everybody will have to cover their own bill from now on, and only a few remain at the table — those who know how it really feels.

My publisher always stays until the last round, and now it's the afternoon, half past two.

He stares at me with bloodshot eyes.

'Resi,' he says, 'you think you're smart, but sometimes you have to let go.'

'Okay,' I say, 'I'll try. Let's go and pee outside.'

He fetches my jacket.

I squat down between two cars. With a skirt on, it's no problem. Some trickles into my tights, but it doesn't matter, it will dry straight away. The publisher is waiting.

'Now you,' I say.

He turns around and pees up against the wall.

Then we stand there for a bit. It's a Sunday in November on Friedrichstraße. But this Sunday all the shops are open, and heated air wafts from store doors, and tourists without scarves can go in buy themselves one.

It's really great not to need the toilet anymore. To never have to go to the toilet again, because you can just pee in the gutter.

'You would never have to breathe in that fruit-scented cleaning fluid they spray in restaurant toilets,' says the publisher, nodding.

'And you'd do a Number Two on the pavement too?'

He nods again. Gestures that he'd like another cigarette.

'And masturbate? And menstruate?'

I don't know if I should believe him. He can't even menstruate, but he nods.

List to self:

Stop waiting for Alexander the Great. You're not

Diogenes in his barrel saying 'Get out of my sunlight.' The sun doesn't even shine on November afternoons here, and although the Berlin Palace has been rebuilt in the meantime, it doesn't house a king that you could shame, let alone foist your modesty on.

Stop trying to ingratiate yourself with people in the literary business. She has her price now, old Resi, and no one needs to comment anymore on the fact that her name isn't short for Theresia, but Parrhesia.

Stop making demands on Bea. There are too many gaps in your advice to her; while you're talking about starving, the number of clinically obese children is rising relentlessly above the clinically underweight.

And, speaking of children, my family doesn't exist. I'm not the type that manages.

'Well, I'll let myself go, then,' I say.

The publisher nods, gives me a fatherly hug, and goes back into the restaurant; I walk down Friedrichstraße.

Diogenes was single, and singly tied up in his own life. He didn't write, he did street theatre, the post-dramatic kind, claiming that roles were not to be played, but to be embodied. That packed a punch, even back then.

He had his greatest moments in front of an audience. These are the only moments we know about, because Diogenes didn't take any notes, and the folklore of his interventions is probably at least half invented. Certainly exaggerated. Unacceptably overstated.

There is some controversy over his death. He knew very well how it felt, but that was his own private business and not part of his work.

He improvised a lot; he was an ad-libbing comedian. Naturally, he thought up and rehearsed scenes and sayings in his barrel, but he couldn't have planned Alexander the Great's visit or known that Alexander would give him the opportunity for his most famous line. It was pure luck, and not the essence of his work. It just happens to be a very clear example.

To be, not to have.

Everybody knows that's the secret!

Having never stops; but it's part of being. You define what is and what you are. That was Diogenes' lesson. If you manage that, you've won. Then you don't need the last word. You are the last word.

Victims

Sven is in the kitchen looking for something he can cook.

There is nothing; I didn't go shopping. But I still could, because the shops are open this Sunday. Instead I sit down at the table, still wearing my rain jacket and brown shoes.

'Finished?' asks Sven.

I nod.

'What's next?'

'Christmas.'

'Oh, God.'

Sven goes to put on a coffee. The espresso has run out too.

'I didn't go shopping,' I say.

Sven shrugs and puts on the kettle for tea instead.

'I got a letter. From Frank.'

'What kind of letter?'

I go into my broom cupboard and fetch it. It's really that easy. I hold it out for Sven.

Sven reads the letter. Twice.

'What the hell's this about?' he says. 'What's Frank's problem?'

'I'm worried,' I say. 'I don't want to move.'

'We can't get far enough away from those windbags.'

I haven't heard that word in a long time. I think of Silas's baby trumpet. Of how Frank wanted Willi to play in the brass band, which Willi predictably refused. And how Friederike wanted to take up flute lessons parallel to Silas's trumpet lessons, and of Ulf's grandma, propped up on her stick next to the grand piano—

'Everything has two sides.'

Sven turns the letter over. 'This doesn't.'

'It's my fault, Sven. I should have known—'

'You did. Otherwise, you couldn't have done it.'

There's a rushing sound in my ears. Tears pour down my face.

'I envy you. You can be proud of yourself,' says Sven.

'But I don't want to live in Marzahn.'

'We're not going to live in Marzahn.'

Sven folds up the letter.

'Then where?'

'No idea.'

We have frozen pizza from the late-night corner shop; the shops still close at five o'clock, even on Sundays, when they're allowed to be open.

Frozen pizza is unhealthy. I buy Cola Orange soda too, which makes it even worse.

'Are we celebrating something?' Jack asks when we're sitting at the table.

'She won a prize,' says Kieran.

'Money?' Jack asks.

I nod.

'A lot of money?'

Bea groans. 'By our standards, yes. But not enough for what you want.'

'What do you want?' I ask Jack.

'What do I want?' Jack asks.

We look at Bea.

'I don't know,' she says. 'A Ferrari for Christmas.'

'Yeah!' yells Kieran.

Sven and Lynn say nothing, as usual, and eat their pizza.

There are six of us. It's like being in a film.

Our flat has been whipped out from under our arses, and we don't know where to go.

There's jaunty Jack, eleven years old, with his stinking dental brace next to his glass of Cola Orange soda. He'd love to be a millionaire rapper, a YouTube star, a football god. He knocks back his drink in one gulp, and his dark eyes flash as he refills his glass right to the very top.

'Stop!' cries Kieran. 'You scumbag.' A fighter whose face is already grim and furrowed. You can see the man he will become, with hunched shoulders and a piece in his waistband, prowling the streets. God help the person who tries to pull anything on him.

Lynn chews on her pizza in silence. Her gaze wanders across the heads of her brothers and sister into the distance. The dining-table lamp dabs her dark-blonde hair with highlights. She's still on her first piece of pizza, unconcerned that somebody might eat her share, or that there might not be enough. She has no food envy.

And Bea, the eldest, self-disciplined daughter, goes without Cola Orange soda. She feeds on the knowledge that one single glass has the equivalent of fifteen sugar cubes—

And then there are the parents. They only have themselves to blame, but in the bosom of the family, they radiate a childish innocence. At least they have produced and reared these four so far. Resi, who seems quite tired in her ugly red tights, and Sven, who says as little as his youngest daughter and is already rolling himself a cigarette. They're basically nice people, and don't deserve to be out on the street in two weeks instead of dragging a Christmas tree up the stairs, a large but crooked one without a proper top, because they were going cheap and it was already shedding its needles.

'Typical,' says Bea, who is in charge of decorating it and has decided that this year there will only be silver baubles. A bummer for the hand-painted play-dough angels from nursery days. Kieran storms out, banging the door, and Lynn secretly hangs one up anyway in the bottom back corner.

We're victims. And we're architects of our own happiness! We can bring it off no matter what the backdrop: we're the main characters of our own lives!

Christmas Eve with no tree. The children carry their personal belongings in a case each and a backpack. We parents are shouldering the kitchen equipment and memories.

In the late afternoon, the InterCity to Hanover has some free seats again, and from there they take the privatised regional train, then the bus. Okay, no one takes buses anymore — so it's a taxi.

Or rather two taxis, or a minibus cab, otherwise they wouldn't all fit in.

Spending Christmas Eve with the grandparents is fine. There might be presents in the backpack. And anyway, it's the holiday season, and the pensioned couple in the living room have spent much too long on their own. Finally, some life in the old place!

There are endless stories about eight-year-old boys who soften the hearts of their seventy-year-old grandpas and bring light into their dark, curtained lives. It's a popular genre: the other six just stay in the background of the story and the living room of a ramshackle detached home in Lüneburger Heide. On a Friday evening, the TV audience won't pay too much attention to details and plotlines—

Perhaps Christmas Eve in K23 around Frank and Vera's Christmas tree would be nicer.

They have driven to Stuttgart with Willi and Leon in their Volkswagen camper van, but they have put up a tree in Berlin anyway to get into the mood. Or for the cats?

Whatever the case might be, there's the tree, brightly decorated and going spare, and around it, their ex-friends' pile of belongings, spilling out of suitcases and rucksacks.

When Frank and Vera return, we'll have to think up something quick. We can write suggestions on a flipchart. Who knows, perhaps there'll be a piece of Christmas cake going spare too?

At least there'll be a decent discussion. Perspectives will be added. What will Frank say, for example, when he can no longer hide behind his stamp but has a speaking role? It could be really exciting: the plot will develop from the confrontation, and even if the end is predictable, the family will make sure they celebrate Christmas outside Zone A too.

Disparaging looks from the old-time residents in the far-flung district of Ahrensfelde. In the unofficial balcony-decoration competition, the newcomers are barely contenders. But next year they'll be initiated, and then they'll be among the best. They'll put up fairy lights and inflate plastic Santas.

The move is a kind of experiment. Resi can write a book about it: what it's like to live outside Zone A or B. What makes the neighbours tick: gruff voices, tender hearts. And the fact that Resi and Sven still smoke makes their integration into the community easier. Jack always has been a top centre-field defender.

The tree is a little smaller because the ceilings in the flat are a bit lower.

A TV set wouldn't be a bad thing.

After the presents have been handed out and everybody has gone to bed, Sven and Resi dare go down to the local pub, just to see who's around. They bring in cold air and conversation, and they begin to have real experiences. It almost starts to feel familiar. It's okay. Over the next few years, many people will go through the same thing.

I can't get rid of it, Bea. Not the worrying, or the shame.

No matter what I think up, it's just a weak, all-too brief comfort.

I decide to give up smoking.

I light a cigarette.